Seven Minutes in Devon

Catherine Gayle

ISBN: 0988335468
ISBN-13: 978-0-9883354-6-2

CONTENTS

Catherine Gayle

DEDICATION

To Melanie, because I still love you so much it hurts. When I started
this story, I had no idea how much this piece of fiction might
become like real life. I had to set it aside for various reasons, and
then I wasn't able to even think about starting work on it again for a
long time. Even with distance, it was almost too much for me at
times. It may always be that way for me. But I will *always* love you so
much it hurts.

PROLOGUE

Late July, 1816—The Year Without a Summer
Heathcote Park, near Topsham, Devon

Aidan Cardiff tore his gaze away from his sister's pallid face, framed by her near-gold hair, to stare out the great bay window. The action, which ought to have been simple, was anything but. It felt like yet another chunk of his heart ripped out as his head turned, but still he chose instead to watch the swollen banks of the Exe Estuary beneath the eternally gray sky. Everything was dark and foreboding, of late: Morgan's demeanor; the out-of-doors; Aidan's own blackened heart.

He swallowed the remnants of his port and scowled upon what once was the most beautiful vista he'd ever witnessed. A few months had certainly changed everything. Once, he would have laughed at such a thought, thinking it an impossibility. There was no more room in his life for laughter, though. Not until Morgan could laugh again.

A firm hand struck his shoulder, jolting him from his sour mood and returning his attention to the house party going on around him.

"The weather has to clear someday." David, Baron Burington, set a near-empty glass on the table and took up position upon the chair across from Aidan, following his gaze out to the mouth of the river. "You'll have to come back sometime and fish with me. Maybe in the fall…" He leaned in and raised a brow in question.

"No."

A deep frown creased David's forehead. "But—"

"But nothing. You've seen for yourself how difficult this has been for Morgan." Aidan choked down a show of emotion to keep it at bay. Not now. Not with so many others watching. Not while the ungainly Miss Hathaway could see, should she deign to look up from her oh-so-precious books long enough to notice anything more than the end of her altogether-too-long nose. Allowing his emotion free rein with witnesses present would be tantamount to granting that loathsome betrayer Stoneham an invitation to view Aidan's own personal visit to hell. "I won't subject her to this again so soon, and I will *not* leave her."

"Your mother will be with her. Not to mention your brother. With Trenowyth, Morgan will be far from alone."

Upon Aidan's glare, one with enough ferocity to level a lesser man, David raised his hands and pushed back from the table, rocking the chair on its insubstantial rear legs like a schoolboy flirting with disaster. It was an action Aidan had seen on countless occasions since their days together at Eton, back when Stoneham was always at their side and in the midst of all of their plans. Even now, David grinned in an altogether familiar boyish way as he balanced on the rear legs of the chair.

Everything, it seemed, pointed Aidan's memories back to Stoneham. He couldn't escape the bastard no matter how he tried. It was little wonder Morgan couldn't, either.

Upon Aidan's glare, David brought his chair down and frowned. "I know. I'm sorry. You all want to be with her right now. I understand, Aidan, I do, but you can't stop living your life."

That was exactly what Mother had said to them all before they left—a fact which ate at Aidan's gut. "I haven't." He hated how everyone seemed to think they knew what was best, particularly when they were all well and truly wrong.

"You have. Ever since Morgan—" David cut himself off, glanced warily over his shoulder to where she sat beside Miss Hathaway, and lowered his voice. "Ever since things changed, you've hardly left her side. Not a single one of you. Come to Heathcote Park again in the fall. Spend a few weeks with us. Try to forget about it all for a little while. Maybe you could work on your sculpting out here—or you could work with oils or pastels if you don't want to sculpt. It would be good for you. Getting back to your art..."

Aidan shook his head. "You could visit us at Tavistock Manor. Bring Vanessa. It isn't too far."

"We won't be able to travel, soon." A sheepish grin spread across David's still boyish features. He leaned across the table, looked pointedly over to his wife, and dropped his voice to a whisper. "Nessa is doing her best to provide me with an heir."

"Indeed?" Even in his current dark mood, Aidan couldn't hold back a chuckle. "I suppose I should offer you my hearty congratulations."

"I'd prefer for you to say you'll come in the fall. How does October sound?"

Before Aidan could refuse once more, a flash of shimmering yellow caught his eye out the window, moving toward the estuary in the distance. Cheerful pink had no place amongst the dreary gray so ever present this summer. *Morgan. No!*

Aidan bolted from his seat, sending the delicate Louis XIV chair splintering to the ground behind him. Ignoring the shouts of dismay left in his wake, he hurtled through the fussy room and into the corridor. At the far end of the hall, almost to the door, the brown hair and gangly limbs of Miss Hathaway sprinted ahead of him, her sunny yellow skirts held up about her knees so she could run full-out.

She flung open the door and careened through it. "Lady Morgan! Stop! Oh gracious heavens, you mustn't." Her panicked voice became muffled as the door slammed closed behind her.

Aidan ought to throttle the chit for allowing Morgan out of her sight. When he finished with that, he'd throttle her again for alerting neither himself nor his brother Niall, the Earl of Trenowyth, that something was amiss with their sister. Surely she recognized the gravity of the situation. Or had she been too engrossed in her bloody books to notice how delicate Morgan was, how volatile her thoughts?

No, she knew. He'd made certain of it before he ever left Morgan in her care. That could only mean Miss Hathaway hadn't cared, that she'd felt her precious books were more important than Morgan's needs.

Reaching the end of the hall at last, he shoved aside a stricken footman who had finally condescended to make an appearance at his post. Aidan almost ripped the door from its hinges in his haste to get to his sister.

His heart thudded to a standstill.

Morgan had already taken several steps into the water. Her curls whipped around her head in a ghastly frenzy, the golden and white hues intensified in the last vestiges of the setting sun that had peeked through the storm clouds as the winter-like winds howled around her.

He'd never get there in time.

The slap of his Hessians against the flagstone drive reverberated in his head. Morgan went deeper into the surge of water, her gown of sunny yellow muslin floating up and enveloping her.

Miss Hathaway leapt in after her, spindly arms and legs flailing in wild tumult. With Aidan's usual turn of the cards, the chit likely couldn't swim and would cause more harm than good. He'd be lucky to rescue even one of them; both would be asking for too much favor from heaven, particularly for someone with such a history of transgressions as he. Although, why should he rescue Miss Hathaway, when she could have prevented this entire situation to begin with? Leaving her to her death would only add to his aforementioned list, damn it all.

The water sloshed about, reaching his ears. Too much distance still. Icy shards pricked the walls of his lungs, but Aidan forced himself to ignore them and ran faster.

Morgan's head went under as he reached the edge of the water. A golden halo floated atop the estuary where she'd just been, nearly halfway to the opposite bank, and then abruptly fell below.

"No!"

Miss Hathaway filled her lungs and dove after Morgan, her dark hair quickly disappearing beneath the water, the yellow of her gown blocking the gold of Morgan's hair from his view. Aidan ran into the riverbed, oblivious to anything but reaching his sister. The force of the water slowed his progress to a near crawl, and he cursed the impediment aloud, uncaring as to who might hear his coarse tongue. Each second that ticked by meant he was a second closer to losing his sister. Forever.

That couldn't happen. He couldn't allow it.

By the time he was waist-deep, Miss Hathaway's head reappeared above the undulating surface. Another breath, and down she went again, leaving only a torrent of ripples behind.

After a few more steps he was deep enough to swim. Aidan took a great breath and pushed off against the mud bank. The weight of his coat and boots threatened to pull him under. Good God, how could either of the ladies manage with their skirts if he was having such difficulty? He fought against the heaviness with all his might while frantically scanning for a sign of Morgan.

Finally, about twenty feet away, he saw them: Miss Hathaway thrashing with the wildness of a trapped hellcat, holding tight to the unresponsive hand of his sister. Despite the ferocity of her kicks, she made no progress. If anything, the two women were heading the opposite direction from what she intended. With all her flailing, they were sinking in an almost whirlpool-like manner instead of rising. What the devil was she thinking?

Aidan swam toward the chaos, the water closing over his head as he dove beneath the surface. When he reached them, he fought through Miss Hathaway's flapping limbs and ripped the fingers of her death-grip from Morgan's arm. She kicked again, sending a foot into his gullet. She reached for him, her fingers desperately seeking purchase in her panic and scratching his arm and face in the process.

She'd be the death of them all if he couldn't contain her hysteria.

He pushed her away with a solid shove toward the surface. Then he wrapped his arm around Morgan's waist and followed after her.

When he broke through, a painful gasp refilled his lungs. Aidan swam for the shore, holding Morgan above the water with one arm and willing her to breathe. A series of shouts and splashes sounded behind him as David reached Miss Hathaway and dragged her to the embankment. Seconds later, David's wife reached the two of them, and then Niall took hold of Morgan's arm to pull her free of the water.

Aidan coughed back tears and river water as he sat on the bank. He draped his sister's unresponsive form over his lap. Her empty eyes stared back at him.

No breath. No sound. No movement.

No life.

Gone. How could she be gone? How could he have allowed it to happen?

Niall sank to his knees before them and cupped Morgan's face in his hands.

A crowd had gathered, as the entire house party had apparently followed after him. Servants rushed through the crowd, carrying blankets. A few feet away, Miss Hathaway spluttered, relieving her lungs of the muddy water. She gasped for breath, but all he could see was her teeth—big, white teeth surrounded by mud and muck.

If *she* had acted more quickly…if *she* had alerted him to Morgan's departure instead of running off alone and attempting a rescue of which she was both incompetent and incapable, none of this would have happened. Morgan would still be alive. Breathing. Warm and safe inside.

That damned girl killed my sister.

Aidan glared across at her, filling his gaze with every ounce of rage and fear and grief and pain that had filled his life these four months, blaming the girl though in truth the blame rested elsewhere.

He needed someone to fault other than himself. Someone. Something.

Anything.

Lady Burington draped a blanket over the shivering Miss Hathaway's shoulders. In his mind, Aidan set it aflame, permanently affixing the image in his mind like a piece of artwork. Even that would not serve as justice for his loss. It wasn't enough. It would never be enough.

Then, inexplicably, Morgan's body jerked in his arms. Aidan's focus lurched back to his sister. Another movement. A flood of water left her mouth, followed by a series of violent, wracking coughs. Her vacant eyes looked first to Niall, then to Aidan as they filled with desperate tears.

She was alive. Morgan was *alive*. Thank God in heaven.

She slowly shook her head, an almost imperceptible motion. Her mouth formed a word, but no sound came out as her eyes bored holes through his. Tears streamed a jagged path down her river-stained cheeks.

"Why?"

CHAPTER ONE

July, 1819

With a somber mien befitting the memories held within, the butler showed Emma Hathaway into the drawing room at Heathcote Park. "If you'll excuse me, miss, I'll inform the lord and lady of the manor of your arrival."

Emma gave him a brief nod, and he backed out of the room. A timid young maid replaced him in the doorway a moment later. She set a tea service on the table, dipped into a curtsey, and then scurried away.

After an agonizing glance out the bay window, Emma scanned the room—the one which had haunted her dreams for many years now, and which showed no sign of ceasing that very activity.

A gradual but thorough change had overtaken the space, and likewise much of the great house, since Emma's sister, Vanessa, had become the mistress of the manor. Now, almost everything inside it was different than it had been upon her arrival—and certainly different than it had been three years ago.

Emma hadn't seen any of the changes take place, herself. She hadn't returned to the Park since that summer. She had only learned of the changes in her sister's letters.

This coming fortnight would mark the first occasion anyone

besides the Burington family and their servants, and now Emma, would step foot inside the room in three years.

Even just walking inside it brought back the rush of memories, the great ache in her chest from all that had happened—an ache that always had her gasping for breath, as though she was being pulled below water again. Perhaps enough change had taken place to erode the abhorrent memories from the minds of most. Surely, that had been Vanessa's intent in making the changes.

Emma doubted anything could ever wash the memory from her own mind. The images were too stark. Too all-encompassing and bitter. The events from that summer were etched in a sea of gray upon the backs of her eyelids, it seemed, haunting her any time she tried to close her eyes and rest. Yet Vanessa had tried to effect enough changes to make this summer's house party at least bearable.

The dainty, too-easily-broken Louis XIV chairs and matching spindly-legged tables were gone, replaced by sturdier mahogany bergère chairs with plush blue and cream cushions—sturdy enough that careless men could likely not shatter them so easily. Scattered near each grouping of chairs, one could find gaming tables, tea tables, quartetto tables, and writing tables, all made of the same solid wood. All designed not only for aesthetics but for durability.

Gone, too, were the elaborate plaster chimney piece and rococo designs which Lady Morgan had so often stared upon that summer as she whiled away the time trapped inside her mind. In their stead, a mural of an autumnal country landscape covered one wall while family portraits dotted the rest of the room, accompanied by framed swatches of embroidery—no doubt stitched by Vanessa. Simple yet elegant mahogany woodwork now adorned the hearth. Though the memories were far from eradicated from Emma's mind, the changes somehow soothed her frayed nerves as she inspected them. It was an odd sensation—not quite at peace, but not as anxiety-inducing as it would have been, had Vanessa made the endeavor.

A bird flew past the bay window, casting its shadow upon the walls and lifting up to the ceiling. Emma's eyes followed the shadow's path. Even the ceiling had undergone a transformation; the ornate plasterwork had been removed and, in its place, it had been painted to look like a cloudy sky, as was all the crack in Town these days. Vanessa had written, upon making this final alteration, that she wanted no reminders of that fateful day three years before. Not for herself. Not for her husband. Not for Emma or any other guest who had been present.

The only thing, as far as Emma could tell, that hadn't changed at all was the Parquet flooring. Since it was already both elegant and serviceable, she supposed there had been no reason for alteration. The Aubusson rugs covering it, however, had been replaced with others to suit the blues and creams which now adorned the walls and the upholstery.

There had been no single moment of transformation according to Vanessa's letters. In the three years since the first and only house party she and David had hosted, Vanessa had simply placed more touches of herself—of the quiet, reserved manner in which the two sisters had been reared—into that room, in particular, and into Heathcote Park as a whole.

Standing here now, so far removed from the dark moment in time she'd prefer to forget, Emma was baffled that almost nothing remained of the frilly, overly opulent décor.

And yet the view outside the great bay window remained untouched. The estuary, which had been the scene of the strongest, most violent parts of the memories, remained thoroughly unchanged—a permanent reminder of all she'd tried so desperately to banish from her memory. Emma supposed only God himself could rearrange that scene. She couldn't very well expect Vanessa and David to rip out the River Exe and build an orangery in its place, after all. If such a feat were humanly possible, she had every reason to expect they would have undertaken the task with similar vigor to that required for the transformation of the manor house.

As though to ward off the biting chill of the river, Emma hugged her arms over her chest and gave her back to both the bay window and the memory. She filled a cup with steaming tea from the service, adding two sugars and just a drop of cream. On such a pleasantly warm day, no fire burned behind the fire screen, but positioning herself there she could avoid looking out the window—something she would prefer to do at all costs—as she waited for her sister's arrival. She sat on the settee by the hearth. With a sigh, she sifted through her reticule for the book she'd brought along for the journey. *Waverley*, again. She'd already read it a dozen times or more, but beggars couldn't be choosers.

A dog's bark momentarily drew her attention outside. The hound raced along the open yard and then out of sight. How odd—she didn't think David had any dogs as pets here at Heathcote Park. Perhaps she'd been mistaken.

Emma pulled her legs up beneath her in a thoroughly unladylike fashion, leaned back, and opened the book to where she'd left off. Edward Waverley had just been accused of both desertion and treason. Highly troublesome, that, particularly since it meant he was to be arrested. Within moments, she was lost in the Highlands again.

"Good Lord in heaven, Emma, you should be thankful David didn't walk in here before I did," Vanessa said.

The intrusion stopped Emma's reading just as Waverley arrived at Holyrood Palace to meet with Bonnie Prince Charlie. She replaced the ribbon between the pages to mark her spot and grinned up at her sister.

Vanessa frowned in return. "I can see half your legs, at least."

"David wouldn't care one whit if he saw my legs. They aren't nearly as shapely or nice to look upon as yours."

"That's hardly the point."

"No." Emma set the book beside her cold, forgotten cup of tea and stood, smoothing her skirt back into its proper place. "But it amuses me to see you in pique."

Vanessa narrowed her eyes, taking obvious pains to keep all trace of amusement from her expression but failing spectacularly. Then she stopped trying and smiled. "You arrived sooner than we expected. I suppose your travel was favorable? David is still meeting with his secretary, and I was in the nursery with Patrick and Danielle when Baxter informed me you were here." She crossed the room and pulled Emma into a full hug, then tugged her down to the settee again. "I miss you."

With a half-smile, Emma pushed against her sister's shoulder. "No one held a pistol to your head and forced you to marry David, you know. *You* left *me* to marry a peer, not the other way around."

"And I made Mama and Father very happy in the process," Vanessa said. Her brown eyes lost a touch of their glimmer. "How are they? I've been worried since the end of the Season. Mama just seemed so…frail, I suppose. Weary."

"Not to mention Father was too indisposed to even accompany us to Town." Emma looked her sister in the eye. "They're both so worried about me, about what will happen to me when they can't—"

Emma cut herself off, pressing her lips together and pinching the bridge of her nose. Saying the words aloud was too much. Her heart broke just thinking of all they had sacrificed to give her a better life, a chance at all of the things they had never had. She closed her eyes for a moment to regain her composure.

"I can't allow them to keep doing this. Mama took me to London for the Season when clearly it was too much for her. She tried to insist on coming with me here this summer, even if Father wasn't well enough to look after himself." Emma choked back a sob, then pressed on. She had to get through this. "If David hadn't sent Fanny with the carriage to accompany me here, Mama would surely have come along, even though Doctor Cary has forbidden Father from being out of bed for more than a few hours a day and he needs her assistance."

Vanessa's eyes widened. "It's that bad? In your letters…"

"He's coughing up blood." Which was not something Emma cared to ever put in a letter. If it were written down, it would be more real. More permanent.

Vanessa took Emma's hand and squeezed, lacing their fingers

together as they had done as girls. "So now what?"

Emma fought down her tears. This was not the time for crying. There were far more important things to be done. "So now I find a way to ease their worries."

Vanessa opened her mouth to speak, so Emma rushed on.

"I know you're going to offer to let me stay here, but that's not what I want. I've been a burden on Mama and Father for far too long. I have no intention of becoming a burden on you instead of them. You have children of your own now, and David to look after…"

Vanessa pursed her lips—a habit neither of them had managed to break—no doubt learned from watching Mama. After a moment, Vanessa gave a brisk nod. "Very well. If you won't come live with us, what will you do?"

"I've thought about becoming a governess. It would be a good way for me to use the few skills I do possess in a productive manner." All her reading had to be good for something other than just her enjoyment.

A wry smile greeted that pronouncement. "You know Father would be loath to allow you to go into service. That would hardly set him at ease, Em."

"I know. Which is why I intend to find a husband. During this house party." *Somehow.* The actual 'how' of the operation might prove to be difficult, particularly since Emma didn't even know which gentlemen her sister and brother-in-law had invited to their gathering. And then there was the fact that she was as comfortable in social settings as an elephant would be drinking from a miniature china teacup designed for a doll.

She used her eyes to plead with her sister. It had always worked, since they were very little. "But I need your help. I'm always so awkward and clumsy. I don't know how to do my hair in the ways that will attract a man's attention. I always say the wrong things at the worst times."

"Or if you don't know what to say, you trip over your own feet to distract everyone," Vanessa said wryly.

Emma cringed. "You make it sound like I do it intentionally."

"Oh, you don't?" Vanessa chided. "It's become such a habit, it's like an illness."

"A pox."

"The Black Death."

Emma wrinkled her nose. "No, I don't think the plague works in this situation. It's more like it's something that is on me. Something I can't get rid of, no matter how hard I try to wash it away. Something you can see, like leprosy. Like my enormous teeth."

Vanessa frowned gently. "They aren't *that* big."

"They're horse teeth. The only thing that makes them look like they could possibly be appropriately sized is the length of my nose."

Never in her life would she understand how she could be so long and gangly everywhere but Vanessa could be so perfectly elegant in every way, and yet they came from the same two parents. The differences between the two had only become more pronounced now that Vanessa had given birth to two of her own children. Her breasts had plumped nicely, and her hips had rounded delicately, and she looked like the perfect example of English beauty. But Emma? Still a giant stick.

"Have you ever looked at a horse's teeth up close?" With a rueful smile, Vanessa chuckled. "I think you might be a wee-bit prone to exaggeration."

"All the same, the point is I need you. Will you help me?"

"I will," Vanessa said without even a moment's hesitation. "But only if you promise to try your very best to make yourself amenable to the gentlemen I've invited. You can't just sit in the corner with a book the way you've always done in the past."

Emma placed her right hand over her heart. "I solemnly swear." She even managed to avoid bursting out in a gale of laughter upon saying it. Likely because she truthfully was earnest about finding a husband this time, whereas she hadn't ever been before. Every last bit of what she'd said was now of the direst import, even though she had as much natural appeal for a gentleman as a goat would.

A corner of Vanessa's mouth turned downward. "I suppose Fanny already helped you settle in to your rooms? She's to serve as your lady's maid while you're here."

"Oh, but—"

A severely arched brow from her sister was enough to silence Emma.

"None of that, now. All of the other ladies will bring their own maids. It won't do for you to be left out. Particularly since you're in need of help with arranging your hair, as you've already mentioned." Vanessa looked pointedly at the limp mass hanging indolently over Emma's shoulders. "Not to mention David wouldn't hear of allowing you to go without, whether anyone else was visiting or not."

She had a point. David had made a valiant effort since marrying her sister to be certain Emma had the best of everything—as long as he wasn't stepping on Father's toes in order to provide it.

"Fine. Fanny can arrange my hair."

A broad smile lit Vanessa's warm, brown eyes. "Excellent. Now, moving on to the rest of the fortnight, I think we should enlist the help of—"

Before she could finish her thought, David knocked at the open door and poked his head inside. "Sorry to interrupt, but the first of our guests have arrived." He moved into the room and helped Vanessa to her feet, kissing her lightly on the cheek.

"I'd say the *first* of our guests arrived almost an hour ago," Vanessa pointed out.

David winked a brilliant green eye at Emma, then offered his hand to assist her. "Emma's not a guest. She's family."

When she stood, he leaned over and planted a similar kiss on her cheek. His sandy-brown hair fell down over an eye and tickled her skin.

"Such flattery," Emma said with a laugh. The ladies of the *ton* were lucky he was already married. The man could devastate a room with a smile. A wink was likely to cause heart palpitations amongst the lesser-prepared debutantes.

"Such *unnecessary* flattery," Vanessa countered. "My husband fails to recognize he won your eternal devotion upon promising to add a proper library to Heathcote Park and stock it to the brim."

Not just any 'proper library,' either. David had set Emma's heart aflutter with tales of books lining every wall of the room from floor to ceiling, of bookcases scattered amongst cozy chairs, and even of a rotating, circular bookcase near the entry filled with her very favorite stories. It was all she could do not to salivate at the thought.

David held out one arm for each of them to hold and guided their way out of the drawing room toward the front entry hall. "Speaking of which, it's finished. Perhaps I can give you a tour after supper?"

"I'd like that very much," Emma replied. She'd like it more to have her tour now but doubted David would share that opinion. He could be a bit of a stickler about things like greeting one's guests promptly upon their arrival. Spoilsport.

They moved past the marbled spiral staircase with iron balusters shaped like lyres and into the main foyer. Baxter signaled for the footmen to swing the doors wide.

"I thought your guests weren't due to arrive until tomorrow afternoon," Emma said. Her brow furrowed in thought. Vanessa wrote that Emma was to arrive on Sunday and the others would arrive on Monday. There had been church bells ringing this morning.

David winked. "Most of them aren't." He led the ladies through the doors and down the stairs to the flagstone entryway lined by a pea-gravel drive. Turning in from the main road, two carriages rolled carefully along, gradually coming into view. Emma immediately recognized the crests they proudly bore as well as the spotless scarlet and silver livery worn by the coachmen.

A faint sense of panic clutched at Emma's chest. "The Earl of Trenowyth?" She looked past David to glare at her sister, who was studiously avoiding her gaze on his other side. Vanessa ought to have warned her. She knew—she absolutely, unequivocally *knew*—that Emma would not have come if there were any inkling of a chance that the Cardiff family would be in attendance.

Vanessa appeared disinclined to answer the unasked question hanging in the air between them.

Emma caught David's eye. "Has anyone accompanied Lord Trenowyth? I do not believe I have seen anyone from the family out in society since…since…"

"Since three years ago? No, I'm sure you haven't."

The carriages pulled to a stop before them, and one of the outriders leapt down from the lead conveyance to set out the steps.

David pulled Vanessa and Emma forward—*pulled* being a disconcertingly literal description of the proceedings, at least on Emma's part, as her feet had suddenly turned to tree roots and her legs to trunks.

"None of the family has been away from Tavistock Manor since then," David continued rather stoically, "other than brief trips into town for provisions and the like. Even then, they've usually sent servants out instead. But they've all decided to begin their reintroduction to social life here."

"All?" Emma squeaked. The panic clutching her chest was no longer merely a faint hint; she felt like she was being crushed between two massive boulders and couldn't sink her nails into anything in order to claw her way out.

"Well, not quite all, I should say," David amended. He lifted a hand in greeting as Lord Trenowyth, the first passenger, descended from the carriage.

In that scant moment, Emma regained her breath. Not quite all of the family had come. Perhaps the odious Mr. Cardiff had better ways to spend his summer than glaring at her from across rooms and making her feel as infinitesimal and welcome as a splinter in the ball of his foot.

David winked at her as Lord Trenowyth waved a hand in their direction in greeting. If he had any sense of her discomfiture, David would have refrained from winking in such a circumstance—it simply caused her to wish to rip his arms from their sockets before running to hide in her chamber, never to return.

"The dowager chose to pay a visit to her cousin in Shropshire instead of attending our little gathering," David said, smiling cheerily, as though there couldn't be a lovelier scenario in all the world than the one currently smacking Emma in the face repeatedly. "She thinks such amusements are better spent on the younger generations." With that, he dropped the arms of both Emma and Vanessa and moved forward to welcome his guests.

When he was safely out of earshot, Emma glared at her sister. "You knew."

"Of course I knew. Mr. Cardiff is David's longest friend. They've been nearly inseparable since Eton. Or they had been until—"

"Until three years ago, yes," Emma said heatedly, cutting her sister off with a dismissive wave of her hand. "But you didn't *tell* me."

A great sigh hefted from Vanessa's chest and she closed her eyes—as certain a sign of a heavenward plea for patience as Emma had ever seen from her sister, though she had seen it countless times from Mama. "You wouldn't have come." Vanessa's matter-of-fact words hung heavily in the air between them as she headed over to the carriage. Emma's eyes followed the same path her sister had just taken.

Mr. Cardiff had stepped out, every strapping, sardonic inch of him, causing nausea to roil within Emma's stomach from her panic. His presence could only mean her nightmares would now come true. For the briefest moment, his mocking blue eyes locked with hers. A flash of revulsion shone in them before being replaced by his usual haughty disdain and the ever-present, smug half-smile he always bore—one which claimed knowledge of just a splash more than everyone else.

Before his presence could affect her any more deeply than it already had, Emma cut her eyes away from him to stare blandly at the scene. She refused to grant him the satisfaction of knowing just how much power he held over her, simply from existing.

He turned back to the carriage. A delicate, gloved hand reached out and took his before halting footsteps descended the stairs in painstaking fashion. Emma tried to ignore the animosity pouring toward her in waves from Mr. Cardiff so she could instead focus on meeting Lady Morgan again.

In that summer, before the incident at the river, Emma and Lady Morgan had struck up an odd friendship of sorts. It would be refreshing to renew it over the next fortnight. Not as invigorating as it might have been without her brother's presence, perhaps, but stimulating nonetheless. And if Lady Morgan's impending return to society was any indication, perhaps the fit of the blue devils that had held her in its grasp for so long had finally relinquished its hold.

Emma certainly hoped so.

Once free from the shadow of the carriage, Lady Morgan took a cautious step forward, holding on to her brother's arm as a lifeline. Her travelling bonnet obscured her face from view at first, but then she stepped into a wide swath of sun between the drive and the main house. A flood of angry, red marks covered her visage, spreading in patches from her forehead to her neck and spanning from ear to ear, standing out against her pale, porcelain skin.

Emma could not contain her gasp. Mr. Cardiff's head snapped up at the sound, his long, sandy hair whipping around where it peeked free from beneath his beaver hat. If sheer hatred could commit murder, she would be dead where she stood. Lady Morgan either hadn't heard Emma's ill-mannered outburst of shock or chose to ignore it. She held her brother's arm as he guided her along to greet first David, then Vanessa.

Mortification stronger than Emma had ever known seized her. How callous she'd been mere moments earlier, comparing her teeth to leprosy and her social ineptitude to a pox. Worse yet, Vanessa hadn't stopped her. She had neither scolded her for her callow insensitivity nor given any indication of what Emma should expect. Vanessa had simply allowed Emma to dig herself into a mammoth pit of unfeeling amusement.

Lesson learned.

Forcing her feet into motion, Emma stumbled forward to join the rest of the group. Lord Trenowyth stepped up to her, and she mumbled an incoherent greeting. Removing her gaze from Lady Morgan was fast proving to be a sincerely difficult task. Not because of the scars covering her. Not any longer.

As Lady Morgan spoke with Vanessa, the path of the young woman's eyes lay somewhere in the vicinity of Vanessa's hair. They held a faraway, clouded expression, as though she wasn't seeing Vanessa at all. Or, perhaps, as though she didn't see *anything* at all.

Emma's jaw dropped, but she quickly snapped it closed. Mr. Cardiff's eyes shot to her with newfound fury.

That couldn't be. Could it? How could she be blind? Emma's chest tightened unbearably.

Vanessa turned to her, guiding Lady Morgan's free hand to take the one Emma held extended. "I'm sure, Mr. Cardiff and Lady Morgan, you'll both remember my sister, Miss Hathaway."

"I can't forget, no matter how much I've tried." Mr. Cardiff's muttered words were filled with acid and vitriol. His cold, blue eyes pierced through her, making her feel as though she had no clothes on to protect her from his raving gaze.

"Miss Hathaway." A smile lit Lady Morgan's features, though it stretched her scarred skin. The smile did, however, ease some of the opacity of her eyes.

She released Vanessa's hand and reached out for Emma. Her gloved fingers explored Emma's hand, as though memorizing the size and shape, learning the contours. Emma had never experienced the like, and she trembled ever so slightly, more unnerved than she would care to admit, beneath the lady's examination. Lady Morgan's stare remained fixed at some point seemingly behind Emma's head.

"I must admit," Lady Morgan continued, her voice tinkling like chimes in a soft breeze, "I was undecided about attending the Buringtons' house party this summer until Lady Burington wrote and assured me you would also be in attendance. Once I learned that, I couldn't possibly refuse." Her voice was haunting in its familiarity, particularly since little of her appearance remained as before.

Her brother grunted at her side, though his expression remained unchanged. Irate. Loathsome. Jeering. Just as he'd always been in Emma's presence, only intensified ten-fold because of his proximity—usually, she only felt his rage from across a crowded room.

She wondered briefly what he must be thinking. The corner of his lip jerked when she stared at him a bit too long, and his eyes narrowed upon her before flashing over to his sister in agitation.

"I'm pleased to see you again as well, Lady Morgan," Emma stammered. "It has been a very long time."

"Too long." The gentle, blonde-haired lady squeezed Emma's hand before dropping her hold on Mr. Cardiff's arm. She took up the same grip on Emma and, with slight pressure, urged her to turn. "Might you and I go for a promenade? I should like to take some exercise after a day spent in the carriage, and it is quite pleasant out today."

"Morgan," Mr. Cardiff interrupted, his voice low and steely, "I think it would be best for you to settle in your room, first. Your *maid* can take you for a walk through the park later. Don't you agree, Niall?"

Without waiting for Lord Trenowyth's response, Mr. Cardiff took hold of Lady Morgan's arm and guided her into the house. The earl followed close behind, as a contingent of servants unloaded trunks from the carriages and carted them inside. The waiting housekeeper directed the Cardiff family to their respective chambers, leaving Emma staring after the lot of them, dumbfounded, mouth agape, and shaken to her core.

Emma felt Vanessa move up behind her.

"You didn't warn me. About any of it. You never said a word. Not even when I got here, when I was making a fool of myself, comparing my problems to those of a leper."

"No."

Emma's eyes filled with hot, ashamed tears. She spun to face her sister. "Why?"

Vanessa pursed her lips and her shoulders slumped. "You wouldn't have come." She made her way up the stairs with David at her side. When she reached the top, she turned around to look at Emma again. "It's been long enough. You've got to face what happened. All of you."

CHAPTER TWO

"You may take Lady Morgan for a brief excursion through the grounds once she has settled in," Aidan said to his sister's nursemaid. "No longer than a half hour, though. I don't wish to overtire her."

Janetta bobbed a brief curtsey. "Yes, Mr. Cardiff."

They stood in the corridor outside Morgan's assigned chamber—on the opposite side of the house from the river, just as Aidan had insisted upon. Not that Morgan could see the water, but she'd undoubtedly hear it. He wanted no reminders for her of what had taken place before.

Almost as an afterthought, he added, "Don't go near the water. Keep her to the other side of the property." Morgan hadn't attempted to harm herself in more than two-and-a-half years, but Aidan saw no reason to tempt fate. "Perhaps today, you should limit her to a walk through the maze to the east of the house. If she wants to explore further than that, I'll take her tomorrow."

The little maid dipped her head and timidly excused herself to return to her mistress's rooms.

After a moment's hesitation of warring with himself over whether to inform Janetta he had changed his mind and would see to escorting his sister outside himself, Aidan spun on his heel and marched through the hall. He had to let go. He had to begin to trust Morgan's sanity again, even if he could only take a small step toward that end at a time.

At the main staircase, he made his way down and headed for David's study. His friend might not be there, but Aidan had no doubt he'd find a good whiskey in the sideboard. Few things in his life could ease the rage which always bubbled under his skin in quite the way a dose of spirits could.

Niall had been right, though it pained Aidan to admit it. They couldn't hover over Morgan constantly; it would only serve to leave them all anxious and Morgan agitated with their interference. She wanted them to trust her. She wanted them to believe she was right-minded now and would not fall into a vast pit of despair as she had done before. She wanted them all to believe, herself included, that she could navigate the world without the aid of her eyes, that she could live her life as it was meant to be lived.

Aidan wanted to believe it, too. Desperately. He'd promised her years ago he would never give up on her, and yet how could he trust her to be all right after all that had happened? The one time he ought to have been unfailingly at her side, he'd left her behind again.

The only way any of them would find out for certain if she truly *could* live a normal life, though, would be to leave Morgan to do as she wished from time to time—or at least with only a servant to assist her when necessary.

Doing so at Tavistock Manor had been nerve-wracking enough, but Morgan had quickly proven herself adept at getting around with the aid of her maid or a walking stick, once she'd learned to count her steps and recognize the feel of things. But now, she wanted to go somewhere other than her home and to be around people again. Around society. Around vain twits like the vexatious Miss Hathaway, who apparently could not bear to see Morgan's scars without gasping in abject horror.

Aidan grumbled something unintelligible even to himself beneath his breath. Just before reaching a side door which led to the rose garden, he pushed open David's study. Empty, as expected, but the credenza was well stocked. Leaving the door ajar in case David wished to join him, he located a tumbler and pulled the cork on the nearest bottle, then sniffed the contents. Rich, aged whiskey. Perfect. He poured a full glass and threw it back, dispatching it in a stinging swallow, then filled it again.

It would take much more than a few shots of whiskey to remove the revolted expression that had covered every blessed inch of Miss Hathaway's face from his memory. With one look, a brief moment of at most a second, every ounce of fury Aidan felt toward this woman, fury which he had kept suppressed over the last three years, came crashing back to the surface with the force of a gale.

Somehow, Aidan's ire toward her felt all the more powerful now than it had before. It was as though all the traumas that had befallen his sweet sister were Miss Hathaway's fault, at least in some twisted manner in his mind.

Not just the incident at the river, but before that summer, when Morgan had thrown herself before a racing carriage in the hopes she would be trampled to death. Alas, Morgan hadn't even met Miss Hathaway yet, so his reaction was entirely unfounded.

But he also blamed her for that time after the river, when Morgan had ripped leafy spurge from the ground and ate it, desperately wishing that it was water hemlock and would be enough to finish her off, and yet unaware that she'd selected the wrong poison.

They had been fortunate that the poisonous plant had not been lethal; however, Morgan's eating it had caused her to collapse into the lot of it, and its sap had left her scarred and blind.

Aidan took another swallow of whiskey and carried his glass with him to the window. David's study looked out over the rose gardens, where a number of lush red and sunny yellow blooms still blossomed, despite the lateness of the season.

How terribly unfair. On Morgan's last visit to Heathcote Park, the sun had never peeked out from behind menacing clouds and heavy fog. The world had been cast beneath a dismal, gray blanket until it felt as though it would never change. The beauty of the place had been tarnished by the year without a summer, and now, when nature had returned to its usual heavenly glory, she couldn't experience it. She couldn't see how the colors of the flowers were bursting with life, or watch a sunset turn the sky first to flame, then pale gold, then soft rose.

For a moment, Aidan's hand itched to pick up a pastel and capture the scene outside the window. It only lasted a moment, though, because then he remembered that he could never share his creations with Morgan again, that she could never experience his artwork for herself. That was why his pastels had become so grim, so gruesome. So rage-filled. He wanted to take his pain out on the one who'd caused it. Instead, he merely drew and shaded what he wished would happen.

It was never enough. *He* could never be enough.

David cleared his throat in the doorway, and Aidan turned to him.

"I thought I'd find you here." David crossed into the study and poured himself a glass, scrutinizing the decanter before taking a swig. "Excellent choice, if I do say so myself."

"That's why I came this summer." There was no masking the droll tone of his voice. "I can always count on you to have the highest quality in everything."

"Don't lie. You're here because you still can't stand to allow Morgan out of your sight—no matter that she seems to be fine now—and *she* is intent on getting out into the world again."

"Fair enough," Aidan conceded. "Allowing her to attempt to live life again has presented the lot of us with quite the riddle to solve."

"At least she's alive to make the attempt," David muttered.

Aidan blanched. Did David believe he wished Morgan had died?

He eyed Aidan quizzically and took another sip from his glass. "Your mother seems to have no such qualms. She's off in Shropshire. I'd say the countess is ready for Morgan to move on with her life."

Being ready for Morgan to move on was only half the tale. "Either that or Mother can't face the possibility that we've all been duped into believing Morgan is…believing she…" Blast, it was so hard to put things in words.

"That she won't try to hurt herself again?"

A clatter sounded in the hallway, and glass hit the floor. An altogether-too-familiar feminine voice followed—the voice belonging to the very woman who had fueled his art for the last three years—and the cords in his neck tightened until he thought his veins might explode.

"Drat."

A fortnight in Miss Hathaway's company would prove far too long for Aidan to maintain any semblance of cordiality if the mere sound of her voice was enough to set his teeth on edge. David caught Aidan's eye and scowled at him before stepping out into the hall.

He must not have hidden his reaction to the chit's reappearance well. He remained near the credenza and sipped from his glass, waiting for her to go on her way so he could drink in peace.

"Oh, David, I was hoping you'd be down here," Miss Hathaway said amongst the clunking of curios and trinkets being replaced on the table just outside the study door.

"Let me help you with this."

"I'm just so clumsy all the time," she murmured.

David laughed—a genuine laugh, which left Aidan seething even more. How could anyone feel anything but rage whilst in Miss Hathaway's presence?

"Perhaps if you watched where you were going instead of trying to read and walk at the same time…"

Precisely the damned problem. Or one of many.

Aidan filled his glass from the decanter again and took a long swallow. This would be an absurdly long two weeks. At least others would arrive tomorrow. Maybe he could find a way to avoid Miss Hathaway—and to keep Morgan away from her as well. Surely there would be other young ladies present, others better suited to befriending his sister.

"Oh, dear. I must have broken this one."

Much as she would break his sister again, if given the chance.

"Don't worry about it, Emma. Why were you looking for me?"

"Oh. Well. I had hoped you would take me to the new library. If you're not busy, of course. I know you said we could do it after supper, but Vanessa suggested you might have time now, and since Mr. Cardiff seems so wholly opposed to me spending any time with Lady Morgan today…"

Aidan couldn't fail to notice the derisive tone her voice took on at that last bit. He slammed his glass on the sideboard and marched across the room. When he reached the doorway, he crossed his arms over his chest, stepped into the corridor, and glowered at the repugnant girl.

She jumped back at his appearance, her brown eyes rounding as far as they could go. "Oh, I…I'm sorry, I…"

David passed a look between them, his eyes flashing with annoyance when they fell upon Aidan, and then he turned to Miss Hathaway. "I'd be glad to take you to the library and give you a tour." His tone had gentled. How was David so bloody well in control of his reactions around her? "Why don't you wait for me in the drawing room? I'll fetch you in a few moments. I just need to finish a word with Mr. Cardiff."

She dipped her head. "Of course. If you'll excuse me." Before either of them could respond, she scurried off down the hall again.

Aidan wasn't sorry to see her go, yet he couldn't stop himself from admiring her retreating form. Good God, when had she gone from being as straight as a tree trunk to having the curves of a woman? And why the devil was he noticing it?

When she had disappeared around the corner at the end of the hall, David spun around and shoved a finger into Aidan's chest. "You *will* remember that Miss Hathaway is my wife's sister and accordingly treat her with the appropriate level of respect."

Aidan rubbed the back of his neck. That stung, coming from David, because they'd learned to behave as gentlemen together. They'd gone to school together, taken their Grand Tours together— become men together. And David would never dream of treating

Morgan with anything less than the utmost respect. "I didn't say anything."

"No, but you said plenty when you arrived. And your eyes just now said far more than you would ever dare to say with words in my presence." David took a breath and let it out slowly. "I have never understood your animosity toward her, and I never—"

"You just—"

David held up a hand and scowled. "Allow me to make myself quite plain. I will not tolerate your behavior. If you cannot find a way to comport yourself in a civil manner with regard to my sister-in-law, or *any* of my guests, you will have to leave."

"In that case, I'll take Morgan with me."

"I said you would have to leave. Morgan is free to stay." David crossed his arms over his chest. "It will be her choice, just as living her life is. Trenowyth will remain, so there is no reason she must go just because you're incapable of behaving as anything other than an arse."

Morgan would never leave with him if given the choice, should he be forced to go. Aidan held no doubt on that score. This was her first foray into society in years, her first attempt to test herself and see how she could get along. He couldn't bear the thought of leaving her behind. He wouldn't be able to watch over her, to guarantee her safety.

That couldn't happen. The family had all promised Morgan a fortnight of enjoyment. Two full weeks of diversions and entertainments, of not thinking about the past.

Well, he hoped she would not think of the past. That was the point of all of this, after all.

Despite the sharp stab of pain it caused his pride, Aidan nodded. "Understood."

"Good. Then I suspect we'll have no problems." David walked away, following the path clumsily blazed by Miss Hathaway moments before.

Aidan stood there for a long while. How could he tamp down the rage that built within him every time he saw Miss Hathaway's face or heard her voice? He would have to find a way.

This might prove to be a very long fortnight, indeed.

Emma took a sip of her chocolate the next morning and placed the cup back on the dining room table, cautious not to overturn anything. Perhaps overly cautious, but now was not the time to make a cake of herself again. She turned the page of her book as quickly as she dared, lest she rip the pages from the bindings.

Damaging the book would not do.

Almost before the page had been settled, her eyes were roving over the words as fast as they would go.

How dreadful, that Sir Walter Elliot and his family must let their estate! Emma had been far too close to similar circumstances in her own life. It felt entirely too real. The authoress, Miss Austen, had Emma hooked into the story, as usual.

Coming to the end of the page, she bent back the spine more than she'd intended in her haste to turn to new words. "Lud," she muttered, earning a snicker from the footman standing beside the door. She frowned up at him. He raised an eyebrow, almost daring her to comment on his reaction.

Instead, she returned her attention to the novel. Yesterday afternoon, she'd selected two from the library: *Mansfield Park* and *Persuasion*. *Mansfield Park* hadn't lasted her the night. Emma had finished with it before turning in to bed. She could quite possibly finish *Persuasion* before any of David and Vanessa's other guests arrived.

After reading about twenty more pages without pausing to take a bite, the footman snapped to attention and his austere expression returned, drawing Emma's notice. She set her book aside and took a now-frigid bite of shirred egg. Someone must be joining her, finally.

Sure enough, Lady Morgan came through the entryway to the

breakfast room with her maid on her arm.

"Good morning, Miss Hathaway," the maid said with a sweet smile. "We imagined most of the house would still be abed at this hour."

"Indeed, most of them are," Emma replied. She cast a surreptitious glance behind them as the maid helped Lady Morgan into a seat across from her. No one else followed. No Mr. Cardiff— at least not yet—and no Lord Trenowyth. Thank goodness. Emma didn't mind the earl overmuch, but she wasn't ready to face the cantankerous grump who was his brother today. It was far too early for such unpleasantness, and no amount of chocolate could ease the way. "Good morning to you both. Did you rest well, Lady Morgan?"

"Yes, quite," the blonde lady murmured with a slight smile, which she then turned in the general direction of her maid. "Thank you, Janetta."

Janetta took a seat beside her, and then she filled two mugs, gently nudging Lady Morgan's hand with one of them.

"Thank you." Taking the cup, Lady Morgan lifted it to her lips, giving a near-imperceptible sniff before drinking. "Oh, chocolate! How lovely." After swallowing a delicate sip, she sent a conspiratorial smile that brightened her features across in Emma's direction. "What book are you reading today, Miss Hathaway?"

Emma's jaw dropped. How could Lady Morgan possibly know she was reading?

Janetta chuckled. "I daresay you've surprised your friend, my lady."

Emma wanted to sink below the table and never be seen again, her mortification was so great. She wished she had somehow learned the art of schooling her features into perfect placidity. At this very moment, her cheeks were heating uncontrollably.

"You've not changed so much in these last few years that you aren't constantly absorbed in a book, have you?" Lady Morgan took another sip and held the dainty china cup between her hands as though warming herself on it. "I'll be highly disappointed if you aren't exactly as I left you."

Was that a hint of humor? If so, Emma may not have changed, but Lady Morgan certainly had. Emma forced her jaw to close. "*Persuasion*, today."

"I loved *Persuasion*. Janetta read it to me several months ago."

The footman placed two plates heaped with eggs, sausages, bread, and fresh fruit with clotted cream before the ladies. Ever-so-inconspicuously, Janetta guided Lady Morgan's right hand to the silver.

She grasped a fork and lifted a bite to her mouth. After she chewed and swallowed, she grinned at Emma again. "And yesterday? What did you read then?"

Emma couldn't contain her chuckle. "*Mansfield Park* last night."

"Only one book? You went an entire day and read only a single book? I'm shocked, Miss Hathaway."

"I started *Waverley* on the journey over and finished it not long after your arrival."

"That sounds more like the Miss Hathaway I remember," Lady Morgan said. She felt for a strawberry and picked it up, then searched her plate for the clotted cream to dip it into. Her movements were slow and meticulous, but also very studied. Not to mention impressive. Any time Emma had to move about in the dark, she invariably stubbed a toe on her bed or spilled water down the front of her nightrail. Lady Morgan didn't have even the tiniest hint of sight to aid her, though.

Heathcote Park's housekeeper poked her head around the doorway. "Oh, good. There you are, Miss Drummond," she said to Janetta. "One of the footmen suggested I might find you here."

"What is the problem, Mrs. Oldham?" The maid dabbed at the corners of her mouth with a napkin of fine silk.

"I was hoping we could discuss any needs your mistress might have this morning, before the house is overrun by the rest of His Lordship's guests."

"Of course." Janetta left her napkin beside her plate and pushed back from the table. "That sounds like an excellent plan. Lady Morgan, will you manage all right without me for a bit?"

"I'm fine. Go." Lady Morgan shooed Janetta with her a hand when the maid failed to leave immediately. "Miss Hathaway will assist me if I need anything. Won't you?"

"Of course," Emma said. She looked over at the hesitant lady's maid, who might actually be more of a nurse in this situation, and tried to offer a reassuring smile. "We'll do just fine on our own."

The maid vacillated for a moment longer, then she gave a brisk nod. "I'll be back shortly, my lady. Wait here for me, if you please."

"Go," Lady Morgan repeated on a laugh. The sound was soft and tinkling, even a bit melodic, like chimes in the wind. Emma couldn't remember ever hearing it before. Had she truly not laughed once during that entire fortnight so long ago?

When the door closed with a snick, Lady Morgan let out a long breath. "I was beginning to think she wouldn't leave me. They have all developed a tendency to hover, lately…especially my brothers. But the servants are no better."

"They are just worried about you, my lady," Emma said, hoping to reassure her.

"They've been worried for far too long. And please, just call me Morgan." She took another bite and spilled a bit from her fork onto her lap. She frowned and her brow furrowed. "Oh, fiddle."

Emma started to run around the table to assist her, but Morgan stayed her with a hand.

"I can manage. I've been managing for over two years. Something my brothers seem to conveniently forget more often than not."

Emma didn't know what to say to that. Surely Morgan recognized that they were only worried about her, that they only wanted what was best for her. Still, they might very well smother her with their assistance if they didn't learn to let go. Morgan seemed entirely capable of doing a great deal on her own, yet from what Emma could tell, someone was with her at every moment, coddling her along like a babe just learning to walk. Granted, she'd nearly done the same herself—but Morgan's family had been living with her all along. They ought to know what she could and couldn't do on her own.

"I'm sure it is quite vexing to never have a moment to yourself," Emma murmured for lack of anything more appropriate coming to mind. "If I'm to call you Morgan, you must call me Emma."

"Emma," Morgan said with a wide grin stretching her scarred features. "Well, this is delightful. I've not had a friend such as you for too long. Do you think tomorrow afternoon we might walk through the arbor? I know today will be filled with greeting the other guests and the like so there won't be time, but I should very much enjoy taking a walk with you tomorrow."

"Of course. If it is all right with your brothers, that is." The last thing Emma needed was for Mr. Cardiff to glare at her again for yet another unknown indiscretion. She couldn't very well attract an unsuspecting, eligible gentleman's notice with Mr. Cardiff looking daggers at her. It would give off a most definitively *wrong* impression.

Morgan frowned. "It will be. They'll be distracted with all of the house party goings-on. We can easily make our escape."

"Escape?" Emma said, laughing. "It sounds as though they might not be so accepting of our plans if we must escape."

Leaning across the table, Morgan lowered her voice conspiratorially. "Won't it be more exciting, though? I dreadfully need a little excitement in my life."

If the girl couldn't take two steps without someone racing to her assistance, Emma could well imagine that to be the case. "Indeed you do," she said slowly. In all the time of their acquaintance, Emma had never known Morgan to have anything worth becoming excited about in her life. Three years ago, she'd been so despondent.

She finished off the last few cold bites of her shirred eggs and followed it with a sip of her chocolate, all the while staring at her new friend across the table. Here, with the morning light coming through the eastern windows, her scars were more pronounced than ever— red and angry, so visible she could almost see the blisters which must have marred her skin. "Morgan?" she asked tentatively. Never, in a thousand lifetimes, should she dare to ask what she was about to. But she couldn't seem to stop herself. "What...what happened?"

"The scars and the blindness, you mean?" Morgan ate her last bite of sausage and wiped her mouth with a napkin. "The same as what happened here three years ago. Instead of trying to drown myself, I thought to try poison, but I picked the wrong weed."

Emma brushed back a tear. "Oh, heavens." All of this, because the man Morgan had loved had betrayed her? Emma racked her mind, trying to be certain that her memory would not fail her on this score. But that had been the cause—an intended who'd come home from the wars already married to another.

All the more reason Emma would never trust her own heart with a man until he was well and truly her husband. Too many ladies in her acquaintance had been left heartbroken because of fickle men.

"It seems I wasn't meant to die yet—three attempts, three failures. There were things I had yet to learn, I suppose. Life I had yet to live."

Three attempts? Emma bit the inside of her lower lip to keep from blurting out anything else untoward. Thank goodness Morgan couldn't see her expression, although it was entirely possible she might sense Emma's tension. Still, even though they were becoming friends again, the degree of their friendship was, as yet, rather tenuous.

She didn't want to push Morgan too far, too soon. Better to focus on those things they'd already begun discussing. "Does it hurt?"

"The scars? Not anymore." Morgan sipped from her cup of chocolate. "Not since a few weeks after that day. I'm sure it pains you more to look at me than it pains me to live with it."

"Oh, no. I—"

"It's all right." Morgan smiled tenuously. "You don't need to apologize for what you see. I did this to myself." Her voice was shy and gentle, and she dipped her head.

The door opened, and the devil himself walked through. His blistering gaze locked on Emma briefly, and her skin crawled with goose flesh. Mr. Cardiff turned his focus to Morgan, leaving Emma shivering in this wake of his stare.

"Mr. Cardiff," Emma whispered, dipping her head to avoid his gaze once more. The intensity of his blue eyes was mesmerizing, even when it was filled with his animosity.

"Good morning, Morgan. Miss Hathaway," he added tersely a moment later. Resentment heavily laced his tone when he said her name, but the hostility seemed to have left his eyes, at least for the time being. "Why has Janetta left you alone, Morgan?" he asked when he faced his sister again. His eyes narrowed to slits.

"I'm far from alone." A thin line creased Morgan's brow—the only outward sign of her frustration.

Emma doubted she knew she'd revealed that much. Likewise, she doubted Mr. Cardiff had noticed his sister's vexation. He certainly showed no indication that he'd noticed any change. Could he truly be so oblivious to his sister, while at the same time being so thoroughly unable to leave her to do things without his interference?

"Miss Hathaway has kept me company since Janetta was called away and has done an admirable job of it. The housekeeper needed to discuss things about my condition with Janetta before everyone else arrived. Surely you can understand the necessity for that."

Mr. Cardiff grunted but said nothing. He sat beside his sister. The footman cleared away Janetta's plate and replaced it with a newly-filled dish.

Before moving away from the table, the footman bowed to Emma. "May I bring you anything else, ma'am?"

She turned her empty plate aside and shook her head. Any thought of eating had fled along with her body heat the moment Mr. Cardiff entered the breakfast room. He'd also stolen her ability to think of anything to say. Why did being near him cause her heart to hammer and her tongue to twist? She felt like such a ninnyhammer. Emma stared at her hands folded together on her lap as the weight of the sudden silence pressed down on her shoulders.

Morgan did not speak, either, but continued to drink from her cup of chocolate.

Mr. Cardiff rapidly broke his fast, not pausing to speak or drink. He continued to stare across at Emma as he ate, the expression in his cold, blue eyes revealing a combination of exasperation and inquisitiveness. Emma felt his gaze more than saw it. He left her fighting off a series of shudders that threatened to overwhelm her because of how unnatural they felt. It wasn't fear or anger causing them. She didn't quite know what it was, other than decidedly unnerving.

Within a few, short minutes, he had finished. He turned to his sister and placed the tips of his fingers on the back of her hand. "Well, shall we begin our day?" He stood and took Morgan's hand, attempting to help her rise.

"Janetta asked me to wait for her here. I shouldn't leave."

Mr. Cardiff scowled fiercely, but his tone remained light. "I'll take you to her. She won't be cross with you for joining her. I'm sure the housekeeper might have some questions that you could answer better than Janetta could, anyway."

Morgan sighed. "Very well." She allowed her brother to assist her to her feet. When they reached the door, Morgan stopped and turned back to Emma. "I look forward to your company again later today—if I am to enjoy it, that is." Her tone was hopeful.

Emma would deny Morgan nothing, but she wasn't so certain about Mr. Cardiff's intentions. She glanced at the gentleman before responding. A muscle jerked in his cheek, but he remained silent.

There could be no doubt—he hated this. He hated every blessed moment of this interaction. She felt it pouring out of his skin and working its way through the thick air toward her, like a serpent slithering toward its prey.

Why was he so angry at her? Never in her life would she understand what she could have possibly done to engender such distaste.

Yet, despite her disquiet from being near him, she couldn't help but admire his tenacity in protecting his sister. True, he was taking things too far in his desire to see her safe. Emma couldn't imagine what he thought keeping Emma and Morgan separated would accomplish. Not only that, but he tried to do every little thing for Morgan when she could seemingly do a great deal on her own.

For a moment, she wondered what it would be like to have someone so fully engrossed in protecting *her*. But only for a moment, because then Mr. Cardiff nearly snarled toward her.

She couldn't be free of his presence soon enough. "I would like that very much, Morgan."

Morgan stretched her scars into a smile. Mr. Cardiff's jaw worked, and his eyes narrowed to steely slits. He nodded to Emma, tugged on his sister's arm, and then they were gone.

CHAPTER THREE

The act of hating Miss Hathaway, regardless of the sheer, perverse pleasure it gave him, was irrational. Aidan knew this all too well.

Blaming her for Morgan's attempts to take her own life was not only unreasonable but delved into the realm of the ridiculous.

Morgan's despair had begun well before she'd ever met Miss Hathaway. It had started when Stoneham—a man with whom Aidan had long been friends, and whom he had suggested court his sister—left her heartbroken by returning from the wars with a bride on his arm. Despite Stoneham's promises. Despite Morgan's loyalty and steadfast patience. Despite any attachment which the man had sworn to feel for Aidan's sister.

Indeed, it would make more sense to lay blame upon Stoneham. Some part of Aidan continued to hate his friend, even though he had answered for his treachery in a duel. Yet, since the viscount had had the decency to answer for himself in such a way, how could Aidan continue to blame him? Despise him, certainly. But blame?

Likewise, it would seem exceedingly more rational for Aidan to cast some, if not all, of the blame upon himself. He'd encouraged the attachment, after all. If he hadn't done so, would Stoneham have ever paid Morgan any notice? Would she have so readily set her cap for him? Would she have fallen so easily and so thoroughly into the darkest recesses of her mind?

But hating himself was not an option, lest he potentially cast himself along the same perilous path his sister had taken. Morgan had always been so steadfast, so levelheaded. Until Stoneham. So if she could fall victim to such desperate thought, wouldn't it also seem reasonable that he would? He'd always been prone to acting rashly and then rehashing his choices interminably in his mind.

And, while she was the one who had attempted to take her own life, Aidan could not bear to place any of the blame upon Morgan's shoulders. They were too frail. Too weighted down already. He would never do anything to add to her burden.

How could he, when he'd sworn back when they were children that he would never give up on her again? He would never forget that day, how when she was all of ten years old, Morgan had chased after them when Aidan, Niall, and David had once again left her behind while they went off to explore the grounds at Tavistock Manor.

She'd raced along behind them, her skirts tangling in her legs, heedless to any danger she might place herself in.

"Go back to your governess," Aidan had called, rushing ahead with his brother and friend, a snicker in his tone. "You can't possibly keep up with us. You're a girl."

Then they'd kept going on their way, assuming she would do as she was told. They climbed trees and walked along the cliffs, doing those dangerous things that boys were wont to do. And they never looked back.

But Morgan hadn't returned home. She'd kept following them, until her half-boot slipped out from under her as she tried to leap across a ridge, and she'd fallen down onto a ledge below. There she'd remained until they made their return journey to the manor. She tried desperately to climb up the rocky wall, but she'd broken her leg in the fall and couldn't manage it.

In the end, Aidan had lowered himself down to lift her out, and Niall and David pulled them both up. As he carried his sister home, he'd promised her he would never doubt her again. Despite her smaller size and the limitations of her skirts, she had kept pace with them far beyond what any of them had ever imagined she could do. She'd proved them wrong.

She'd proved *him* wrong. That was the most important part. And so Aidan could never again believe less than the best of her. That was what he'd told her—what he'd promised her. What he intended to do. What he *wanted* to do. It was easy to have good intentions. He was discovering, more so now than ever before, that it was far more difficult to follow through with those good intentions.

Still, he couldn't possibly blame *her* for the situation she'd found herself in after Stoneham's betrayal.

Stoneham, Morgan, himself…Aidan couldn't blame any of them. That left only Miss Hathaway, since she was the only one involved, in whatever small way. He'd trusted her. He'd placed his already fragile sister in Miss Hathaway's care and trusted that she could perform the simple task of keeping Morgan from hurting herself again, and *she* had failed.

These last three years he'd spent countless hours at his easel, trying to ease the rage he felt billowing up from his gut. Even if he couldn't take the time and effort to sculpt his marble as his heart yearned to do, he'd made the attempt to return to his art in some manner. Yet, instead of creating portraits or landscapes with his pastels, he often found himself creating depictions of his rage. Against Miss Hathaway, more often than not.

These were not pieces of art he could ever share. Not with anyone. Certainly not that first one—the one with the brown-haired, brown-eyed woman. It had been all long limbs and sleek curves, with her hand reaching out past her buttery yellow dress as though to rescue—

No. Not rescue. She wasn't going to rescue anyone. She couldn't save anyone, not even herself. She just lured him into thinking she was something other than what she was. Aidan had tossed that first piece into the hearth at the dower house, watching until the last licks of the flames ate the canvas away. Yet he couldn't burn the image from his mind, no matter how hard he tried to do so.

Most of his artwork since then depicted women, dead beneath the glassy surface of water, burning trapped in buildings...all sorts of awful things that he could never actually do in life. Despite the direction his thoughts had begun to travel, he was not a monster. He would never be a monster.

He was just a man who wanted to protect his sister from all the atrocities in the world.

And none of them eradicated that first one from his mind.

But in art, he could do anything. In art, he could take all the abominable ideas that kept assaulting his mind and act them out, to see if they actually helped. If only Morgan had had something like that—a way to exorcise the demons that had haunted her and led her to hurting herself. What might have changed then?

He'd never shown even a single piece he'd created in these past several years to Niall or Mother. They'd think him mad beyond repair or redemption, deranged even. Surely they'd send him off to Bedlam without batting an eye, though they had never allowed Morgan to suffer such a fate.

She was innocent, after all. He wasn't always certain about his own innocence. Some nights, he awoke in a sweat, thinking he had actually committed the revenge he so often depicted upon canvas.

He'd crafted so many of them that they filled nearly the entirety of the dower house at Tavistock Manor, where he'd been living since returning to the family estate. With these dark works interspersed so completely through his living quarters, he couldn't possibly be free of the thoughts which led to their origin.

Even now, as he tried to force a smile for Morgan's benefit and greet David's guests as they arrived, the images burned in the back of his mind. They seared him with their intensity, leaving his mind scarred and with open, seething wounds.

Today, his animosity only grew when he saw Miss Hathaway standing off in a corner of the great hall. She wore a lemon-yellow gown far more fashionable than anything he'd seen her in before and had her hair done in a style that could almost be considered pretty.

Yet still, her nose remained buried in the crevice of a book.

She hadn't changed, so why should his hatred of her have diminished, even somewhat?

Yet with her sitting there, looking so fashionable and pretty, and wearing yellow again for Christ's sake, he couldn't hate her. He couldn't see her as anything other than the girl he'd tossed into the flames and watched until the last ember had died. The piece of art he couldn't bear to look at…but why?

He swallowed hard, trying to force the images away. But even after he turned away from her, he could see her reaching out her hand to him from the flames. That hand had been the last bit of her to burn.

Morgan cleared her throat gently at his side, and he refocused on the present. He was here for her. So she could meet the other houseguests. He could do this.

Aidan stood fully across the room from Miss Hathaway, near the hearth with Morgan by his side. His sister's delicate hand, covered by a kidskin glove in order to hide as many scars as possible despite the warmth inside the grand house, rested just over the back of his hand. She wasn't holding onto him for dear life, as she'd so often done in the first months after her blinding. Yet he knew she preferred to have some contact, however slight, so she could sense when she might need to move.

In truth, he preferred it too. He worried less when he could see her.

A veritable parade of ladies and gentlemen had been brought over and introduced to them over the last hour—some familiar, others not—and still more continued to arrive. As Lady Burington crossed over to them once more with a gentleman at her side, Aidan leaned down to Morgan's ear. "Our hostess is bringing another gentleman our way. Do you wish to meet him, or have you tired?"

Part of him hoped she would have grown so tired by now that she'd beg off. Niall had stood with her to begin the day, but now he was off mixing with the other guests, making himself amenable to the lord of the manor.

Aidan would prefer to leave entirely, to escape out of doors, but he wouldn't leave Morgan if she desired to stay. His needs no longer mattered. That was what he'd told himself all along. He was determined to hold true to that.

"I'm perfectly all right, Aidan," she said softly, a twinkle lighting her eyes in a way he'd so rarely seen these many years. She wouldn't be ready to move on until the very last guest had come to her, that much was clear, and he couldn't bear to take that from her. Morgan had been hidden away at Tavistock Manor for so long now he could practically sense her excitement radiating from her skin.

He patted over the back of her hand. "Of course you are." He hoped his tone did not betray his lack of confidence in that statement. Not that he didn't want to believe her. He did wish to, more than he could possibly ever explain. Yet she had been in such a dark place for so long, it was difficult to ever truly believe she'd come back to the light.

"Lady Morgan," Lady Burington said, her smile melting through to her tone. "May I introduce Lord Muldaire? Lord Muldaire, this is Lady Morgan Cardiff and her brother, Mr. Cardiff."

Muldaire. Something niggled at the back of Aidan's mind with the name, but he brushed it aside as Morgan brightened considerably, her shy smile and blinking eyes making it next to impossible for Aidan to see her flaws.

The man couldn't be a total degenerate, since he wasn't looking at Morgan's scars as though she was a leper. Better than could be said for a few of the others present who'd already had their introductions. Finding appropriate ladies and gentlemen for his sister to interact with would have to become Aidan's new personal mission, given the scarcity of people who could look upon her without wincing.

"It's a pleasure to make your acquaintance, my lord," Morgan said. With each new person who came to her, her enthusiasm grew. She couldn't see the disgust on their faces. She couldn't know better than to think they were all as eager to meet her as she was to meet them. Her naïveté was both a blessing and a curse.

"Hardly as pleasant as making yours, my lady." The smooth-talking man bent his dark-haired head low, leaning in as though to share a conspiratorial moment. "I can assure you, I'm a far better person to know than my brother."

She laughed, drawing several scandalized eyes around the room. "And is your brother here? I can't say I've had the pleasure of an introduction, so I can't speak to the truth of your claim."

Slowly but surely, the others who, moments ago, had been so scandalized by her daring to laugh, resumed their own conversations and forgot about Morgan at least for the time being.

For several moments, Aidan stood there watching the two without really hearing them. His participation seemed unnecessary, and he was not one to interject himself where he was not wanted.

Watching her thus felt so odd. Morgan acted as though she'd hardly spent a day outside the influence of society. She was talking with ease, even flirting, however much Aidan hated to be present to witness such a thing. She seemed natural in this setting, despite her disfiguration and blindness and isolation. How natural would she seem if she were aware of the hushed voices and averted gazes that followed her every movement?

Blast, but he had to learn how to trust her again. How to let her go.

Since she was otherwise occupied with Muldaire, Aidan allowed his attention to stray to Miss Hathaway again.

A blond-haired gentleman walked over to her. Who was he again? Aidan remembered meeting him, but he'd already almost banished him from his mind. Sir…something or other. A man with kind eyes and a gentle spirit…one of the few like Muldaire who had not blanched upon realization of Morgan's disfigurement. Perhaps he was a man Aidan ought to encourage in that regard.

But no. He'd already encouraged Stoneham to take an interest in Morgan, which was more than enough of such a thing for one lifetime, and it had not resulted favorably.

Never again.

He needed to let Morgan make her own choices, do as she wished. She didn't need his involvement.

Still, he did not like seeing the man with Miss Hathaway, which was quite a bothersome discovery. She set aside her book—something she'd rarely ever done three years ago—and smiled up at the gentleman. They talked, and her face became animated, her eyes alight with enthusiasm which did not appear to be feigned.

Her response left Aidan seething, for whatever inexplicable reason. He hated that she had such an ability to bring out the worst in him—the anger which went so far beyond mere anger as to touch upon rage. He hated that simply her presence here was enough to take such control over him, rendering him a vengeful, loathsome shell of a man. Well, more of one than he already was. It left him feeling inhuman.

At his sides, his fists clenched until his knuckles must have turned white. Then he forced his attention away from Miss Hathaway and back to Morgan and Lord Muldaire. Morgan deserved his attention far more than Miss Hathaway did.

After a few minutes, another man who looked almost the same as Muldaire, though with a certain harshness to his presence that the marquess did not possess—clearly a brother—and a third, with many of the same features but less of the darkness, drew alongside them. Morgan's head turned to the side, as though she could sense their presence even though she could not see them.

Muldaire glanced over at the intruders with a hint of a scowl, but made a polite introduction. "Lady Morgan, have you met my brother, Lord Jacob Deering? And our cousin, Mr. Charles Deering."

She smiled again, all lightness and goodness and air—all of the things Aidan was not. "It is a pleasure, gentlemen."

Aidan thought it anything but a pleasure, particularly with the dark look that had passed between the brothers, yet he held his tongue—almost bit down on it, so as not to say anything untoward. For Morgan's sake, even if she did seem to no longer need his help as much as she had for so long. He didn't want to draw any more attention to her than she already drew upon herself.

At least none of these men seemed overly concerned about his sister's appearance.

Blessedly, a moment later, David interrupted them. "Won't you all join us in the drawing room? It is time for tea."

Serena Weston, with her sharp nose and high cheekbones and perfect English rose complexion, smiled kindly down at Emma. "Might I join you?" She spoke softly as though to avoid drawing much notice, yet her voice almost lilted in the crowded drawing room despite her efforts. It rose and fell, like the music of a harp. What was more, everything in her eyes said she was equally as lovely inside as her voice and appearance were on the outside.

Emma could stand to have more kind, lovely people in her life during this house party. She needed their positivity in order to negate the less savory sensations she received from Mr. Cardiff's stares.

She nodded and moved over, making room upon the silk brocade sofa. Then she set her book on the occasional table beside her, vowing silently to ignore it for the rest of the evening. She'd made a promise to Vanessa, and so she would follow through with it. Besides, if she was going to catch a husband…well, being lost in a story wouldn't exactly help with that endeavor. As the room had filled with David and Vanessa's guests, none of the others had come over to sit with her—not until Miss Weston arrived. Emma had been worried that, even with her proper gown and coiffure, and with trying to comport herself as a proper lady ought to do, she still wasn't coming out successfully with her plans. She needed to be present in the here and now.

But Miss Weston had chosen to sit with her. Perhaps all hope was not already lost. Perhaps Emma could pretend to be a proper young miss who might be interesting to a gentleman for long enough to fool him into a besotted state. She couldn't allow herself to think about the alternative. If she were to fail so spectacularly as that, much as she'd always done, this would quickly become a very, very long house party.

"I love that shade of yellow on you," Miss Weston said as she took a seat. "You look as lovely as a daffodil. I can't wear that particular hue unless I want everyone who sees me to cast up their accounts from the sheer horror of my complexion."

Emma tried but failed to hold back a smile. "I rather doubt that."

"Oh, truly." Miss Weston took Emma's hand in hers. "I would never lie about such a thing." She leaned closer and dropped her tone to a conspiratorial whisper. "Father's forbidden me to ever wear a yellow gown again. He says it turns my skin a sickly shade of green, and he thinks it will mar my chances of obtaining the match he desires. Which will be difficult enough, given that he's in trade." Her pert nose wrinkled slightly.

The way she said it, with her very specific facial reactions, one would think Miss Weston felt ashamed of her father's need to work for his living. But when Emma looked more closely at the girl, she found no self-reproach evident in her eyes. Her lips *were* downturned, however, and she *did* try to avert her gaze.

And then it became clear.

Miss Weston was trying to make it appear that she was embarrassed, so that she would be accepted by those within this set, but she wasn't *actually* ashamed in the slightest.

Nor would Emma be if placed in Miss Weston's circumstance. Her own father had been a farmer all his life, and had only been knighted upon a chance occurrence on the occasion that the King had needed a place to sleep when the local inn had burned to the ground. If not for that unexpected event, neither Emma nor Vanessa would have had the opportunities they'd been granted. There would be no house parties and peers and social engagements. There would only be the hope of finding some kindly country gentleman to marry or going into service.

Still, it was rather unfashionable amongst this set to have the necessity to work. Money was to be handed down from generation to generation, not earned through one's labors. Because of the strictures of society, Emma could well understand the reasons for her new companion's attempts to seem discomfited by her father's livelihood.

How truly refreshing to discover someone who would reveal such plain truths, whether it was intended or not.

"That may be, Miss Weston," she murmured. "But I doubt it. With your beauty, you'll have countless beaux falling at your feet before the end of tomorrow, if not sooner."

Miss Weston pursed her lips in a very matter-of-fact sort of way. "Well, perhaps with my dowry I might."

Morgan finally came in on Mr. Cardiff's arm. He scanned the room, passing his eyes over every person present, as though determining where it might be safe to take his sister. His gaze burned when his eyes locked momentarily with Emma's, but he quickly moved on. He would never allow Morgan to be in Emma's presence, if he could avoid it. He'd made that perfectly clear on numerous occasions.

When he guided her toward a group of the other young ladies, those same ladies who'd looked at Emma with disdain before moving on to sit on the opposite side of the room, Miss Weston squeezed Emma's hand. "Would you mind if Lady Morgan sat with us as well? I think I would like to get to know her. She seems so very nice, and I'm sure she could use a few friends."

Emma had only managed to say, "I wouldn't mind at all, but—" when Miss Weston darted to her feet.

"Lady Morgan? Would you care to sit with Miss Hathaway and me?" Her previously soft voice carried throughout the room, and silence descended all around them as everyone turned to stare at Morgan.

Their stares caused Mr. Cardiff's gaze to burn more darkly. His lips set into a thin line and his jaw hardened, and he gripped his sister's elbow as though to guide her out of the room.

But Morgan apparently had other plans. "I'd be delighted," she said with a true smile. Heedless of the heated whispers sounding around her, Morgan headed toward them. Her brother tightened his grip on her elbow, but she shook him free and kept coming.

When she paused nearby and held out her arm for Morgan to take, Emma felt the weight of Mr. Cardiff's stare settling on her. It never left her as she helped Morgan to sit between her and Miss Weston. It never diminished as they struck up a conversation.

The rest of the guests resumed their own discussions and began, yet again, to ignore the three ladies. At the same moment, Mr. Cardiff took up a seat near the massive window in perfect position to keep an eye on everyone and everything taking place in the drawing room, yet it seemed most of his focus lay on Emma and her friends. Despite Morgan's growing animation, the palpable tension of Mr. Cardiff's full attention upon them fell over Emma as though to swallow her whole. It seemed to be more on *her* than it was on *them*.

A flash of heat raced to her face, and she fought to ignore it. Why was he always staring at her? What was it that always drew his attention? Were he another gentleman, she might welcome it. But since it was Mr. Cardiff, she'd prefer he turn it elsewhere.

She had no business feeling warm and tingly from any gentleman's attentions, let alone those of a man such as he. Warm and tingly feelings would be perfectly acceptable once she was well and truly married, and not a moment before.

The two ladies she sat with talked, seemingly oblivious to Mr. Cardiff's perusal from across the crowded room, yet Emma could focus on nothing else. She tried to pay attention to her friends' chatter, particularly since they'd begun discussing a new gothic novel Miss Weston had been reading, but every time she looked up, Mr. Cardiff's eyes bored more fully through her. Within minutes, she was a trembling, agitated mess.

Morgan took Emma's hand into her own, drawing her back into their conversation. "Perhaps tomorrow you could take Serena and me to Lord Burington's new library."

Emma blinked at first, trying to sort out who Serena was. Then she remembered that was Miss Weston's name. The other two must have already decided that they'd all be the best of friends while she'd been otherwise occupied with worrying over Mr. Cardiff's interest.

"I'm sure we could do that," she spluttered, hoping dearly they wouldn't think her a simpleton for her odd behavior. "I'll make certain it is all right with Lord Burington, and then we can form our plans."

But at the moment, the only sort of plan wishing to take root in her mind was a means to avoid Mr. Cardiff at every turn.

CHAPTER FOUR

Seated as she was with Sir Henry Irvine on her right, Lord Jacob Deering on her left, Lord Jacob's cousin Mr. Deering occupying the seat across from her, and Mr. Cardiff so far down the table that she couldn't see him at all, Emma couldn't help but say a silent prayer of thanks to Vanessa. In the last day, she'd had as much of Mr. Cardiff's rancor as she could handle.

Emma needed to start making herself amenable to the eligible gentlemen at the party at once, which was a daunting task, but at least she now had three of them surrounding her. Granted, Lord Jacob was equally as sullen and brooding as Mr. Cardiff, or perhaps even more so, but at least he didn't glare at her as though she had concocted the plague all by her lonesome. He was rather handsome, with his dark hair and eyes. He would not be a difficult man to look upon day after day, should a lady be granted that honor.

And his cousin, Mr. Deering, was an affable fellow. Not only that, but he was probably someone she would do better to focus her attentions upon…a gentleman on a far less lofty strata of society. He had a kind smile and a gentle air to go along with Lord Jacob's dark appearance.

Sir Henry, likewise, was the sort of gentleman Emma ought to be setting her sights upon. He was a baronet, so still above her station— but not nearly so far above her as Lord Jacob. Still, he seemed quite at his ease among his betters here. She would do very well if she made him as her match.

Vanessa knew very well what she was doing when she'd arranged the seating for supper.

Right that moment, Emma made up her mind that she would do everything she could over the course of supper to get to know both Sir Henry and Mr. Deering. She shouldn't set her cap upon a gentleman who would never deign to notice her. It was best to aim for a target she had at least some small hope of hitting.

A footman held a bowl of split pea soup beside her while she placed some in her bowl, and the scent of it wafted up to warm her nostrils. It was all she could do to refrain from letting out a sigh of contentment. Once everyone had been served, she picked up her spoon and filled it, then gingerly moved it toward her mouth so as not to spill a drop.

Up and down the length of the oak table, the sounds of silver meeting china and polite conversation swelled.

After they'd been eating for a bit, Sir Henry turned to Emma and smiled. "I couldn't help but notice you were reading *The Bride of Lammermoor* earlier, Miss Hathaway. Tell me, have you read any of the author's other novels?"

Bother if she hadn't already garnered attention for her reading. She'd prefer to draw notice for her lovely coiffure or commendable deportment. Emma forced her agitation with herself aside and turned more fully to Sir Henry. "I've read *Waverley* more times than I ought to have done, but this is only the second of the author's novels I've had the opportunity to read."

Mr. Deering leaned across the table slightly, as though joining a secret discussion. "You've not read *Rob Roy* yet?" His incredulous tone left her near giddy. When she answered in the negative, he continued with, "Promise me you'll read it next so we can discuss it"

He wanted to discuss novels with her?

Perhaps she wouldn't have to leave behind all parts of herself in order to gain a gentleman's notice. If he were the *right* gentleman.

"I'll have to see if Lord Burington has it in his library," she said with more confidence than she felt.

"Surely he does," Lord Jacob drawled. He took another spoonful of his soup, and then passed a glare over to his more enthusiastic cousin. "Burington must have five copies of every book ever published in that room. It's hideous."

Hideous was about the last term Emma would use for such a grand library, but she kept her opinion on the matter to herself. This fortnight was to be about ingratiating herself to as many gentlemen as she could in order to relieve her parents' worry, not about alienating either those very gentlemen or herself.

Instead, she smiled across at Mr. Deering. "If he has a copy, I would love to discuss it tomorrow."

"Tomorrow?" He sat up straighter, his brows lifting inquisitively. "Surely you couldn't read an entire novel so fast as that."

"On the contrary," Serena put in from next to him. Emma couldn't be certain, but she thought Serena gave her a little wink before she continued. "I have it on the highest authority that Miss Hathaway reads two books a day. Three, I'd wager, if she's not too engrossed with other goings-on."

Emma couldn't decide if she should be pleased with Serena's interjection or if she ought to be mortified to have her reading habits set out so plainly before the party. She blushed slightly, and it then intensified when Sir Henry gave her an appraising look, his friendly, brown eyes sparkling.

"A lady after my own heart. I've not had the time to devote to my own desire to read of late, but when I took my Grand Tour, I spent more time reading than I did anything else…much to the chagrin of my companions."

"And to those who must listen to you discuss it now," grumbled Lord Jacob beside her beneath his breath.

Emma glanced around, but no one else seemed to have heard his comment. She decided to ignore it, to pretend she hadn't heard a thing. It seemed the wisest course of action at this juncture. To keep from doing or saying anything inappropriate, she placed another spoonful of soup into her mouth.

Mr. Deering let out a hum of assent. "Much of my time is now spent reading legal tomes, when I'd rather read for enjoyment."

"Legal tomes?" Serena queried. "Are you a barrister then, Mr. Deering?"

"In my second year." He brushed the corners of his mouth with his napkin while a footman lifted away his bowl of soup. When the servant backed away, he went on. "I do have a bit more time for pleasure reading now than I did during my schooling, but only just."

"Pity," Lord Jacob said amiably, which took Emma by surprise. He'd not seemed one to pity anyone for any reason, up to that point. Or to be amiable, for that matter. But then he looked down at the plate being placed before him, with roast squab and parsnips, and the previous glower returned to his features. "Pity you ever decided to return," he added so low, Emma was certain that no one could have heard him besides her.

She'd think he was deliberately trying to shock her or be provoking if she didn't believe she rated as low on his scale of notice as a slug.

Sir Henry then struck up a conversation with Mr. Deering about their tours of the Continent, granting Emma a moment to regain her bearings. Having a few things in common with these two gentlemen would only serve to aid her cause. Perhaps she could glean more of their interests throughout the course of their meal. Even if she couldn't, there was at least some connection between them now, so she wouldn't feel quite so lost in a conversation—if she ever got up the nerve to start one.

Sir Henry and Mr. Deering both looked expectantly at her then, and she chastised herself for not paying attention. She opened her mouth to apologize for her lack of attention, but a voice at the far end of the table carried to her over the din.

"I can't imagine why they have brought her into society again. Her skin is ghastly with all those scars! She'll surely ruin the appetite of anyone in her general vicinity, simply from her presence." The biting words came from Lady Portia Hemmings, a dark-haired, sharp-tongued debutante who had made Emma's skin crawl upon their first meeting. "Clearly it has already affected Lord Jacob's appetite."

This diatribe only justified Emma's premonition about the woman. She glanced down to the other end of the table, where Mr. Cardiff sat, but he clearly hadn't heard it. Nor had Lord Trenowyth, who was in mid-conversation with a debutante whose name Emma couldn't remember.

She bit down on her lip, halting her apology to the gentlemen she'd been ignoring. Serena gave her a brief shake of her head, questioning her with her eyes, and then spoke, drawing the two gentlemen's attention onto herself. She mustn't have heard what Emma had heard. There would be no need to question if she had.

Surreptitiously, Emma turned her gaze to where Morgan was happily chatting away with Lord Muldaire, oblivious to the fact that another lady was boorishly denigrating her character.

Whether Morgan had heard it or not didn't matter. Emma had. It left her mouth dry and her chest tight and caused hot, stinging tears to form behind her eyes.

It was all so unfair. No one deserved such treatment. Certainly not Morgan. And for that matter, Emma didn't deserve the treatment Mr. Cardiff so readily handed to her.

Lord Jacob brushed the back of his hand against Emma's knuckles with a touch so soft she almost thought she'd imagined it, but it was enough to make her realize she had clenched both hands into fists. She forcefully loosened them, and then met Lord Jacob's gaze.

He was staring at her almost kindly, however ridiculous that notion might be. Lord Jacob Deering was a great many things, but her initial impression of him did not lend itself easily to *kind*. He dropped his voice again to where no one but Emma could hear him. "Don't grant them the satisfaction of seeing what they do to you. Lady Morgan does not."

Before she had wrapped her mind around what he'd said, Lord

Jacob cut off a bite of quail and filled his mouth with it, turning to his other side to take up a conversation with the lady seated there.

He was right, of course. She'd not do herself any favors by delivering the gossips at the other end a set-down with a full dining room looking on. Emma was here to become a perfectly biddable, perfectly agreeable miss—one whom a gentleman might wish to pursue. Not a single gentleman of her acquaintance wished to pursue shrewish harridans who acted inappropriately in social situations. Mother had done her best to instill in both Emma and Vanessa a sense of proper decorum, and Papa had shown them time and again that keeping silent while amongst one's betters was often the proper course of action. She needed to simply keep her thoughts to herself until such time as she could reveal them to someone she trusted, or she'd let both Vanessa and David down.

Yet when she tried to return her focus to her meal, another voice floated down the table, a masculine timbre this time, assaulting her ears with more vitriolic comments about her friend.

"Pity she was unsuccessful in her attempts. One would think, after three tries, she could have gotten one of them right."

"And it's a pity your nursemaid was unsuccessful at teaching you simple manners and basic human decency." The words were out of Emma's mouth before she could stop herself. Indeed, she'd overturned her chair in her fury to gain her feet. She must have knocked over a glass of wine as well, as Sir Henry and two footmen desperately tried to mop it up with napkins before it spilled over the table's edge.

Every eye in the room had turned to her—in shock, in awe, in admiration. None seemed inclined to look away.

Heavens, what had she done? Her entire body shook from head to toe, but she couldn't bear to see the censure she was sure she'd find in Vanessa's eyes, couldn't possibly handle witnessing the dismay David's expression was sure to bear. Worst yet, with one simple action she had certainly destroyed any possibility of making a match at this house party. She might as well pack her trunk and return to

Knightsbridge, tucking her tail between her legs as she left.

But if she'd already destroyed any chance she had at securing a husband, she might as well finish the job at hand.

Taking a calming breath, Emma turned to Lord Roxburghe, the man who'd so callously wished Morgan had successfully taken her own life, and stared him through. He had the gall to stare back at her, without even the slightest hint of shame coloring his expression. Lady Portia, at least, had the sense to look down at her lap. She appeared contrite. But Roxburghe's supercilious gaze never wavered.

This was hardly the time to back down from her stance now that she'd taken one. Emma ignored the trembles that coursed through her body. She straightened her spine and forced herself not to waver, not to cower in fear of what she was in the midst of doing.

"Lady Morgan is a guest of Lord and Lady Burington, just as we all are." With more bravado than she actually felt, Emma passed her gaze along the length of the table, pausing for a moment on each eye that dared to meet hers. When she paused upon Mr. Cardiff, she nearly stopped at that very moment and ran from the dining room, so censorious and disapproving was his expression. But finally, she moved her gaze on to the others. "She deserves the same basic courtesies we all do. She does *not* deserve to have anyone speak ill of her, for any reason whatsoever."

The clatter of silver dropping back against the table was the only sound in the room, aside from a few scandalized breaths or gasps of shock.

Faintly, Emma felt the back of Lord Jacob's hand grazing against her knuckles in warning again, but she ignored them, despite the impetuousness of her actions. He was trying to warn her against making a fool of herself, but it was far too late for that. Or perhaps he was warning her against raising Lord Roxburghe's ire. Roxburghe was a peer, after all. Not the sort of man one ought to go about trying to put in his place—particularly not if one was the mere daughter of a knight.

But she couldn't stop herself if she tried. Now that she had a full head of steam built up, she had to let it release. If she didn't, she might very well stamp her foot and cry, or dump a tureen of soup over Roxburghe's head, or something else equally horrifying. She didn't do any of those things, however, because she heard a sniffle coming from the other end of the table.

That sniffle could only have come from Morgan.

Vanessa rose and placed a placating smile upon her lips, clearly trying to stop Emma before she'd gone too far. "Ladies, why don't we all excuse ourselves—?"

Blast it all, Vanessa ought to have tried sooner. She knew how Emma could be when she lost her temper, far better than anyone else in the world. Vanessa shouldn't have let her go as far as she did.

Emma spoke more loudly than she had been, making certain everyone heard her over her sister's voice. "I will not excuse anyone until Lord Roxburghe has apologized to Lady Morgan for being a vile excuse for a gentleman."

With a fierceness in her brown eyes he never imagined she possessed, Miss Hathaway straightened her shoulders, tossed back her head, crossed her arms over her chest, and looked as regal and certain of herself as the queen. "We shall also wait for Lady Portia to apologize to Lady Morgan. I'm prepared to wait as long as is necessary."

Aidan could do nothing but gape at her. He had never felt more conflicted in his life.

On the one hand, he wanted to stand up and applaud Miss Hathaway for daring to take such a stand—particularly one in favor of his sister. Yet she was still the woman he loathed more than anything or anyone else in this world, the one whom he had cursed for nearly three years, the one he'd so often depicted in the throes of his revenge whilst using his pastels.

He preferred to use vellum with his pastels any time he was creating his vengeance. It left the images crisper. Clearer. More exact.

There was nothing left to the imagination when he used pastels on vellum.

And right this moment, he wished he had an easel and some vellum, not to mention his pastels. He wanted to capture her as she looked just at this moment. She was like an avenging angel, come to teach the mere mortals such as himself a lesson they clearly hadn't learned in the rest of their lives. Never in his life had he seen such fire coming from what he'd once thought to be dull, brown eyes.

Here, amidst a room filled with lords and ladies, men and women with enough power and social standing and narcissism they could crush her in an instant—more permanently and readily than Aidan could ever do in real life or on canvas—here, Miss Hathaway laid aside all thought of self-preservation and thought only of protecting Morgan.

And he couldn't catch his breath.

He hadn't heard what Lord Roxburghe or Lady Portia had said about his sister. They were far at the other end of the table, well away from him and his siblings. Frankly, he couldn't imagine what they could have said to elicit such a response from Miss Hathaway. She'd always seemed so meek before. Docile, even. He'd never imagined her to care for anyone or anything but herself and her damned books.

But clearly she cared for Morgan, and that left Aidan with quite the conundrum.

Damnation.

He wanted to stand beside her. Right this moment, he wanted to kiss her so deeply and so thoroughly she would tremble in his arms, and not stop kissing her until she agreed to never pick up a bloody book again. He wanted things he had no business wanting, because he'd as good as burned her at the stake in his artwork for three years without feeling even the tiniest inkling of remorse.

So he stayed where he sat, unable to do more than close his jaw and stare, memorizing every detail of her form.

The room remained silent. Everyone stared at the daring miss, then turned to either Roxburghe and Lady Portia, or to Aidan, Niall, and Morgan, as if trying to gauge their reactions in order to facilitate their own.

Roxburghe's eyes flashed with fury, his leer turning fully upon Miss Hathaway, a dangerous sign if ever Aidan had seen one. "I am the Earl of Roxburghe," he spat in her direction, standing to tower over them all. His hands clenched into fists at his sides.

Aidan turned to Niall, trying to determine what his brother would do. Now that Miss Hathaway had brought their treatment of Morgan to light, the two of them would have to ensure Morgan's honor was protected. Niall gave him a slight nod—not nearly enough for Aidan to know what he intended.

"And Lady Morgan is the sister of the Earl of Trenowyth," Miss Hathaway countered. She lifted an eyebrow as though in challenge.

This was not going well. Not at all. Aidan started to push back from his seat so he could call the bastard out, but he was apparently too slow.

"You'll apologize to both Lady Morgan *and* Miss Hathaway, or you'll answer to me at dawn." The voice rumbled, deep and dark. A vicious threat hung in the air after the pronouncement, one which made all of Aidan's imaginings over the last three years seem like child's play. Aidan could do nothing but gawk at the ladies' unlikely defender.

Lord Jacob Deering did not rise, did not look up, did not make any outward sign that he'd been the one to issue the challenge. But there could be no doubt it was him from the manner in which Miss Hathaway flinched at his side and looked down at him. She gave an almost imperceptible shake of her head, but it didn't matter. She couldn't stop him from doing a damned thing.

David stirred from the head of the table. "I'm sure there will be no call for that," he murmured softly, but everyone in the room was bound to have heard him. They could have heard a single grain of rice falling to a china plate, it was so silent.

"If there is," Niall put in, "I'll be the one Roxburghe will answer to."

"You may be my second," Lord Jacob said in an offhanded manner which only served to leave Aidan seething, inexplicably, in his seat.

It made no sense. Why was he so angry with this man? Jacob Deering was not the one at fault here. He did not deserve to feel the brunt of Aidan's rage. He was trying, as was Miss Hathaway, to protect Morgan's honor.

And then it struck him—would have bowled him over, were he not still seated at the table. They were taking from him the one thing he'd allowed himself to assume as his responsibility these last several years. They were taking upon their shoulders the protection of Morgan.

It left him feeling unmanned. Useless. What was he, after all, if he did not have his sister to guard and protect and coddle as if his very life depended upon it?

An artist whose work no one would ever wish to purchase.

A younger son of a peer with no direction in life.

A wastrel. Nothing.

His head felt suddenly heavy, and he dipped it down so his chin rested upon his chest. A sheen of sweat covered him. How had he let his life become what it was?

Lost within the dark thoughts of his own mind, Aidan felt as though he was watching the scene unfold around him—not as a participant, but as though he were somehow floating among them.

Eventually, Lady Portia gave a tearful apology and rushed from the room, her face red and splotchy. Lord Roxburghe grudgingly offered a few words to Morgan and then to Miss Hathaway. As one, the ladies rose and then filed out of the dining room, with Morgan firmly ensconced between Miss Hathaway and Miss Weston.

When they left, it was the first time since the incident started that Aidan had dared chance a look at his sister. She didn't appear flustered in the slightest. On the contrary, she seemed almost…whimsically happy. That couldn't be, could it? What in God's name could possibly have made her so damned happy in what had just taken place?

After the last of the ladies had gone, the footmen came through with glasses of port, settling them before the gentlemen.

Roxburghe downed his in a single swill and then quit the room. That seemed an excellent idea, all things considered. It seemed even more so when David turned to Sir Henry Irvine, the deuced bore, and asked him about the hounds he'd been breeding, as if nothing out of the realm of the ordinary had just occurred.

"Just had a new litter a few weeks ago," the baronet responded jovially. "Four females and two males."

That was all the inducement Aidan required. He swallowed the last of his port and pushed back from the table. "If you'll excuse me," he muttered. Before anyone could stop him, Aidan barreled through the doors of the dining room and made his way out to the park.

If he was going to sort out what had just happened, he needed air. He needed space.

Had he thoroughly misjudged Miss Hathaway? And Morgan? And if he had...now what?

Tensions ran high the rest of the evening in the drawing room, despite David and Vanessa's best efforts to distract everyone with parlor games. They had an area set up near the hearth where people could play cards, and a group went off near the Bornholm clock and played charades, while a third grouping of guests situated themselves by the bay window to simply talk.

Emma had no desire to play charades with such horrid people. Nor did she want to play cards with them, or sit around and gossip. Instead she sat with Morgan and Serena, and they made plans for Tuesday, and generally tried to forget about the scene she had caused at supper.

At various moments, Sir Henry or Lord Muldaire or Mr. Deering would come over to them and try to coax them into participation.

Emma and Serena always declined, since Morgan couldn't see to play cards or charades, and Morgan was all too content to spend her time in their company and not with the others. Lord Trenowyth kept an eye on them from afar but never interrupted them. Emma did not see Mr. Cardiff the rest of the night.

Not that she was upset over such a realization. Far from it, in fact. Even with the tension in the room between her and Lord Roxburghe and Lady Portia, she felt lighter than she had at any time in Mr. Cardiff's presence.

The exact reason for this newfound lightness wasn't readily available to her.

There was the fact that he'd stared at her, but for the first time, she hadn't felt as though his stare was quite a scowl or a burning hatred. It was more... Certainly shock, which shouldn't be all that surprising. Emma had shocked even herself, so she had no doubt that everyone in the dining hall right down to the footmen serving their meal had been shocked. But there was more. Admiration, perhaps?

Whatever it was she'd seen in his expression, it left her near giddy. Which was the absolute *wrong* reaction for her to have. She was here to find a husband. Mr. Cardiff might be many things, but he would never be a husband for her.

The three girls made their escape from the drawing room early that night, well before the rest of the party had begun to dissipate. Emma knew she ought to take Vanessa aside and beg her forgiveness for what she'd done. But she wasn't sorry she'd done it—only that she'd caused such dissent and tension amongst their guests. Even now, even knowing what a mess she'd caused, she would do the same all over again if someone were to make such comments about Morgan within her hearing.

The awkward heaviness in the air had not yet evaporated by the next morning when the party broke their fast. Lady Portia and her friends kept glancing over at Emma, casting her snide looks and then whispering to each other. At least their attention was now on her, and not on Morgan. If it diminished Emma's chances at making a match while she was here, she could always revert to her alternative plan of becoming a governess to some aristocratic family. It wouldn't be ideal, as Mother and Father would prefer her to marry a gentleman who could provide for her, but it would suffice. At the very least, she still had her integrity.

That wasn't a very good excuse for the scene she'd caused at supper last night. An apology was most certainly in order.

As she left the morning room with Serena and Morgan, still without Mr. Cardiff in sight, Emma stopped beside Vanessa and David, allowing the other two ladies to go on ahead of her.

"I'm so sorry. I've ruined your house party," she whispered. And she had. How could it possibly ever recover from the horrid scene she'd caused last night? No one seemed to be having a good time. It wouldn't surprise her in the least if several of their guests had urgent matters suddenly arise, calling for their immediate departure, and it would be all Emma's fault.

But David smiled at her, which left her confused all the way down to her toes. "You didn't do anything I wouldn't have done, had I been in your position. In fact, I think you handled yourself rather well, all things considered. I'd have called the bastard out right then and there, and then your sister would have been upset with me."

"Scared," Vanessa corrected him. "But proud."

"You aren't upset with me?" She could do nothing but shake her head dumbly, grasping for any reason this could be.

"We wouldn't stand for anyone treating any of our guests that way," Vanessa said.

"Of course not," Emma murmured, blinking far more than was necessary. "But I can't help but think you would have gone about handling the situation in a very different manner."

David grinned, then shooed her with his hand. "Off with you, then. Your friends are waiting, and there's no telling how long Lady Morgan has before one of her brothers discovers she's gone missing and decides to rectify the matter."

"Just be back before luncheon." Vanessa smiled at her, and even gave a wink. "And then be prepared for an afternoon of painting watercolors and the like. Or reading," she added, almost as an afterthought.

David was right. There was no point in standing around waiting for the sleeping bear that was Mr. Cardiff to wake. She darted out the door behind Morgan and Serena without further delay, catching up to them just as they slipped out into the park.

Morgan held out her arm, and Emma put hers out so Morgan could grasp it. It was a light touch, which left Emma slightly unnerved. Shouldn't Morgan hold on a bit more tightly? Didn't she need more assistance? But she was coming to learn that her friend was far more capable than anyone seemed to believe.

Emma vowed to keep all of her doubts to herself, to never voice them…and to do her very best to eliminate them completely. She'd be doing Morgan no favors by trying to help her when no help was needed. In fact, she'd be just as bad as Lord Trenowyth, and even Mr. Cardiff, if she were to succumb to such a line of thought.

They were well away from the main house when Serena broke the silence. "Sir Henry is quite handsome." Her tone said far more than her words did.

Emma felt a flush creeping over her face. Thank goodness it was just the three of them. "He is," she murmured. "But I can't imagine he'll seek me out after the way I behaved last night."

"If he doesn't, you are better off without him," Morgan put in.

Serena nodded. "I don't think you need to worry about that. You clearly didn't see the admiration in his eyes during supper."

She'd been so caught up in determining just what sort of expression Mr. Cardiff was passing in her direction, she couldn't have possibly noticed a thing about Sir Henry's. "No, but I did notice his lack of attention *after* supper."

"It was only the first day," Serena said. She turned them in order to take a footbridge over a creek—one that hadn't been there on Emma's last visit. "There is still plenty more time. He's got to make himself amenable to the whole party…he can't focus all of his attention solely on you so soon. It would give the wrong impression."

An impression Emma had no doubt he would never in a million years wish to give. She bit down on her tongue to avoid saying that aloud as they followed a trail leading to a fragrant, vibrant rose garden.

It was like seeing the entire estate with new eyes, despite the fact that, up until a few years ago, she'd seen it many times. Vanessa hadn't left anything as it had been before, it seemed, not even the out of doors.

"Oh! Roses," Morgan said suddenly, lifting her face high into the air. She pressed her eyes closed and sighed with contentment. "Can we stop? I'd like to sit by them for a bit if we could."

How had Morgan noticed the roses? Emma had hardly seen them herself, and she certainly hadn't been able to smell them. It seemed even she was discounting her friend's abilities.

Scanning the area, she found a stone bench in the midst of the garden. "There's a bench we can sit on off to the right," she said. That simple statement, and a slight nudge in the proper direction, was all it took for Morgan to start moving straight toward it.

Once they were settled, a mischievous grin overtook Morgan's features. "So, tell me, Serena. Which gentlemen have caught your eye?"

Serena blushed fiercely and looked at Emma, then shook her head. What on earth could that be about?

"I don't know that any of them have caught *my* eye—"

"Liar," Morgan cut in, her eyes twinkling in the morning light.

"But it seems *my father* is rather interested in Lord Muldaire."

Morgan pursed her lips. "Your father has high aspirations for you. But Lord Muldaire seems to be a very kind man. And his cousin is, as well."

Emma couldn't stop herself from chuckling. "I notice you didn't mention his brother, Lord Jacob."

"And *I* noticed that Lord Jacob seemed to pay you more attention last night than he paid just about anything," Serena chortled, causing Emma to join her in blushing profusely. "Not that that is saying much."

"I think I might prefer to escape the notice of Lord Jacob," Emma mumbled. After spending supper seated next to him, she still hadn't quite determined what it was about him that left her feeling…well, cold.

That statement caused Morgan's eyebrows to knit together. "Why is that? I know he's…well, he's a bit…"

"Caustic?" Serena suggested.

Emma bit her lip in thought for a moment. "I'd say more abrasive."

Morgan huffed, and her breath sent a stray tendril of her blonde hair flying. "I thought it was more that he's troubled than either of those things."

Emma and Serena burst into giggles.

"Well, he is," Morgan protested, which only caused them to laugh harder than they already were.

"You're just determined to see the best in everyone, aren't you?" Serena said once they'd calmed a bit. She threaded her fingers through Morgan's and held tight. "I think that's why I like you so much."

That was what Emma liked so much about her, also, not to mention Serena's ability to see things exactly as they were.

She linked her fingers with Morgan's other hand, bonding the three of them physically as she felt they already were internally. Emma continued talking with her friends, sharing her impressions of the other guests and listening to the other girls' opinions. She laughed until her belly ached, right up until the very moment they had to go back to the main house for luncheon.

CHAPTER FIVE

Emma settled on a blanket spread over the lawn with the copy of *Rob Roy* she'd found in David's library. She did her best to ignore the titters and rude looks coming from the ladies around her. Painting with watercolors would hardly serve to garner her any favor with any of them, so why should she bother with it? Her painting skills were rather putrid, and such a description of them was possibly being more than kind.

The ladies could paint all they liked, and she'd never say a word against a single one of them for it, however much they deserved it. Not even Lady Portia. So why should they care that she shunned the activity and chose to read instead?

She and Serena had begrudgingly left Morgan with her brothers, who claimed they would find an appropriate entertainment for her.

While Morgan would have likely gone along with the rest of the ladies without complaint, sitting in the warm, clear weather outside as they painted, she couldn't very well participate in the activity herself.

Not only that, but the gentlemen planned to take some of David's boats out to the estuary and try their hands at fishing today. Morgan couldn't go along with them and be the only lady present for such a thing. That just wasn't done.

Besides, Emma doubted either Lord Trenowyth or Mr. Cardiff wished to allow their sister to encounter any more reminders of what had happened there than absolutely necessary.

She didn't know what they intended to do with her this afternoon, but she and Serena couldn't very well keep Morgan all to themselves during this fortnight. And if they did, how would Emma possibly find a husband? She'd be forever surrounded by the two other ladies, forming a bit of an impenetrable shield which would inadvertently keep the gentlemen away.

Serena set up her easel near Emma, placing a canvas upon it in a position which should allow for her to have a nice view of the folly. Emma smiled at her and then delved back into her book.

She'd read a few pages and was almost fully engrossed within the story, when a disturbance coming from the main house interrupted her reading. A footman was carrying yet another easel and a board of some sort. Not too far behind him, Mr. Cardiff had one hand full with vellum and a box of pastels, with Morgan holding the other.

Emma frowned and then turned her eyes back to her book. It was one thing for her to be out with the other ladies while they were painting. After all, she *could* choose to pick up a brush and try her hand at watercolors. It would be disastrous, but that would be her choice.

But Morgan couldn't see, so she clearly couldn't paint. Unlike Emma, she couldn't read to entertain her mind. If they were just going to bring Morgan out to sit with the ladies, why had the brothers insisted on separating her from Emma and Serena?

And then it struck her. It hadn't been the *brothers* who'd insisted, but just *one* brother. Mr. Cardiff. He'd done it because he didn't want Morgan to be with her, without a doubt. That rankled more so now than it had before, because of supper last night.

Emma attempted to concentrate on her book, but she couldn't focus on it. Her eyes roved over the same paragraph at least four times, and still hadn't even the slightest inkling what it said. She could only think about how Mr. Cardiff seemed to hate her so much, and yet he also seemed to be watching her in a different way, as well. His manner of expression left her bewildered, to say the least. But did she want him to change his mind, to stop hating her? She didn't know any more.

Looking up again, she saw that Mr. Cardiff had situated his easel to where Emma was directly in his line of vision. But surely he didn't intend to do a portrait of her. No, he must be preparing to sketch the vista behind her.

Morgan sat on a blanket at his feet, well away from the other ladies. She fidgeted with a flower she'd plucked from the lawn. She pulled a petal free, and it floated out of her fingers to land next to her feet. Emma had never seen Morgan look so bored. Distraction had always been common for her—she'd stared off into the ether all of those years ago, far more often than she did anything else, but her mind had been fully engaged in her wayward thoughts. One couldn't simply pull her out of her head back then. Now, it seemed even the slightest little provocation would allow her some excitement.

Yet her brother had brought her here, sat her down, and left her with nothing to engage her mind save plucking the petals from a flower. Insolent man.

Emma was overly tempted to give him a piece of her mind, but she had already caused enough damage by speaking plainly last night. She bit her tongue—literally—when a dog's bark broke through her thoughts.

Her head whipped around behind her just in time to see a mangy, brown mutt loping toward her with its tongue lolling out of its mouth.

A chorus of screams and scandalized squeals sounded all around her, and two easels fell to the ground as the other ladies rushed to move out of the dog's path.

"Does Lord Burington have a dog?" Morgan asked tentatively.

"No," Mr. Cardiff growled, even as he hauled his sister to her feet and stood between her and the animal. He ignored Morgan's indignant huff, simply shoving her behind him…and within moments, almost every lady present had followed her of their own accord.

71

All of them but Emma.

"Emma, do come this way," Vanessa called out from her position of safety next to Morgan. "It could be rabid."

"Could be might be the understatement of the century," Mr. Cardiff grumbled.

Emma's head shot up to stare at him. "For all the indications you've given, Mr. Cardiff, you *could be* rabid as well."

He leveled her with a stare and placed himself between all the other ladies and the dog.

The animal didn't seem even the least bit dangerous to Emma. Dirty and unkempt, certainly, and possibly a bit flea-ridden. She'd been rather unkempt more than she ought to have been in her life, too, and she wasn't even remotely dangerous. Granted, she was a human and not a wild animal. But still. Emma held out her hand as the animal came closer to her. He shoved his head into it straightaway.

She scratched behind his scraggly ear, and he let out a whining sort of sound.

"Do you like that?"

Of course, the dog couldn't answer her, so she scratched harder. He shoved his head into her hand more insistently than before. Emma dropped her book and used both hands. Within moments, he was happily panting and rubbing against her.

"He's harmless," Emma called out to the other ladies, hoping that they'd relax and resume their painting once they realized he wouldn't hurt them.

Instead, she heard them all talking beneath their breath.

"If she considers fleas harmless…"

"I can smell the mutt from here."

"It'll serve her right if he bites her."

Good heavens, they were being ridiculous. Emma kept petting the dog and scratching him, and within minutes he'd curled up at her side, calm as could be.

"I think he's decided to join us." She almost laughed at the horrified expression on Lady Portia's face. "I don't think he has any intention of doing anything but sitting next to me. You'll all be fine."

Serena was the first to venture out from behind Mr. Cardiff, who'd been scowling in Emma's direction the whole time with his arms crossed over his chest like a disapproving papa.

"Miss Hathaway is right," Serena said authoritatively. "He just wants a little affection. I'm sure he won't cause any harm." With that, she made her way back over beside Emma, bent down to give the dog a scratch, and then took up her spot behind her easel.

Slowly, the other ladies returned to their spots. Morgan tried to move forward, but Mr. Cardiff put out his hand, perhaps in an effort to stop her. She skirted around him, as though she'd felt his interference. "Miss Hathaway?" she called. "Pray tell, are you reading a book this afternoon?"

"*Rob Roy*," Emma replied. "I haven't gotten very far into it yet. Would you like me to read it aloud to you?"

The smile that lit Morgan's face could rival the sun...until her brother said, "I don't want you to go anywhere near that dog." Then Morgan's expression fell into a near pout.

Vanessa stepped in and offered her arm for Morgan to take. "Come along. I'll sit with you both and be sure you're safe from the dog."

The simple suggestion yet again visibly lifted Morgan's spirits, and Mr. Cardiff relented. They sat, the three of them with the dog, in the middle of the circle of ladies, reading and petting the dog, and laughing each time he'd nuzzle one of their hands.

Even though Mr. Cardiff had forced his way into her day when he brought his sister to paint with them all, Emma felt it had somehow turned into a pleasant one.

Kingley.

She'd named the damned mutt. One more bit of proof that Miss

Hathaway was absolutely not the sort of chit Aidan wanted his sister spending much time with, and yet she was precisely the one Morgan seemed drawn to. Well, one of them. Miss Weston wasn't so bad, and Morgan had spent time with her as well. But Miss Weston, likewise, spent altogether too much time in the vicinity of Miss Hathaway. And now, Miss Hathaway thought she needed to make this beast into a pet.

The dog surely had fleas and it stunk to high hell, and yet she'd allowed it to curl up beside her as she read aloud to his sister, and he was supposed to find this in some manner acceptable?

It had even ruined the delicate pink muslin of her gown! Not even the best laundry maid in all of England could possibly save the fabric after the beast had rubbed its filth and grime all over her, slobbering and drooling on her to boot. It wasn't until he saw the stains against the pink of his vellum that he realized he'd been doing her portrait, which only infuriated him more. He'd been putting her to canvas, as he'd done time and again, and all she wanted to do was sit with a mangy dog curled up at her side instead of—

Aidan stopped himself before he completed that thought. It was ludicrous. He needed to move on from that. It was better for his sanity's sake to think about how she'd given the beast a name. Like a pet. Like an animal she intended to keep and coddle and croon over.

When Aidan and the ladies had all packed up their easels and supplies to go back into the house, it took every ounce of restraint that he possessed to refrain from reminding her that the animal was not welcome inside. And it wasn't even his home! He had no right to make such a pronouncement, and yet it nearly fell from his lips as easily as his own name.

At least she'd left her dear *Kingley* outside, where he belonged. The last thing Aidan needed was for Morgan to become overly attached to a wild, mangy dog. When she became attached to things and then lost them, nothing good came of it.

Once the ladies went off to whatever they were to spend their afternoon doing, he made his way into David's library. He flipped the page of some massive tome on animal husbandry he'd picked up, not that he'd read a single word of the last page, or the page before that, and not that he intended to read even one word on the new page…but if a servant were to walk into the library and find him doing nothing but brooding with a murderous glower upon his face, he surely would hear about it later from David. Or Niall. Possibly both of them.

Aidan already had enough things plaguing his mind without his brother or his friend adding their voices to the ever-present voice in his head.

He'd been alone for a good half an hour or more after the ladies retired inside. The other men were still out on the river. It was likely for the best that he'd stayed behind with the women, despite the taunts a few of the men had sent his way when he'd informed them he would prefer to work on some art with the ladies. It had allowed him to keep an eye on Morgan and that dog.

He trusted Lady Burington well enough. But it was a large beast. All of the women combined might not have been able to pull it off, should it decide to attack one of them, which only made Miss Hathaway's befriending of it all the more troubling. How could she know it was tame? How could she guarantee it wouldn't harm anyone? What would she have done if it had attacked?

Devil take it, why was he thinking about Miss Hathaway again?

When Aidan turned what must have been at least the tenth page without having read a single word, the door to the Heathcote Park library swung open and David stepped inside, then stopped abruptly.

"What are *you* doing in here? I thought I might find Miss Hathaway."

"So terribly sorry to disappoint you," Aidan drawled, unable to hide his irritation at hearing her name on David's lips. Good God, it was like she followed him everywhere here, even if she wasn't present. "I needed somewhere to think. Your library was quiet and, for once, empty."

"Too many ladies out on the lawn chattering? They can be a little overwhelming when they're all together in a flock like that."

Aidan scowled. They had actually been rather quiet, all things considered. Well, aside from the shouts of dismay when the mutt had come upon them. That part was enough to leave him with a ringing sensation in his head, like church bells that never ceased.

He shook his head. "They weren't so bad as all that."

David strolled in. The door closed behind him, and he moved closer to the armchair beside Aidan, then peeked over Aidan's shoulder. "Christ, what are you reading?"

"I'm not." No one would believe he had an interest in such a thing, so there was no point in pretending otherwise. "I'm just holding it so I give off the appearance of being occupied."

"You're giving off the appearance of being a sullen, angry fool." David dropped into the chair and crossed one ankle over his knee.

"That's hardly an act or a mere *appearance*."

"It's good you recognize the truth for what it is."

Aidan gave a wry grin. "One must call a spade a spade."

"True." David narrowed his eyes. "So what is your foul mood really about?"

But he couldn't give voice to that. He hadn't sorted it all out in his own head yet. All Aidan knew was that he wanted to let Morgan live again, but he couldn't seem to find the fortitude within himself to trust her to do it all alone. He knew that, no matter how he tried to twist things around in his head, somehow he was always at the crux of every matter…and he hated that. He knew he wanted to continue to hate Miss Hathaway because it was what was comfortable and familiar. At certain turns she made such a task entirely too easy, and at other points she made it as impossible as removing his own heart from his chest and somehow continuing to live. He'd begun to notice things about her, such as her kindness to Morgan, and the way she seemed to attract outcasts and then take them under her wing, and how she didn't look altogether ungainly any more when she wore such pretty frocks. Yet he didn't want to notice any of those things at all—which begged the question: why didn't he want to notice?

The only answer which came to mind was that it was easier to continue hating her than it was to admit she hadn't done anything to deserve his hatred. The more he noticed how pretty she was or how kindly she treated Morgan, the closer he came to being forced to admit that, at least to himself.

But he couldn't tell David any of that. Not until he'd worked it all out within his own mind. So he blew out a breath. "I'm frustrated, is all."

"That much is obvious."

His cheek and lip pulled at one side, almost in a grin, despite himself. "I think it would be best for everyone if I tried to separate myself some. Get some space."

"You could have distanced yourself from the people who are frustrating you so much if you would have come out to the river with us. You could have left Morgan with the ladies, and everything would have been just fine."

That was the problem. Trusting that she'd be all right without either him or Niall to look out for her...it was too difficult right now. It might always be too difficult, though he didn't want to allow his mind to dwell on that possibility.

When he remained silent, David stretched out both legs before him and loosely crossed his arms over his chest. "I have an idea," he said thoughtfully, "that might grant you some space and allow you to sort through whatever it is that's plaguing you."

Aidan didn't know what to think of that tone. It was like David was being cautious with him. Like he was afraid of what Aidan's reaction might be. In all the years they'd known each other, he'd never experienced the like.

Good God, had he become so despondent now that even David, who'd known him since they were boys, feared what he might do? Lifting his brows, Aidan said, "Go on," though he half dreaded what his friend might suggest.

"I've got an area set up for you in the hermitage, on the far side of the estate."

"Devil take it." He'd be damned if he locked himself away in seclusion while Morgan tried to find her way in society again without him. Even as he started to voice that very thing, though, David held up his hand.

"You'll have everything you could possibly need. Chisels, hammers, marble…even the piece you were working on when you left your studio."

Sculpting. The mere thought of it had his hands rubbing together involuntarily until he felt the calluses still lining his fingers and palms. Yet he shook his head. "I can't."

"You can. I sent my men to London, and they brought everything you left behind. It's all in place. All it needs is you."

He shook his head, baffled by the suggestion, by the mere thought of it. All it needed was an Aidan Cardiff who could devote the time, and energy, and emotional wherewithal to something of that nature. He was no longer that man. Since the day he received an urgent letter from home, telling him that Morgan had thrown herself before a racing carriage and was inconsolable over Stoneham's rejection, he'd invested every ounce of emotion he had in caring for her.

To renew sculpting would require far more than he had to give.

And it would keep him locked away, in seclusion, for hours and hours at a time. So often, back when he allowed himself the opportunity to sculpt, he would lose his grip on time and space, until he'd been at work for hours or days, without stopping for anything but the barest of necessities.

Yet his pulse kicked to life in his veins at the thought, and he couldn't deny that the thought of sculpting again was calling to him. Drawing him closer.

To what? To the life he'd thought to lead, once upon a time? He'd turned his back on that long ago. He couldn't possibly allow himself to become so sidetracked by anything. Not now.

How could he live with himself if something happened to Morgan and he wasn't there? He couldn't. Never again.

Something which so thoroughly absorbed him had no place in his life ever again.

David stood, dragging a hand over his jaw before looking down at Aidan. "Niall told me you'd react this way. I think I knew you would, too. But I had to try."

"Why?" Aidan croaked, no longer recognizing his own voice.

"Because I miss my friend." He let out a mirthless chuckle as he made his way to the door. "It's all there. No one else will go to the hermitage. It's locked, so even if they went they couldn't get in. If you change your mind…"

David dropped a key on the table just inside the door, and then he was gone.

CHAPTER SIX

Emma rushed down to the drawing room at midmorning the next day, reminding herself to walk at a decorous pace once she got close enough to the entryway that someone might see her. She'd allowed Fanny to construct a new coiffure to go along with her lovely periwinkle walking dress, but she wouldn't have agreed to it if she'd had any idea how long it would take to dress her hair in such an elaborate manner.

Despite all of Fanny's efforts, Emma must still wear a bonnet while outside, so it wouldn't matter anyway. Not in the grand scheme of things. What gentleman who might wish to form an attachment with her would see this fashionable coif while it was buried beneath straw and fabric and ribbons and flowers? Taking the time to let Fanny do her business had been a grand miscalculation on Emma's part.

By the time she rushed into the corridor leading to the drawing room, everyone else was already on their way out. In fact, a good half of the other houseguests had split off into smaller groupings and had made their way to the grand entryway, and now they were heading out of doors.

Serena Weston moved past Emma on the arm of Lord Muldaire, alongside Lord Trenowyth and a very frothy young brunette—Miss Selwyn, if memory served. Turning to look over her shoulder, Serena mouthed, "I'm sorry," before they were gone. Her eyes had been quite pained. Understandable, given the circumstances. While Mr. Weston was intent upon making a match between his daughter and Lord Muldaire, Serena had other ideas.

Still, she was sorry? Why? About what?

Vanessa and David came out into the corridor from the drawing room alongside Lady Portia and Lord Roxburghe, interrupting Emma's ruminations. The expression on Roxburghe's face turned sour at the sight of Emma, but Vanessa smiled as brightly as the sun.

"There you are. Lord Jacob?" she called over her shoulder to Lord Muldaire's perpetually sullen brother. "I promised she would arrive momentarily, and she has." Then Vanessa faced Emma again, her eyes bright and cheerful with the anticipation of taking a promenade through the grounds on the arm of her husband. "Since you were late, everyone else is already paired off. I'm sure you won't mind walking this afternoon with Lord Jacob, Lady Morgan, and Mr. Cardiff."

Emma felt her jaw drop, but quickly set it to rights. Spending the morning with Morgan would be no hardship, and while she wasn't entirely certain how she ought to feel about Lord Jacob and his grim visage, she was certain she could manage. But Emma had no intention of willingly placing herself in the path of Mr. Cardiff. Not when he still sent fiery glares in her direction at every opportunity he was given. Not when he could hardly bear to say a civil word to her. Not when he was so bound and determined to treat Morgan as though she were completely inept and unable to do anything by herself.

But then again, he *had* seemed to respond favorably to her outburst at supper, and until Kingley had come along while they were painting, she'd imagined he might be doing a portrait of her.

Blast, why did the man have to present her with such a conundrum?

Without giving her the chance to argue, Vanessa and David kept moving. When they reached the door leading outside, Mr. Cardiff and

Morgan had appeared at the threshold coming from the drawing room.

Lord Jacob stood in the hallway, his ever-present glower darkening his already dark features.

Goodness, this was shaping up to be a very dissatisfying morning. Emma hadn't thought anyone capable of being more brooding and irritable than Mr. Cardiff until she met Lord Jacob. Now she was beginning to rethink her previous assumptions.

Lord Jacob held out an arm to her. "Shall we?"

There really was no option left available to her. Emma reached to take his arm, but Morgan somehow got there first, wrapping her hand deftly into the crook of Lord Jacob's arm and giving him a pleasant smile. He merely scowled down at her in return, proving yet again that he was as impenetrable as a London fog.

"Please don't force me to spend the entire day on my brother's arm," Morgan whispered quietly, but vehemently, to only Emma. "He hardly lets me out of his sight as it is. He wouldn't join anyone else today…"

"Of course," Emma said in response, though on the inside she wanted to scream her frustrations from the rooftops. She had no more desire to spend the day with Mr. Cardiff than his sister did.

Lord Jacob started off with Morgan at his side, leaving Emma and Mr. Cardiff in their wake. Tentatively, she looked up at him. His lips jerked downward in response, but he silently held out his arm.

And what choice did she have? Emma took hold of his proffered arm, biting down on her tongue in the process to avoid saying anything untoward. Although on second thought, letting Mr. Cardiff hear a few of her somewhat less-than-friendly thoughts might not be the worst thing that could happen today.

He followed after his sister, moving with an intensity of purpose that left her shuffling her feet along hastily in order to stay with him.

Indeed, he didn't slow at all until they were a scant two steps behind Morgan and Lord Jacob, within a short enough distance that they could hear every word spoken between the two. Not that they were saying much at all. For that matter, Mr. Cardiff seemed perfectly content, at least for now, to spend the morning without saying a word to her.

It certainly wouldn't hurt her feelings if she didn't have to hear him deride her for some misstep or another.

"Tell me, Lord Jacob, where are you leading us?" Morgan asked sweetly after they'd been walking for nearly ten minutes. Her tone made it seem as though she were unaware that she was on the arm of a man more frosty and less congenial than even her brother. Could the inability to see into his eyes have so thoroughly clouded Morgan's judgment? "My feet don't seem to recognize the path we're on."

Only then did Emma chance a look at her surroundings. She'd been too caught up in her discomfiture over having to spend the morning with Mr. Cardiff that she hadn't paid even the slightest bit of attention to their direction.

Good heavens.

Lord Jacob had led them off in a direction Emma had never before traveled at Heathcote Park, so there was little wonder that Morgan didn't recognize it. The trail they'd taken was woody, thick with maples, willows, poplars, and birch. The trees lining the path were overgrown, as though the path itself hadn't been in use for a great many years—but occasionally, they'd pass by a large limb that seemed to have been freshly broken off. Someone must have been along here not too long ago. What their purpose might have been remained a mystery. Emma couldn't imagine what anyone would do out this way, so far from the great house. So far from anything of use to the civilized world. Why, there were hardly even any animals about—birds and the like. Just how deep into the woods had they gone?

"I'm not entirely certain," Lord Jacob said in response after a few moments. For that matter, he didn't sound as though he cared in the slightest where they were going.

Still they stumbled along, never slowing or stopping, and certainly never coming across anyone else. Emma couldn't imagine that any of the other groups had gone in this direction. Surely, if they had, they would have turned back long before now.

With each step she took, the tension in Mr. Cardiff's arm grew. The strong, corded muscles beneath Emma's fingertips clenched tighter and harder, yet never released. He was as wary about their journey as she was, and yet he did not put a halt to it. Why wouldn't he say something? Why didn't he stop Lord Jacob?

Wasn't he concerned about Morgan's safety, with the uncared-for path and the deep woods surrounding them and Lord Jacob leading them with no clear direction in mind? The man was infuriatingly persistent with hovering over his sister at every opportunity which presented itself. So why now, when there could truly be a problem, was he ignoring it?

Emma could well imagine he had no such qualms about *her* safety and, perhaps, might even hope something untoward might overcome her. But he was always so overprotective of Morgan that she couldn't understand why he wouldn't insist they turn back.

Where could they possibly be going? If they didn't stop soon, they might just walk all the way to London or some other equally as unlikely place.

When the path narrowed further, and the trees grew so thick there were only faint traces of the sun's light peeking through the branches, and *still* Lord Jacob led them on in monotonous silence, Emma finally had had enough.

She planted her feet where she stood, causing Mr. Cardiff to jerk to a sudden and unexpected stop. He rounded on her, his eyes flashing with steely determination in the dappled light, giving her a moment of hesitation.

"What is the problem?" His tone made clear the impatience she sensed in the tic along his jaw line.

Emma refused to cower beneath his glare. She'd allowed him to intimidate her far too much in this lifetime already. No more. Not when Morgan's safety could be hanging in the balance. "Where in God's name is Lord Jacob leading us?" She loosed her grip upon his arm and crossed both of hers over her chest. "This path clearly is not in use and hasn't been for some time. I cannot imagine where he thinks to take us. You can't truly think we should keep going."

Mr. Cardiff pierced her with his scowl before turning to look over his shoulder. When he faced her again, his jaw was working in frustration. "I don't know where he thinks he's going, but he's got my sister with him and *they're* still moving." He again looked over his shoulder toward where Morgan and Lord Jacob were disappearing into the woods. His brow furrowed, and a single muscle flexed along his jaw.

"Feel free to go with them, sir. I'll make my way back to the main house alone."

Emma spun around to do precisely that, but he gripped her on the upper arm, halting her escape.

"Unhand me," she demanded.

"You're putting me in a truly impossible situation, Miss Hathaway."

For the first time that she could remember, Emma felt slightly sorry for him. He sounded utterly miserable, as though he couldn't stand the thought of allowing her to walk back on her own…as though it were equally as impossible a thought to him as leaving Morgan alone with Lord Jacob.

How laughable.

Were he any other gentleman, Emma might believe such a thing to be true. But she had no such delusions where Mr. Cardiff was concerned.

Were she any other lady, she might think him less a cad and more concerned about her welfare. She knew better than to harbor such lies within her heart. She'd seen the truth of his feelings for her in his eyes.

"I can't imagine it is as impossible for you as you imply," she said coolly. "Go make certain your sister is well. I'll do just fine on my own."

Again she tried to leave him, yet his hand remained improperly and firmly attached to her upper arm in an unyielding grip. He tried to pull her along with him, dragging her despite her desire to go back.

Emma tugged against him until once more, he jerked to a stop.

He spun to face her, his eyes flashing with ire. "It is unsafe for you to be out here alone, Miss Hathaway."

"Pardon me." The acidic tone dripping from her tongue was unfamiliar even to her. Good heavens, Emma didn't recognize herself in the slightest. It was bound to be his fault. No one else could possibly rouse such negativity from her, not in all the three-and-twenty years of her life. Yet she was powerless to stop it. "I never thought you to be concerned for my safety before. Indeed, I never thought you to be concerned for anyone save yourself."

"Myself?" he barked back at her, his jaw grinding his teeth together unnaturally. "In all the time of our acquaintance, you think I've been concerned for myself? When have I ever done anything that was not for Morgan?"

"You can't possibly think you're helping her. You smother her. You never allow her to do anything for herself. We all do, everyone in her life! How is that helping her?"

Mr. Cardiff took a menacing step toward her, tugging her closer by the arm he still grasped. "And you think you know better? Better than her relatives, her blood?"

Despite her every inclination to back away, her stomach flipped about from his proximity. She wanted, irrationally, to be closer. Good heavens, what was coming over her? Emma took an involuntary step toward him as well, crossing her free arm over her chest as though to place some sort of barrier between them. "Yes, I do. You're hurting her by trying to help her so much."

A muscle in his cheek jerked. His eyes darkened, and his lips pressed tightly together, and for a moment she thought he might do something more completely mad than even he had done before, like kiss her. But then his grasp lessened just enough that she could pull her arm free.

What was she thinking? Mr. Cardiff, *kiss* her? Perhaps she was the mad one of the two of them. She certainly didn't want him to kiss her. Did she? But no matter how she tried, she couldn't stop staring at the thin line of his lips and wondering how it would feel to have them pressed against hers. Oh, blast, what was happening to her? She took two quick steps away, needing desperately to put more distance between them so she could clear her thoughts.

He reached as though to stop her again, but froze in place at the sound of a dog's bark.

Emma spun her head in the direction of the bark to find Kingley bounding toward her, his tongue lolling from his mouth. If she didn't know better, she'd think the dog was actually grinning. But dogs couldn't grin—could they? She didn't think they could. But then again, perhaps she just didn't *know* they could.

He didn't stop until he was at her feet. Emma bent down to scratch behind his ears, and he yapped happily.

"You'll be as flea-infested as that beast is if you don't stop," Mr. Cardiff grumbled.

But Kingley's arrival had come at precisely the right time. A moment longer, and she feared she would have done something incredibly stupid like kiss him instead of wondering if he wanted to kiss her.

"I suppose we can discover if you're right, Mr. Cardiff. I'll walk with Kingley back to the main house, and you may chase after Lord Jacob and your sister."

Emma didn't give the boor an opportunity to stop her. She patted a hand against her thigh a few times and took off. Kingley trotted at her side as though he had walked with her thus every day of his life, never moving too far away from her. He was the perfect companion.

Certainly far more perfect a companion than Mr. Cardiff. It was too bad gentlemen couldn't be as agreeable as canines.

When he'd finally returned Morgan to her maid that afternoon, thereby ensuring that she was no longer in the clutches of Deering and his madcap schemes to take them on a seemingly pointless journey through the woods, Aidan stomped through the corridors of Heathcote Park until he found an empty room in which to brood until luncheon.

The only positive to come from the jaunt was that they'd come upon the hermitage where David had set up a studio for Aidan. And, as promised, it was well off the main path. No one would possibly come across him there, if he were to choose to sculpt again. Well, other than perhaps Lord Jacob Deering.

And why in God's name did Deering want to go out there in the first place? What was his intention? In all likelihood, Aidan would never learn.

The entire morning, he had felt the necessity to protect not only Morgan from Lord Jacob's aimless meanderings, but Miss Hathaway as well. If there was one person on this earth he had no desire to ever purposefully protect, it was Emma Hathaway. Yet, with her on his arm as they tromped through the woods, he'd been unable to stop himself from feeling the need to turn them all around and return *both* ladies to safety, post haste.

It was maddening. Infuriating, even. Particularly since he didn't know what it was about Deering that set his teeth on edge. True, the man was more sullen than even Aidan by half, but what had he done to engender such anxiety for the ladies' safety. He'd never had a violent outburst. The worst he'd done was to challenge Roxeburghe to a duel.

Far more troublesome, however was the compunction Aidan felt to see to Emma's safety.

None of it made any sense, least of all the strange urge he'd felt to kiss her at the very moment she was suggesting he was handling Morgan improperly. She'd stared up at him with the same flash of brilliance in her eyes as she'd had when she defended Morgan at supper the first night of the house party, and he'd been taken aback by her gumption. Nevertheless, how would *she* possibly know what was best for his sister? She was hardly more than a mere slip of a girl, a lady who spent more time in the fictional world of her books than she did in the real world around her. What could she know about how best to aid Morgan and to help ease her back into society? What could she know of his sister's needs?

What Morgan needed was her family around her. She needed to know they loved her. She needed guidance and assistance as she learned to live life again without the use of her sight. She needed people to protect her from all the cruelty that could and would be heaped upon her by the heartless world of the *ton*—those who would see her scarred skin and blind eyes, and choose to mock her for them.

Anyone could see that was what he was trying desperately to give her. Anyone could see he only wanted what was best for her. It irked him to no end to have Miss Hathaway, of all people, try to tell him he was doing his sister a disservice by assisting her in every single way he could.

Hardly more than two minutes had passed since he'd closed the door and flopped down in an elegant silk brocade armchair before the door opened. Aidan scowled as he looked up, and his scowl only intensified when he saw his brother standing in the doorway.

"I thought that was you I saw skulking through the house and coming in here," Niall said. He pulled the door shut behind him and then moved through the room, taking up the matching armchair across from Aidan. "Why did Miss Hathaway return alone?"

That question was absolutely and unequivocally the wrong question for Niall to ask at the moment, though he couldn't possibly have known such a thing.

Aidan felt his lips twist against his will. He shook his head, as though the slight action could perhaps clear the ugly thoughts chasing through his mind. "She wished to return," he muttered. "I couldn't very well leave Morgan alone with Deering in the woods, could I?"

"But it was acceptable for you to allow Miss Hathaway to find her way back all by herself?"

Aidan lifted a brow, which earned him a scowl from his brother.

"Burington is rather displeased with you, and I can't say I blame him for it. You seem to have forgotten how to act like a gentleman in the last several years. Lord knows it would have to be an act…"

That stung, coming from his brother. He winced. "What would you have me do?" Aidan asked. He couldn't very well act on his own impulses, lest he end up kissing the chit. Yet another thing that would cast him in the light of a villain.

Niall crossed an ankle over his knee and relaxed a bit. Apparently, he had no intention of leaving Aidan in peace any time in the near future. "Perhaps you could start by apologizing to Miss Hathaway."

Apologizing to her? The deuced chit had been the one who'd forced him to choose between protecting her and protecting his sister! He'd been placed in a position where he couldn't possibly make the right decision—there'd been no *right* decision available to him, save tossing Miss Hathaway over his shoulder and dragging her along with them. Which, now that he thought about it, held rather more appeal than he'd care to admit.

But no, if either of them ought to be apologizing for the situation, it was her. He started to tell his brother precisely that, but Niall cut him off.

"I don't want to hear any excuses, Aidan. You're the gentleman. You've got to make her see reason if she places you in an awkward position." He stood, straightening his coat, which had only been mussed slightly all morning. "Just imagine if it had been Morgan with some other chap, and he'd allowed her to walk off alone."

"No one would do that," Aidan bit off. She was blind, for God's sake. He couldn't imagine anyone who'd allow her to separate herself from the group in the midst of a strange wood.

Niall held up a hand. "But what if someone would? Miss Hathaway doesn't have two older brothers with her, protecting her at every turn, you know. Burington is looking after her, but it's hardly the same." He headed for the door, but stopped just before going through. "You owe it to Morgan to look after her friend, if nothing else," he said quietly, without turning his head.

Then he left, pulling the door shut behind him.

You owe it to Morgan... Niall's words hung heavy in the room, repeating in Aidan's head over and over again, as though they were bouncing off the walls of his mind and creating an echo.

He owed Morgan more than he could ever give her. But this might be asking too much.

CHAPTER SEVEN

Emma sat on a sofa with Serena and Morgan on either side. Sir Henry stood beside them, his hands clasped behind his back and a kind smile tugging at the corners of his lips. Emma studied him, trying to catalogue each of his features and attributes and reason out why he would make an excellent match for her.

Sir Henry was adequately handsome, though she was almost as tall as he was. Not that that should hinder her affections toward him. She couldn't allow something so petty as physical appearance to cloud her judgment.

He was a good man. Thoughtful. Affable. Congenial. And, perhaps more importantly than any of his other attributes, he seemed interested in her. That alone ought to be enough for Emma to set her sights upon him.

Not to fall in love with him—but she had no intentions of falling in love with any man until she was well and truly married to him. Morgan's heartache a few years ago was more than enough warning for Emma to decide she'd never allow any man such power over her own feelings, at least not until he was irrevocably the only man for whom she ought to have such feelings.

Yet she couldn't help but think of Mr. Cardiff again, and the tiny flutters he seemed to always engender in her stomach, and the way he made her heart race at the most inopportune moments. Those were precisely the sorts of reactions she ought to be avoiding with any gentleman.

Thankfully, Sir Henry did not inspire any such flutters. The way he was smiling down at her at the moment made her think he might wish he did.

"If you truly want a dog as a pet, Miss Hathaway, allow me to train a pup for you," he said, laughing.

She smiled up at him then. "A pup?" He wanted to train a pup for her. How utterly charming, despite the fact that she hadn't truly considered having a dog for a pet. Yes, Kingley had chosen to follow her around quite a bit, but that didn't mean she wanted a pet. Did she? "And where might we find this pup?"

"I breed hounds, you know," he continued as Mr. Deering and Lord Muldaire made their way over to join them. Deering clapped a hand on his shoulder, which caused Sir Henry to jump slightly. He recovered himself quickly. "For that matter, one of my bitches delivered a new litter a few weeks ago. You could come to Seton Court later this summer and make your choice, and then before the next Season I could have it trained and ready to go home with you."

Morgan gasped at her side, but tried to cover it by coughing delicately into her hand. Serena hurried to pick up a cup of tea and hand it to Morgan, her surprised eyes locking onto Emma in the process.

He was inviting her to his home. Goodness, she hadn't expected that. Not by any stretch of the imagination. Wasn't that a bit forward?

"Of course, that would all depend upon Lord and Lady Burington accompanying you," he added after a moment's hesitation. Sir Henry looked a bit flustered, shifting from one foot to the other. "I wouldn't—"

"He's good with them," Lord Muldaire put in, interrupting before Sir Henry could make a total cake of himself. He took a seat in the armchair directly across from them and set his glass of port down on the mahogany occasional table beside him. "I bought a pair from him

After Aidan's inexplicable desire to kiss Miss Hathaway while they'd argued in the woods that morning, and then Niall's insistence that he find some way to repent for his behavior or at least apologize to her for it, Aidan could do nothing but brood over the fact that he couldn't keep his mind anywhere but on the vexing woman.

Indeed, he'd spent the rest of the day with little else on his mind but the impertinent girl who seemingly had no regard for his sister's safety. Even now, as he sat by himself near the hearth after supper, nursing the glass of port which he'd brought with him from the dining room, he was bewildered to find himself watching her.

Perhaps more befuddling was the fact that she, likewise, was watching him. Yes, he'd made an arse of himself when he'd arrived in the drawing room by tripping over the chair upon which he was now sitting. He'd only done it because, for whatever reason, he couldn't stop staring at her. Couldn't focus on where his feet were moving. Couldn't think of anything but how perplexing it was that he was suddenly so fascinated by her: the intensity of her gaze, the plumpness of her lips. And the flush that was delightfully creeping over her skin. That flush made him think all sorts of inappropriate thoughts.

At least he hadn't spilled his port when he'd tripped.

She sat well across the room from him, her blue gown the precise shade the morning sky had been when they'd gone off on their promenade through the woods. Morgan sat on one side of her and Miss Weston on the other, and the three of them were surrounded by gentlemen—a thought which left Aidan with very muddled thoughts. Miss Hathaway was turned at a slight degree so that her attention remained squarely on Sir Henry Irvine. Her legs were angled and bent, crossed at the ankles, and the slightest hint of her slippers peeked out beneath the hem.

His unfocused thoughts moved along with his eyes, which trailed over those long, ungainly legs. He thought about how she always seemed on the verge of falling down, as though her legs would not cooperate with her mind and do as she wished them to do…and then he started thinking about those legs wrapped around his waist while he drove himself inside her repeatedly.

That line of thought absolutely wouldn't do.

So then he forced both his eyes and his thoughts elsewhere, only to discover himself looking at her lips that were too wide for her face, and which were far from society's idea of beauty. Her eyes flickered away from Aidan for a moment and she smiled up at Sir Henry, stretching those lips wide. But then Aidan's mind turned to thoughts about the feel of them suckling against his earlobe or stretching over his cock—and the cock in question hardened to the point of pain in his breeches.

This time, he repositioned his body, facing the opposite side of the drawing room and doing his best to hide his erection from view until he could gain better control over himself. Good God. What was wrong with him? It was Miss Hathaway, for Christ's sake, not some piece of Haymarket ware or opera singer. He didn't find her attractive in the least. Did he?

A grouping of gentlemen that included both David and Niall was situated in his line of sight now, blocking his view of Miss Hathaway and her lush lips and delectable legs. Much better.

How had one entirely inappropriate thought about one very inappropriate kiss with a thoroughly inappropriate lady turned to this madness?

Until today, every thought he had of Miss Hathaway that involved an image of her had been linked to somehow punishing her for the slights he'd perceived. Now the images coursing through his mind were punishing him instead, almost begging him to take out his pastels and vellum.

Niall caught Aidan's eye and worked his way through the room to join him. Blast, but he didn't want to talk. Not now. Not while he had a mind filled with lustful images that he was trying, unsuccessfully, to banish...not to mention the proof of those lustful thoughts pressing against the flap of his breeches. He tried to cross his legs and somehow hide the evidence, but managed only to draw his attention more fully to the growing problem. The dog. He should think of the dog and all the fleas. But that thought only led him back to thoughts of Miss Hathaway.

There was no stopping his brother when he set his mind to something. Aidan had never met a more single-minded person in all of his life, nor one more driven to set things right. Or at least *right* as he perceived *right* to be.

They didn't always see eye to eye on that score.

Nevertheless, there would be no stopping Niall from joining him. After stopping briefly to discuss something with Lord Roxburghe in a far more civilized manner than Aidan would have managed, Niall finished crossing the room. "Have you apologized to Miss Hathaway yet? I can't help but notice you've hardly taken your eyes from her the whole evening."

"I've been watching Morgan," Aidan lied.

"And I've been dining with Alexander the Great. You've never looked at Morgan that way before, and the very instant you start, I'll send for someone to cart you off to Bedlam."

He ought to have come up with a better lie. Looking at their sister with lust in his eyes? Christ, he ought to voluntarily commit himself to Bedlam just for making the suggestion, but now was not the time for such an endeavor. He grunted for his brother's sake. At least it could be considered some sort of response.

"So you haven't made your apologies yet, then." A statement, not a question. His brother had always been too readily able to discern the truth from Aidan, even when he had no inclination to divulge it. A damned annoying trait.

"When would I have had time to do that?" he bit off. It was damned near miraculous he could say even that much while he was so otherwise occupied.

"I won't march you over there holding you by the ear and watch over you while you do it," Niall bit off. "Not even Mother would do something like that anymore. You're a grown man. Act like it. I'll trust you to do what is right."

What is *right*. Such a perplexing concept, yet one that Niall spoke of as though it were the simplest thing in the world. He always saw things in strict black and white, never a shade of gray.

Aidan was not so lucky as that. In his world, not only were there infinite combinations of grays, but every other color under the sun as well. Waters were much murkier in his head than in his brother's—always had been. Some days, he wished he could see things as plainly as Niall did.

Those days were rather rare, of late.

Lucky for him, Niall didn't wait around for a response. He turned and made his way to a table where Mr. Weston sat with several other gentlemen playing whist, and took up a chair…leaving Aidan alone again. Blissfully, blessedly alone.

The conversation with Niall *had* served one purpose. The raging lust that had previously been coursing through his veins had cooled, at least a small degree. He thought, perhaps, he could yet again turn around without his erection making itself known to all and sundry.

When he did, Miss Hathaway's warm, brown eyes immediately found his. She looked away, staring out the window, and Aidan couldn't miss the hint of a blush creeping up her cheeks.

Why would she be flustered? He knew why *he* was—it was a damned nuisance to be physically attracted to a woman upon whom he'd harbored such hatred for so many years. But why would Miss Hathaway join him thus?

He'd given her no cause whatsoever in all the time of their acquaintance to even be able to stand the sight of him. She clearly had no desire to be in his presence. Why would she flush from being caught staring at him? Indeed, why would she be looking at him at all?

There seemed to be no end to the complexity of their fledgling, ill-fated relationship. He ought to do them both a favor and banish her from his mind. Ignoring her would serve far more purpose than either entertaining his lustful thoughts or those of vengeance.

But…

For all his best intentions, Aidan could not remove his eyes from her if he tried.

Every now and again, she'd turn back to the group surrounding her, laughing with Morgan and Miss Weston, or answering Sir Henry or Lord Muldaire with a smile that could warm even the coldest of hearts such as his own. Her eyes might flicker over to Aidan again before she hastily returned her gaze to the window—the great bay window overlooking the estuary.

He wondered what she thought of when she looked out that window…when she saw the riverbed where their lives had altered so drastically. Well, his had been drastically altered, at least. He could only imagine that Miss Hathaway's life had been changed in some manner as well. Those few minutes when Morgan was drowning—five minutes perhaps, or maybe seven—had been the worst of his life.

It must be high tide now, like it had been that day. The water would be up against the banks, pulsing with the life of the ocean. Threatening to take anything within it out into the sea, never to be seen or heard from again.

And yet, Miss Hathaway sat there and watched with no discernible emotion taking over her visage. The desire to know what was going on inside her head became so strong within Aidan that he almost had to force himself to leave. All he could think of doing was marching over to Miss Hathaway, gripping her shoulders, and shaking her until she told him everything he wished to know before kissing her senseless.

He was still trying to calm himself, making an effort to slow his pulse and return his breathing to that of a sane person, when Miss Hathaway's lips parted slightly. Even though the room was crowded and there was no way he could have possibly heard anything coming from between those lips, he imagined he heard a soft, "Oh."

Then she was on her feet and making her excuses. She placed a hand to her forehead, feigning a headache or illness or being overly tired—he couldn't be certain which, since he was fully on the other side of the room from her.

She made her way to the door. Sir Henry followed her, holding out his hand as though to offer her assistance. Miss Hathaway shook her head, using her hands to gesture him back to the rest of the group they'd been seated with.

Then she darted through the doors and was gone.

Once the drawing room doors closed behind her and she was certain no one had followed her, Emma raced through the corridors in the direction of the kitchens. They'd had a lovely roasted quail for supper, and if there was any of that left, it would do perfectly.

No servants stopped her on her way. Thank goodness. More than likely, many of them were occupied with either seeing to the guests' current needs or preparing for their future needs, which served her purposes quite well. While she had no qualms about pretending to have a headache in order to escape the drawing room, there was no call for her to have to explain her deception should word somehow reach guests in the drawing room.

Emma hadn't really thought through all of that before setting her plan into motion. She'd just seen Kingley pawing at the window and imagined she'd heard him whining with hunger, and then she'd decided to act.

When she turned the final corner and discovered the stairs down to the kitchens, still without being stopped, she let out a sigh of relief. Lying had never been a particular skill of hers, so she did it as sparingly as possible. She took the stairs as quickly as she could, and then came to an abrupt stop when the cook and all of the various kitchen maids looked up at her, startled.

Perhaps she was a bit mad, but this was no time for her to worry about it; nor was it time to allow the servants to deter her.

"Can we help ye, Miss Hathaway?" Cook bustled around a table, wiping her hands on an apron as she came. "Ye could ha' just rung for a maid, ye know. They'd be glad te bring ye anything ye need, should ye just ask." She tucked a graying strand of hair that had escaped her mobcap behind her ear and put a hand out as though to indicate that Emma should follow her. Before she knew what was happening, the cook had turned her back around and guided her back up the very steps she'd just raced down.

Blast, that wouldn't work.

"Yes, I know." Emma stopped moving and turned yet again to face the cook. "But what I need must be kept secret."

Based on the expression on the older woman's face, one would have thought a murder had just taken place right before her eyes. She planted one hand on each hip and gave Emma a scowl that would have put Mr. Cardiff's to shame. "I keep no secrets from Lord and Lady Burington, miss, and I won't be changin' tha' for ye or anyone else, mind."

But Vanessa and David wouldn't be bothered in the slightest if she fed Kingley, Emma was sure of it. "It needn't be kept secret from Lord and Lady Burington," she hastened to say, grateful when the cook's eyes softened by a minuscule degree. "Just the rest of the guests, you see."

This caught Cook's notice. Her bushy eyebrows rose in question and a decided gleam struck her eyes. "And wha' secret might this be?"

A few minutes later, Emma was being shuffled through the servants' stairways and corridors so as not to be seen by any of the other guests, her hands filled with a plate of quail, carrots, and peas.

When she arrived at the door leading out to the west side of the house, near the bay window that overlooked the estuary, the scullery maid who'd been sent to guide her gave a little curtsey as she opened the door. "We'll send Horner to lock it after you come back in, miss. Just bring the plate back to the kitchens." She scurried away through the wending halls before Emma could properly thank her.

Carefully, Emma made certain the door was closed, so as not to rouse unnecessary suspicions, but that she could still open it. Then she moved around the corner until the bay window was in view. Candles lit the drawing room inside, casting the others aglow in dancing flickers. With the light of the moon the only thing illuminating the out of doors, she was certain no one would be able to see her. Certainly not if she didn't go close to the window.

Taking cautious steps, she made her way along the side of the main house. It wouldn't do to fall into an unexpected hole or trip over an unseen plant. "Kingley?" she called out softly. Perhaps a bit too softly, since he didn't come to her. But she couldn't risk anyone inside hearing her, so she daren't shout.

"Kingley," Emma repeated with a bit more heft behind her voice. Surely, with all of the noise in the drawing room from the revelers, they wouldn't hear her.

He still didn't come.

Having the forethought to have brought a lantern with her to light her way would have been the intelligent thing to do. Instead, she had to rely solely on the light of the moon. Emma reached out her free hand, using it to guide her path along the side of the great house until she feared moving any closer to the bay window.

"Kingley!" she called out once more, growing in confidence that she'd never be heard through the massive stone walls. "Kingley, I've got some food for you."

And then she heard his bark, off on the other side of the house.

Without a thought, she dashed off to meet him, nearly sprinting in her haste to move past the window. Her slipper caught on a root or something, and she jolted forward but only just managed to avoid falling flat on her face. Kingley barked again as he raced around the side of the house, making a mad dash to reach her. "No, Kingley, not here." She was still directly outside the bay window! They couldn't stop there.

What had she been thinking? Anyone inside the drawing room could have noticed her at that proximity. Emma chanced a look inside to see if anyone was peering out.

Mr. Cardiff's cold, blue eyes locked onto hers for a moment, piercing her with their intensity, but just as quickly he looked away.

Her heart came to a standstill and she broke out into a cold sweat. Had he truly seen her? He couldn't have. It must have been her own fears that had planted such a thought into her mind. Besides, it wasn't as though Mr. Cardiff would care one way or another. Emma brushed away the notion that he'd noticed her and then rushed on to meet Kingley—out of view of the drawing room's occupants.

When they came together, he dashed in circles around her, jumping up and down while his tail wagged from side to side.

Emma took care not to stain her gown as she took a seat on the grass, and then laughed at herself. Heavens, she'd already fallen. Surely it was already stained. She set the plate down beside her. Kingley was so excited to see her that he kept nudging her hand with his head and licking her fingers instead of eating.

"Silly dog," she said with a laugh. Then she picked up a bite of the quail and held it out in her palm beneath his nose.

Kingley sniffed it and then ate it. Soon enough, he found the plate and worked his way through his meal without another sound, aside from his jaw working. When he finished, he curled up beside her and dropped his head on her lap, letting her pet him and scratch behind his ears.

"You're really a very sweet dog, you know?"

Of course he didn't respond to that. She stayed out with him for as long as she dared. At last, she realized she must go back inside. If someone were to search for her, to see if she'd recovered from her headache or if she needed anything…well, she shouldn't be missing.

Kingley came with her, guiding her in the moonlight, as she took a wide berth in front of the bay window. Once they were past it and she could see her way to the servants' door ahead, Emma patted him on the head. "Be a good pup, and I'll be sure to sneak you some more food tomorrow."

He let out a whining sort of sound that she took as acquiescence, and then he darted off into the distance. Emma watched him go, laughing at his exuberance. Dogs were such honest creatures. All one must do to earn their eternal devotion was show them a little care. If only men were so easy to handle. Once he was out of her sight, she turned back toward the door and took a step—but walked straight into the very solid expanse of a man's hard chest.

CHAPTER EIGHT

What in God's name am I doing outside following after Miss Hathaway? It shouldn't matter to him in the slightest what she was doing, let alone why she was doing it. But when he'd seen her stumble and nearly fall while skulking around outside the bay window, he had been unable to stop himself from making his own exit. He'd gone off to search for her outside to demand an explanation for just what, precisely, she thought she was doing outside alone at night.

And now he had her. Quite literally, as a matter of fact.

She'd bumped head-first into his chest, her pert nose brushing against the hollow at the base of his neck, and his arms had instinctively shot out to steady her, as though they had a mind of their own. Indeed, they must have. He wouldn't have attempted to save her from a fall, would he? Yet even though several moments had passed since her initial stumble, Aidan had yet to release her.

It was unfathomable, really. While his head told him to let her go and return to the house, his hands wouldn't cooperate. They remained firmly affixed to her upper arms, as though they'd become permanently attached. Her heartbeat pounded against his chest, and her breaths · came out feather-light but fast, tickling against the underside of his chin much as the light scent of lemons tickled his nostrils. Instead of pushing her away and putting a reasonable distance between them, he wanted to draw her closer. To drink her in. To drown in her scent.

More and more, Bedlam seemed the perfect destination for him.

Miss Hathaway scowled up at him, her brown eyes glinting in the moonlight. "Kindly let me go," she finally said into the charged stillness between them, her haughty tone making him want to draw her closer still, which was nothing short of befuddling. "I shouldn't want to be missed."

But she'd already made certain she wouldn't be missed. Before she left the drawing room, she'd claimed a debilitating headache—that was what Sir Henry had informed Aidan when he'd gone over to investigate her sudden departure.

Why had she claimed illness and yet gone outside alone to stumble about in the darkness instead of to her chambers to convalesce?

"What in God's name have you been doing out here alone?" Aidan demanded. "In the dark, no less!" He hadn't intended for his tone to be so gruff, and he halfway regretted it when she flinched against him.

Granted, he hadn't intended any of this.

For a moment, he thought he saw a glimmer of tears forming in her eyes. But that couldn't be. The Miss Hathaway of his memory had always been an unfeeling girl, more concerned with what happened in the pages of a novel than what happened to the people around her. Such people did not care about anything enough to warrant tears in Aidan's experience.

The way she looked after Morgan would seem to contradict the impression he'd had of her from before, though. Did ladies who would toss their own good reputations aside in defense of a friend often cry? He didn't know.

"What I'm doing is of no concern to you, sir," she said a moment later. The tears were gone. They must have been a figment of his imagination—something flittering through his mind despite the fact that it wasn't real.

She pushed against his chest, and only then did he realize she'd been holding a china plate in her hands. A plate? She was outside, alone, at night, traipsing around and losing her footing…carrying a plate. Yet Aidan was certain she'd been present for supper. He'd hardly been able to keep his eyes from her the entire meal, confound it all.

A dog barked in the distance, and then he understood. "You've been feeding that mutt, haven't you?"

"What if I have?" Miss Hathaway's lips turned down in a frown, and his eyes fell to them against his will. Being so close to those lips did nothing to help eliminate his earlier vision from his mind. They were far more lush than he'd realized from across the room, more supple. They looked to be as smooth as silk.

This was no time for his thoughts to stray back to all of the delightful things her mouth could be doing. He'd already spent far too much time thinking of such things when he never should have allowed his mind to travel that path in the first place.

Aidan gave himself a mental shake, willing the unbidden lust away. "If you feed that dog, Burington will never be rid of it. It will bring its fleas and whatever else it might have with it to infest all of the animals here. Is that what you want?"

"Kingley doesn't have *that* many fleas," she muttered.

"Not *that* many," Aidan repeated, mocking her tone. Damn, but he needed to rein himself in.

This was going altogether poorly. Emma Hathaway's presence this summer was wreaking havoc on him in a way he'd never imagined. He could no more stop his thoughts from drifting to inappropriate places than he could remove his foot from his leg, but surprisingly he didn't want to. It may not have been his plan to fall in lust with her, but lust was rarely something he wished to avoid.

He bit down on the inside of his cheek before going on, hoping the small amount of pain would help him remember himself. "Meaning he has fleas, much as we all expected."

Aidan wanted to shake some sense into her, not that he really thought such a thing were possible. She'd gone off alone in the night without a thought other than to feed a mangy cur. She was little more than a brainless twit. He had no doubts on that score. That didn't mean she deserved to be mocked as he'd just done. She'd caused him to lose all sense of his reason, all sense of decorum.

Miss Hathaway granted him no opportunity to apologize for his rudeness. "I don't know why it should matter to you one way or another. You seem to be here for no reason other than to stalk Morgan's every move and to remind me how much you despise me at every turn." Somehow, her frown deepened, yet again drawing his eye and his thoughts to a place they had no business being. "Speaking of Morgan, shouldn't you be in the drawing room with *her* instead of out here with me? Surely you can find a reason to get in her way right now, imposing yourself upon her instead of upon me. I can't imagine you have nothing more important to do than stop me from feeding a starving dog."

Only one bit of her speech resonated with him. It stuck in his head and refused to leave. "I don't get in Morgan's way." It left him more irritable than normal that this infuriating woman was trying to redirect their conversation. "And your feeding that hound matters to me because Burington is my friend. I won't have you doing anything that will cause him problems."

"No, I've already caused enough problems for the people in your life, haven't I?" she shot back.

"Yes, as a matter of fact, you have."

She pursed her lips together, which only served to make her look like a prim governess. Her eyes flashed a mere moment before she stomped one of her slippered feet down on top of his boot.

He would have laughed at the lack of pain it caused him, were it not for the instant flood of tears that hovered just on the brink of spilling down her cheeks. Good God. She was the one who'd assaulted him, and she was behaving like he'd tried to ravish her.

"Blast!" Miss Hathaway hopped on her other foot, trying to reach down to the one she'd just harmed, but he hadn't released her arms. She flailed about, kicking out her legs while her arms flew at anything and nothing. "Let me go. You are impossible."

"Be still," Aidan grumbled. The blue muslin of her gown whipped about from all her exertions, entangling both his limbs and hers even as he fought to contain her struggling. It was no use, particularly since she fit so perfectly against his frame, like she was made just for him and no one else. In her innocence, she couldn't possibly have an idea of the effect her movements were having upon him, but Aidan was entirely too aware of certain parts of his anatomy. He'd have to be mad to let her go.

"Callous, unfeeling, insensitive…" The litany of her insults rang out into the empty night air, echoing in his mind. She kicked again, this time connecting with his calf, and the swirling fabric of her gown tightened around both of their legs. With a jerk, she tried to disengage herself, but she only succeeded in shifting all of their weight until he fell with her beneath him.

Somehow, he twisted mid-fall so he hit the ground first with her on top. Her gown was trapped beneath him, and she couldn't move an inch.

Aidan wrapped his arms fully around her torso, entrapping her arms and keeping her still against him. With all of the fury she had built up, now was not the best time to release her—lest he end up covered in scars from her scratching at his eyes or something else of the sort.

A furious woman was not to be underestimated.

"Insufferable, churlish, despotic, tyrannical…" The stream of her contempt seemingly had no end, and her voice continued to rise in pitch.

If he didn't quiet her, and quickly, someone from the main house would hear her and come out to investigate. And while his cock was rather accepting of their current position, with her squirming atop him, being discovered thus was far from what either one of them wanted. The last thing they needed was to be leg-shackled.

Aidan didn't know what else to do. The need for silence grew heavier upon his mind. He moved one hand to the back of her head, pulled her down, and kissed her.

Emma was in the midst of calling Mr. Cardiff a scurrilous, indecent cad, following a litany of other insults, when his lips pressed hard against hers—further earning every name she'd called him and more. Her eyes flew open at the contact, only to find his boring into her as though he was trying to etch every detail of the moment permanently into his brain.

He would do something like that, too. Emma had no doubts on that score. It would be just like the loathsome cur he was to take such delight in the moment that he ruined her that he would wish to relive it in his mind over and over again. For that matter, he might be committing it to memory so that he could recreate it in a piece of artwork later.

The licentious brute.

Even as his lips moved over hers, deftly maneuvering in such a way that he could slide his tongue across her tightly closed lips, he readjusted the hand against her nape and angled her head. His touch was almost punishing, falling just short of potentially bruising. And yet, while it was absolutely nothing at all like what she'd imagined a kiss would be, she couldn't help but part her lips for his questing tongue and shudder in delight at the sensation of his invasion.

She'd always thought her first kiss would be sweet and tender, thoroughly romantic. She'd imagined herself so in love with the man kissing her that she'd lean in and one foot would lift up behind her, toes pointed, oblivious to everything but the man she was with.

She *was* oblivious to everything but Mr. Cardiff, but in such a different way. His kiss was demanding, aggressive, needy. It was perhaps because of how different it was from her imaginings that she was so lost within it. Within him.

For what it was worth, she did lean in, seeking more. More heat. More pressure. More of his roving hands and heated lips, which were now traveling along the length of her neck, his tongue dipping out to taste her.

Just more.

Which was all wrong. This was the path to disaster, and they were racing along it neck-or-nothing. She had to slow him down. She had to separate herself from him before they were caught in such a compromising position.

Before she lost her heart.

Emma squirmed against him, desperate to stop him, but her efforts were pointless. Short of ripping her gown, she couldn't escape his vise-like grasp on her. She screamed her frustrations, but the sound was muted against his mouth even as her fisted hands were tangled in knots of fabric against his angular, dangerously muscled chest, rendering them useless in her struggle. Her fists pressed back into her so hard it almost hurt.

As he worked his tongue between her lips once more to stroke inside her mouth, he let out a groan of sorts. His eyes darkened in the pale moonlight—twin pools of lust that undulated with a need she'd never witnessed before—pools that mirrored what she knew must be evident within her own eyes.

He tasted dark, a perilous and inadequately masked feast of sin.

His tongue swept over every inch of her mouth, tasting and exploring and kindling something wanton and delicious and, to this particular point in her life, left unheeded.

With one arm still holding her tight to his chest, Mr. Cardiff shifted her higher over his body until her lips were at a level with his and he could plunder her more freely. The friction of shifting fabrics and hard muscles against her breasts left them feeling heavy and needy, and somehow aching.

Without realizing what she was doing, she opened her fists and flattened her palms against his chest, mimicking his actions and exploring the hard angles of his muscles.

He let out a growl, feral and inhuman—her only warning before he left her mouth to ravage the path leading from her jaw to her earlobe with his lips and tongue. Breaths coming in rapid bursts, pulse pounding loud in her head, Emma's entire being swam with unfamiliar sensation.

She didn't know how she came to be on her back with him above her and the cold, hard earth beneath her.

She couldn't have possibly determined when he'd stopped suckling against her earlobe and nibbling the spot just behind her ear to move lower.

All she knew was that her hands remained trapped between their bodies, kept immobilized by his superior size, and Mr. Cardiff's hot, searching mouth had moved perilously close to the edge of her bodice. Her back arched up as though her traitorous body welcomed his assault upon her senses, and a storm of anxiety-laden pinpricks rattled against her core from the inside.

It was too much. Too wrong.

Too needy.

A moan tore from Emma's lips when his questing fingers drew down the cap sleeve of her gown and his tongue dipped beneath the fabric, the moist heat of it sliding over the sensitive flesh of her bosom in a way that left her trembling in both terror and desire. She couldn't want him like this—so needy and raw. She couldn't let herself feel such a deep well of sensation. Not until she had a husband. Not until he couldn't rip all her hopes and dreams out from beneath her and leave her a shattered mess.

Thus, it was the terror that broke through the haze of sensation first.

"Stop. Stop this." Emma thrashed her legs, startled at the discovery that she could move them again. The moment of realization halted her struggle long enough that Mr. Cardiff was able to reposition his thighs and trap her legs beneath him.

But he did stop kissing her so intimately even if he remained atop her, staring down with a wild look in his eyes and frayed breaths spilling from his lips. She reached out her hand to cup his cheek—an instinctive gesture—but pulled back before making contact.

In an instant, his eyes filled with profound remorse. As fast as it arrived, it was replaced by sheer panic.

He removed his hand from her sleeve and placed it over her mouth, but must have thought better of it only a moment later. Pulling it down to rest beside her body, he lifted some of his weight from her, situating it on his strong forearms.

"Promise me you won't call out." His words were a prayer in the night. "I doubt that being discovered in such a thoroughly compromising position is what either of us wants."

At the moment, Emma didn't have the first inkling how to voice what she wanted. She wanted him to go on, to take her further than she'd allowed. She wanted to be as far away from him as she could possibly be. She wanted never to be too long outside his touch. She wanted a kind man to marry her, and only *then* to fall in love.

Everything she wanted was a convoluted mess in her head.

But he was right. If anyone from the house party were to find them, there wasn't a doubt in her mind what David would insist upon. Her brother-in-law was too honor-bound by half. She'd be married to Mr. Cardiff within a sennight, if not sooner.

The mere thought of it was enough to send a tingle racing over her spine. "I won't call out," Emma repeated, though her voice shuddered and threatened to give way before she'd gotten even the first of the words out.

Taking more of his weight onto himself, Mr. Cardiff carefully extracted his legs from Emma's skirts and then rolled aside. He stood, brushing grass and dirt from himself before holding out a hand to assist her.

When she stood again, trying to regain the ability to breathe, the moonlight allowed her to see just how much damage had overcome her gown. There were grass stains and a few small rips along the skirt, and the bodice was completely crushed. The muslin was ruined. No laundry maid would ever be able to salvage it.

Clearly Mr. Cardiff was experiencing those very thoughts. He looked over at her and his lips quirked down into a frown. "I don't suppose there's much hope for it, is there?"

"None. But don't trouble yourself over it." Not that he would, anyway, but that was beside the point. "I'll tell my maid about feeding Kingley, and that I fell down in the dark. No one will ever know about…" She gave an empty gesture with her arms toward the place on the ground they'd been tumbling about.

"I wasn't…" Mr. Cardiff stopped himself short and pressed his eyes closed for a moment. "I shouldn't—"

"You should go back inside before you're missed, sir. I need to return this plate to the kitchens before Cook sends someone out searching for me." And before she could do that, she'd have to calm herself enough that her lies would be believable. Not an easy task, that was for certain. Blast, she wished she were a better liar.

A muscle ticked in his cheek, and he started to nod, but then he shrugged and muttered an oath. "I do not understand how you have such control over me, Miss Hathaway, but I do not like it. Not in the least."

Mr. Cardiff took three steps in the direction of the main house, blessedly heading toward a different door than Emma would use to return to the kitchens, but then stopped and spun around, grimacing something fierce. "I am everything you called me and worse. You would do well to stay away from me so I am not tempted to repeat tonight's performance."

Emma stood on the grounds for long moments after he left, trembling—though she couldn't decide if the trembles were due more to fear or anticipation.

She pressed a finger to her swollen lips and winced…but then she pressed it harder, as though she could recreate the sensations he'd caused within her, which only confirmed her fears. She wanted more.

CHAPTER NINE

Aidan chose not to break his fast with the rest of the household the next morning, thinking it might be a better option to avoid seeing Emma Hathaway so soon after he'd nearly ravished her on the lawn. Instead, he sent his valet, Cochran, down to the kitchens to fetch a tray, and then ate in his chambers alone so he could brood.

Brooding always seemed to calm him, at least somewhat, and he certainly needed something to provide a calming effect. The whole night, he'd scarcely slept a wink. He couldn't stop thinking about the flicker of passion she'd given him in return before he terrified the ever-loving life out of her.

Each time he did manage to fall asleep, he awoke in a tangle of sheets. The memory of her taste haunted his tongue, and his cock seemed destined to be permanently erect. He couldn't stop thinking of the wild look in her eyes. Miss Hathaway had been more responsive than he'd ever dreamed possible, and he hadn't even been the slightest bit gentle with her. Yet, she was an innocent. She didn't deserve the callous treatment he'd given her, even if she'd responded favorably to it.

The worst of it was he couldn't convince himself he'd been trying to ruin Miss Hathaway out of spite. Some small part of him had wanted her, wanted all that he'd done and more, and it hadn't been to obtain revenge for the perceived slights against Morgan.

He was far from fit to be good company for David and his houseguests. They were far better served by him keeping his distance.

Aidan grew more confused by the moment.

After he'd breakfasted and sent Cochran to return the tray, he paced through his chambers, trying to decide how he ought to go about the rest of this house party.

In light of his highly inappropriate behavior toward Miss Hathaway—and considering he wasn't entirely certain he wished to avoid taking it further—he thought it might be best for all concerned if he were to leave. Go back to Tavistock Manor and forget all of this had ever happened. Separate himself from the problems. Or temptations. Whichever the case may be.

Except that would mean leaving Morgan.

As much as Aidan wanted to find the strength to trust her recovery, to believe that she would truly be able to live her life without falling so desperately into despair again, Aidan wasn't certain he had it within him.

But Niall would be here with her. It wasn't as though Aidan must leave her alone.

He'd talk to Niall straightaway and inform him of his decision.

Except…damnation. His departure would alter Vanessa's numbers for the party, and David would not let him cause his wife damage so easily.

Good God. *Vanessa.* Would Miss Hathaway have run to tell her sister what he'd done to her? An intelligent chit wouldn't let a cad such as he go unpunished. If she had even a slightly good head upon her shoulders, she would have gone straight to the first female she trusted and sought advice on what to do.

If that was the case, he'd be a dead man before luncheon.

He'd been pacing for close to half an hour when the door to his chamber opened without warning and Niall barged inside.

"You're being a poor guest. Why were you not at breakfast?"

"So kind of you to announce your presence and request an audience," Aidan shot back. He was in no mood for Niall's high-handed manner.

Standing sheepishly in the doorway, Cochran looked over for instruction. It wasn't his fault that Niall had pushed past him. The valet couldn't very well tell the Earl of Trenowyth what he could and couldn't do, particularly when the earl in question paid his wages.

Niall reacted before Aidan could. "Leave us, Cochran."

"Milord," the man murmured, and he pulled the door closed as he went.

Once they were alone, Niall crossed the room and sat in the armchair by the hearth, gesturing for Aidan to take the seat opposite him.

Feeling a stubborn streak rearing its head, Aidan folded his arms over his chest and raised an eyebrow. Let Niall try to force him into a chair. They both knew that, while Niall was taller, Aidan was by far the stronger of the two. It didn't matter that he hadn't done any sculpting in a number of years. The muscles built from wielding his chisel and hammer had not abated in the slightest, despite the loss of some of his harder earned calluses.

Niall scowled, but he left it alone. "You sat alone last night, looking as happy to be here as one on the brink of being murdered. Then you left the drawing room early without even begging Lady Burington's forgiveness for such an affront. You still haven't shown yourself downstairs today, even though it is well past the breakfast hour and everyone is preparing to go into Topsham for a shopping excursion. Your presence is both expected and required."

He stopped there, and silence fell between them. Aidan kept waiting, expecting his brother to deliver the verdict on what his punishment ought to be for his adolescent behavior, or for him to add another crime to the growing litany.

But nothing else came.

"And?" Aidan finally said, as the silence between them grew more than just a bit uncomfortable. He couldn't shake the sense that he was yet again standing before his father as a ten-year-old boy, when he'd been caught ripping holes in Niall's clothing out of jealousy—

Niall was to be sent off to school, and Aidan had to stay behind with Morgan. He still didn't know why he'd done it. Maybe he thought if Niall had no proper clothes to wear, then he would be forced to stay, as well?

Niall's lip ticked further downward. "*And,*" he said, drawing out the word for emphasis, "I suspect your inability to behave like a gentleman and do as your hostess requires of you has something to do with Miss Hathaway."

"Did you see—" Aidan stopped himself before he dug his own grave. "Why would you think that?" His innocent tone sounded laughingly feigned, even to his own ear.

"Did I see what?"

This was not going well. "It doesn't matter. Forget I said anything." This seemed to be becoming a habit. He hadn't meant to say half of what he'd said to Miss Hathaway last night, and yet it had all come from his lips. And then he hadn't even bothered to retract any of it. What would be the point? It had been the truth, devil take it.

Niall's eyes narrowed, but he let the matter drop. "You're to come along on the shopping excursion. You're to make yourself seem the perfect gentleman. You're to apologize to our host and hostess for your coarse manners, if they can even be called that."

But he couldn't. Aidan would only make matters worse if he were to try to insert himself into the day's festivities while he was still so unable to control his own thoughts, let alone the words that came from his mouth. "I need more time." It came out as a plea. He never pleaded for anything, least of all with his brother.

Perhaps that was why it caught Niall's attention. He leaned forward, propping an arm on his knee. "Why?"

Why, indeed? Aidan searched his mind, trying to sort out the answer for himself before revealing it to his brother. He might need to alter the truth for Niall's ears. Lord knew Aidan was the furthest thing from a proper gentleman, so his behavior shouldn't shock his brother—but for the second time this week, he felt the urge to

119

protect Miss Hathaway. Even if what he was protecting her from was himself.

His efforts didn't matter, in the end. "Because it does have to do with Miss Hathaway, but I'll be damned if I can determine just *what* it has to do with her." Aidan snapped his jaw closed lest he say anything more.

Niall sat back in his chair, drawing one leg up to rest his ankle over the opposite knee. He nodded, his eyes softening a bit, as though suddenly he understood everything Aidan didn't. "You finally have an interest in her that goes beyond seeking revenge for something no one else could possibly understand."

"What? No."

How did Niall know he wanted revenge? He'd taken great pains to keep his pastel renderings locked away in the dower house so no one would ever see them—so no one would ever know just how sick and depraved and twisted his mind had become. He'd never allowed anyone in while he worked. Never.

"You don't do a very good job of hiding your feelings, particularly not when you're around Miss Hathaway."

Aidan let out a pent-up breath, which caused Niall to raise a brow. But at least he said nothing. Since Aidan still hadn't sorted everything out in his own mind, he really didn't want to have to explain such reactions to his brother.

"All right," Niall went on, "I'll make your excuses today. I'll tell Lady Burington you've taken ill and plan to stay abed for the day, and you can have the whole day to sift through all the mud in your brain. Tomorrow, you'll take responsibility for your own actions."

"Of course." Aidan nodded, silently giving thanks for being able to gain Niall's cooperation without revealing more than he had.

Niall stood and made for the door, but stopped just before leaving. "But Aidan? If your interest in Miss Hathaway is genuine, you'd best make up your mind to court her properly. I won't have you causing a scandal around her. This family has already seen too much scandal for one lifetime."

Courting her, whether properly or improperly, had never even crossed Aidan's mind. Why the devil would he want to do something inherently mad such as that? Had he gone mad, like Morgan had? That might explain his otherwise unexplainable behavior outside.

Thank God Niall didn't know about what had already taken place last night on the lawn. He was typically slow to anger, but once it had been sufficiently roused—well, Niall would stop at nothing to right a perceived wrong.

Aidan nodded for his brother's benefit, and then Niall left.

For the next hour, Aidan paced around his chamber, waiting for the house to empty of guests. Once it was just him and the servants, he sneaked through the corridors and outside. He needed fresh air and to stretch his legs more than he could within the confines of his chamber.

So he started walking. And kept walking.

Aidan had no true destination in mind. He just needed to move, to get distance...perhaps a bit of perspective. He lost all sense of time and place as he traversed the woody area to the east of the great house. At some point, he recognized that he was heading toward the hermitage that he'd passed with Lord Jacob, Morgan, and Miss Hathaway yesterday.

The hermitage where, supposedly, David had transferred everything from Aidan's studio.

It had been more than three years since he'd picked up a chisel. More than three years since his hand had gripped a hammer and carved away a piece of marble.

The lure of his tools pulled at him—a stronger force than he'd felt in so long he'd almost forgotten the sensation creating used to provide him with.

But he didn't have the key that David had left him. Since he hadn't planned to go anywhere in particular, he hadn't bothered to think of such things. He couldn't get in. He couldn't run his hands over the smooth, cool surface, letting the shape of it seep into his fingers and spread through his body. He couldn't go to work.

Yet his feet kept propelling him forward, closer and closer to the hermitage.

He couldn't turn back to the main house now to fetch the key. The last thing he needed was for some servant or another to spot him out and about, and fully hale and hearty. Niall had lied to the rest of the houseguests, not to mention to David and Vanessa, about him falling ill. Aidan might not always see eye to eye with his brother, but he wouldn't intentionally put him in such a position.

Before he had fully made up his mind whether to stop by the hermitage or not, it appeared through the thicket of trees before him.

Aidan's gait turned to a purposeful stride, and in mere moments he stood before the structure.

It really *was* the perfect place for him to occasionally escape to— out a good walk away from the house, where no one would hear the sounds of his working. Where no one would come upon him unaware.

Well, no one but perhaps Jacob Deering. It was still unnerving, the thought of Deering coming upon the hermitage that day. What was his purpose?

But why would Deering return here? He hadn't been inclined to stop and discover anything about it yesterday, so what reason would he have to come back?

Aidan moved closer and peered inside a window, and his mouth nearly started to water at the sight before him. Chisels and hammers in various shapes and sizes, buckets to collect water from the stream, several untouched pieces of marble—and the piece he'd been working on before word arrived about Morgan's mishap with the carriage.

The overall shape of it was done, but the finer details remained. He'd yet to craft the feathers of the wings, the particular expression of the face, or the lines of the angel's gown.

A desire to pick up the nearest chisel and hammer and set to work became so strong within him that, without realizing what he was doing, Aidan stepped closer to the door and tried the latch.

It opened.

When Sir Henry stopped just before crossing the main road in Topsham and turned to grant Emma and Serena a broad smile, Emma nearly ran straight into him. As she'd just done that very thing with Mr. Cardiff last night, and she recalled entirely too clearly how that situation had ended, she was quite glad she'd somehow stopped before doing so with Sir Henry today.

"Where shall we go first, ladies?" he asked jovially, rubbing his hands together. "I understand the bakery has a delicious lemon scone we could try with tea. Or the haberdasher might have some ribbons you'd like."

Emma's mind was far from scones and ribbons. At every turn, something would remind her of last night's encounter. Thank goodness Serena had taken her arm when the houseguests had sorted themselves into groups for a shopping excursion. Serena had then promptly found Sir Henry and Lord Muldaire to escort the two of them. It would have been just Emma's luck to be stuck with Mr. Cardiff again, and Lord only knew where that might lead.

As it was, her knees were wobbling just from the memory.

She was here to find herself a husband, and Mr. Cardiff was not the marrying sort. Spending time with him would hardly aid her in that cause. Being in his presence only left her with a head filled with anxiety and a series of flutters in her stomach.

A shopping excursion with Sir Henry Irvine and Lord Muldaire was certainly more in line with how she ought to spend her time. The two of them were at least possibilities, Sir Henry in particular, even if his friendly eyes did not leave her all aflutter like the intensity in Mr. Cardiff's did.

In fact, it was decidedly better that they didn't. Emma had no intention of losing her heart to a man who might then leave her heartbroken. Let him marry her first. Then he could have her heart.

It was true they might never love one another in such a case, but wouldn't that be better than being as distraught as Morgan had been? Emma had love in her life. She loved her sister and her parents. That could be enough. She would make it so, if necessary.

It was only after they'd left Heathcote Park in Lord Muldaire's carriage that Emma discovered Mr. Cardiff had begged off of the day's outing, claiming some minor illness or another. Lord Trenowyth was confident that his brother would be fit as a fiddle tomorrow.

Illness, indeed. He likely was still as shaken as she was from their encounter.

"The scones sound delightful, Sir Henry," Serena said, drawing Emma back into the present and saving her from the necessity of forming an answer.

"Excellent." He repositioned Emma's hand on his arm while Lord Muldaire did the same with Serena's, then he checked to be certain they could cross safely and headed out into the road.

Moments later, Emma and Serena were situated at a small table just outside the bakery while the two gentlemen headed off to fetch their treats.

Serena leaned over and took Emma's hand. "Are you still feeling unwell? I'm certain I could convince them to take us back early if you want. No point in trying to have a good time with a headache." She gave a tiny grin and dropped her voice even lower. "Father would be most upset that I wasn't spending enough time with Lord Muldaire, but he can go hang on that score."

Emma nearly choked on a laugh. "Your father, or Lord Muldaire?"

"I'd hate to say anything unkind about the marquess, because he is a perfectly nice gentleman," Serena whispered, checking over her shoulder, "but he is rather dreadfully boring, don't you agree? Yet Father is set upon him."

"There's no changing his mind?"

She shook her head with a sigh. "I'm afraid not. I tried to tell him

I'd be happier with Lord Trenowyth—and he's an earl, so it isn't as though it's such a massive fall down the social ladder, particularly for the daughter of a commoner—but he would hear none of it. I think they might have already agreed to terms, though Lord Muldaire hasn't yet asked me to marry him."

Sir Henry and Lord Muldaire's imminent arrival as they made their way back to their table prevented Emma from responding. Just as Sir Henry set a tray with a scone and a teacup before her, Emma glanced out the window. The scene before the bakery caught her attention.

Morgan was crossing the main road on Mr. Deering's arm, alongside Lord Trenowyth and Miss Selwyn. Heading the other way, a gentleman had a dog on a rope lead, and Morgan's face lit with joy as she bent in the middle of the road to scratch the dog behind the ears.

And that was when the idea struck her.

"Sir Henry," Emma said. She straightened, suddenly focused. "When you train your dogs, what sorts of things can you train them to do?"

He and Lord Muldaire took their seats, and then he turned his attention to Emma. "I've trained dogs to do any number of things. What sort of thing would you like your dog to do?"

Serena turned a questioning gaze on Emma. "What do you want...?"

Emma gave a slight shake of her head before turning back to Sir Henry. "Well, could a dog be trained to help a person? To walk on a lead with them and guide them away from dangers?"

"Like with Lady Morgan, I would imagine," Lord Muldaire surmised. He inclined his head pensively.

"Yes, precisely." Emma gave a firm nod. "Like with Lady Morgan." She picked up her scone, but didn't take a bite. Her mind was far too occupied with thoughts of how she could help her friend become more capable of doing things on her own to worry about something as mundane as eating.

Sir Henry took a swallow of his tea and narrowed his eyes. "I suppose the right dog could learn such behaviors. Lady Morgan would also have to learn how to handle the dog. They could learn together."

"Oh, this is brilliant!" Serena clapped her hands and bounced in her chair. "She'll love the idea, I just know it."

Whether Lord Trenowyth or Mr. Cardiff would love the idea was another matter entirely, but Emma forced that concern aside. "Would you be willing to train a dog for Lady Morgan and teach her what she needs to know?" After all, if Sir Henry wouldn't agree to the plan, it wouldn't matter in the slightest what Lord Trenowyth and Mr. Cardiff thought.

Lord Muldaire gave her a placating smile that grated on her nerves. "There is still the matter of finding the right dog for the task, Miss Hathaway."

"Indeed," Sir Henry said with a nod. "And that is no small task, I can assure you. I wouldn't trust it with one of my pups. At such a young age, they're too unpredictable. We'd need an older, more sedate dog, I'd think. Perhaps a collie…"

Emma got the distinct impression that he would have gone on interminably, sorting through his thoughts aloud. She returned her still-uneaten scone to her plate. "Oh, but I already have a dog in mind."

Sir Henry frowned. "Well, I'd have to evaluate—"

"You can as soon as we return to Heathcote Park. I'm sure Kingley will be perfect."

She ignored the dropped jaws of the two gentlemen.

A sly smile came across Serena's countenance. "You may just be right, Miss Hathaway. And I'll help."

Emma sat back, picked up her scone, and finally took a bite, more at peace than she'd been since the Cardiff family's arrival. Even if, for whatever reason, Kingley was not the right dog to aid Morgan, at least the time they spent trying would have her getting to know Sir Henry better, as long as he allowed her to help, and it would help to keep Emma's mind off Mr. Cardiff.

And that was most decidedly a good thing. Less time thinking about him would mean less time worrying about silly fluttering sensations.

CHAPTER TEN

When Emma and Serena pulled Morgan aside to tell her their plan, her smile was bright enough to light all of Heathcote Park at night.

"Oh, but Niall and Aidan won't allow it," she said a moment later, after the initial glow of the moment had worn off.

"Sir Henry's talking to Lord Trenowyth right now," Emma said. "He'll be far better at convincing your brothers than we will. He's a very accomplished breeder and trainer. If anyone can teach Kingley how to help you, it's him."

Serena took Morgan's hand and squeezed. "And Lord Muldaire is with them, too. He has some of the very dogs that Sir Henry trained on his own property. He can reassure Lord Trenowyth that Sir Henry is the most skilled and knowledgeable gentleman around."

Emma nodded, but then remembered that Morgan couldn't see her action. Morgan seemed so capable so much of the time that Emma often forgot she couldn't see, despite the fact that she was planning to train Kingley for that very reason. "Besides, Mr. Cardiff is unwell, and so by the time he learns what we're doing, it will be too late. We'll already be well into the process, and he won't be able to change anyone's mind on the matter any longer." At least Emma hoped that would be the case.

Morgan rocked forward onto the balls of her feet, as though she was ready to take off running with Kingley by her side at that very moment. "All right. I'm willing to try it. When can we start?"

Sir Henry was already walking across the lawn toward them and slid into place behind Morgan. "We can start as soon as Miss Hathaway convinces this Kingley to join us."

Emma put her hands to her mouth in order to do just that, but then Sir Henry held up a hand to stop her.

"On second thought, perhaps you three ought to go inside and have your maids assist you in changing into something more suitable. There's no call for you to ruin such lovely gowns."

And he didn't even know about the one she and Mr. Cardiff had destroyed just last night. Emma nodded and fought back her blush, hoping no one would notice. "Right you are. In we go, ladies."

Fanny had insisted she could repair last night's gown, but Emma held sincere doubt on that score. Nevertheless, the lady's maid had pulled it from Emma's hands before she could toss it in the fire and run off with it. Heaven only knew where she'd taken it or what she'd done with it.

Half an hour later, they reconvened on the lawn wearing more serviceable frocks they'd borrowed from Vanessa. Not one of the three had thought to bring anything of the sort with them, but then again, none of them had been planning to spend their afternoons frolicking with a dog.

"Kingley!" Emma called as they made their way back over the field to join Sir Henry.

He wasn't alone—Lord Muldaire, Lord Trenowyth, Lord Burington, and Mr. Deering had all taken up seats beneath a shade tree, watching over the scene. Several of the ladies from the party had gathered together, as well, seated together on a blanket spread over the lawn with several parasols shading them from the sun. A great iron tub had been carried out and waited on the ground beside Sir Henry, and a series of footmen were carting out buckets of water to fill it. He held a piece of soap in one hand and waved them forward.

If they were to bathe the dog today, they should all thank the heavens they had changed their gowns. Emma was more thankful than before that Vanessa had been able to spare some for them to borrow.

Before they reached Sir Henry's side, Kingley had bounded around the side of the great house from the direction of the woods, racing straight for them with a series of happy barks.

Emma held out a hand to him, and he shoved his head into it in an effort to both nuzzle her and smother her with affection. It seemed he loved her even more each time she saw him. Soon, he'd be the same way with Morgan, since she would be the one giving him time and attention.

"Right, then." Sir Henry took off his coat and rolled back the sleeves of his shirt. "Miss Hathaway, Miss Weston, if you two will stay with Lady Morgan off to the side, I'll give Kingley a bath to rid him of his fleas."

Emma felt a twinge of disappointment that she wasn't allowed to participate in every aspect of today's lessons, but she grudgingly nodded her assent. She had no intention of doing anything that would cause Sir Henry to change his mind.

He tried to take Kingley by the scruff of his neck and guide him into the tub. *Tried* being the important part of that sentiment, because Kingley would have none of it. He growled low in his throat and snapped his jaws menacingly at Sir Henry each time the baronet made an attempt to move closer to the group of them. Within moments, Kingley had situated himself between the three ladies and Sir Henry, and barked warning after warning.

"Oh, dear." Emma hadn't expected this sort of reaction. She reached down and drew her hand along Kingley's back, trying to calm him.

Again, he nuzzled the palm of her hand. How odd, that Kingley could be so gentle with her, and yet so menacing toward Sir Henry. She chanced a glance over to Lord Trenowyth and the other men and couldn't help but notice the looks of apprehension upon their faces.

They didn't think this would work, blast them. Emma straightened her spine and steeled her nerves.

Well, most of them appeared to feel that way. Mr. Deering gave her a brief nod, his kind smile as apparent as ever. Then he started across the lawn to join them.

Emma turned back to Sir Henry, and she noted the same disdainful expression deep within his eyes. Blast, but she refused to let them make a mockery of her. Not now. Not when it was something that could mean such a difference for Morgan.

She gritted her teeth and straightened her spine, determined now, more than ever before, that she would teach Kingley to aid Morgan—with or without Sir Henry's assistance. "I think it might be best if I assist you, sir."

He started to shake his head, as though he would refuse her, but Emma snapped her fingers and started forward. Sure enough, Kingley came along right by her side, as did Serena with Morgan on her arm.

"I'll assist as well," Mr. Deering said confidently. And, oddly enough, Kingley stopped growling when the barrister came near.

Emma nodded, then bent down and put both arms beneath Kingley, one near his front legs and the other near his hind legs. She straightened her legs to lift him, buckling slightly under his weight. Mr. Deering added his arms to the job, and Kingley allowed him to do so. Moments later, the dog was in the tub and shaking, spraying the lot of them with water.

Morgan gasped, but then laughed with true joy. "Kingley, you rascal."

When Emma looked up again, Sir Henry stared down at the scene before him, slack-jawed. "Well then." He bent with his soap and started to lather it upon Kingley's fur, but stopped with the growl that came from the animal.

Serena held out a hand, and Sir Henry placed the soap within it.

A chorus of laughter echoed over to them from the direction of the other gentlemen.

Emma and Serena set to work scrubbing Kingley all over while Mr. Deering kept him in the tub. The dog tried to climb out on multiple occasions, but Mr. Deering managed to keep him inside the confines with Morgan's help. She had knelt on the ground beside the tub and scratched him behind the ears while talking nonsense to him, which seemed to keep him fairly well occupied and entertained.

It was only right that she should take part in this, after all. He needed to come to know her and care for her. To trust that she would take care of him in return.

Growing the bond between them, creating the degree of trust that would be required on both their parts, was quite possibly the most important thing they needed to do in terms of training Kingley and teaching Morgan how to work with him.

Not that Emma was any sort of an expert on these things. She just had a sense for the outcasts of the world. They seemed to always flock to her like sheep. She ought to know them better than most; she was one of them.

Several minutes later, Emma, Serena, Morgan, and Mr. Deering were each easily as wet as Kingley, but he had successfully been scrubbed and rinsed. Once freed from the restraint of the tub, he raced over the lawn like something was chasing him, trying to dry his fur in the wind he created. Thank goodness the air was not too chilled.

"Now, Sir Henry?" Emma turned to him even as she tried to dry her hands on her gown, but with it being wet also, her efforts were essentially pointless. "What is to be our next step?"

He gave her a wry grin. "Now we teach him to obey. But I thought you might have already known that…since you seem to be the one leading today's lesson."

A flush raced up her cheeks, but it might not have been noticeable due to her exertions in bathing Kingley. Perhaps no one had noticed.

Nevertheless, she called for Kingley again and he raced back to her side, looking up at her with his tail wagging so hard that water flung out in all directions.

Emma sincerely doubted training Kingley would be half as difficult as Sir Henry seemed to believe. Already, the dog would do anything she wanted. She scratched him behind the ears, and Serena and Morgan followed suit.

Now she just had to determine what she wanted him to do, so she could convince him to do it.

The light in the hermitage had begun to dim faster than Aidan was prepared for. The whole day couldn't have already passed him by, could it have? But when he looked up from the angel and scanned the horizon out the window, he knew he only had limited daylight left. He'd need to return to the main house soon.

Not that he doubted his abilities in navigating the dark, but it wasn't ever a good idea to go off traipsing through the woods without a lantern.

Still, he was loath to stop working now. In just the single day, he'd begun to shape the angel's face into something recognizable, with penetrating eyes seeking something off in the distance and high cheekbones and a narrow nose. He could see her, not only in his mind, but also in the marble.

And in the all-too-familiar blisters covering his hands. If he'd never stopped sculpting, the blisters wouldn't feel so unnatural. They'd just be part of him, like the calluses and scars, the cords of muscle formed by years of his labors. But now they were new and fresh, and bloody painful.

They only made him want to continue—to build new calluses and break new skin, all in the name of creating the masterpiece he knew was buried within tons of marble.

Yet, if there would not be enough light for him to safely return to the main house, there certainly would not be enough for him to see his creation. He couldn't risk making a mistake with his chisels—digging too deep, striking too hard with his hammer. This was a delicate part of the work, where each motion added character and depth. Take off too much here, angle the chisel slightly wrong there, and his angel would permanently bear the wrong expression. It would be tantamount to ruining the whole piece, and he might as well scrap it entirely and start over, should that happen.

A cursory search through the hermitage revealed no lanterns, no candles—not even a tender box. If he didn't leave now, he'd be stuck here alone all night, whilst incapable of working even, or he'd be forced to attempt the ill-advised journey along the not-yet-familiar path with nothing to guide his way.

With that in mind, he cleaned up the mess he'd created as best he could while still leaving his supplies in a manner in which they'd be ready for a new day's work, and then he closed the door behind him.

The next time he came, be it tomorrow or some other day, he'd have to be certain to bring the key with him. He doubted anyone would stumble upon the hermitage and do anything to harm his work, but there was no point in risking it. Particularly not since he knew Muldaire had found the place. If he had, Lord only knew who else might.

He hated to be disturbed while he worked. Disruptions splintered the mood in his work space, shattering the muse in his mind.

As he traversed the woods, heading back toward the main house, he sorted through several possible excuses he could offer Niall as to why he would become scarce for the remainder of the house party, ever hopeful he could stumble upon one which would satisfy his brother's moral compass.

Not an entirely simple prospect. Niall's moral compass always pointed true north. There was only one option in any situation that was right, and thousands which were wrong. To him, they were all guests, and therefore must always take part in every activity offered by their host and hostess for the guests. To Niall, David's suggestion that Aidan begin sculpting again would not fit within those confines. That would be one of the many grays in Aidan's world, but for Niall it was pure black.

Nothing had truly struck him yet by the time he exited the woods and started across the open expanse of the yard—and then he found himself incapable of thinking of such things entirely.

Morgan was wearing some ill-fitting gray gown that looked in dire need of laundering, alongside Miss Hathaway and Miss Weston, each in similar attire. Sir Henry Irvine and Mr. Deering were with them—as was that damned mutt Miss Hathaway had been feeding and coddling and treating like a pet.

Aidan walked faster—nearly taking on a militaristic march—in an effort to reach them and discover just what in God's name they thought they were doing.

The laughter coming from the ladies and gentlemen was ludicrous. They were flopping around the lawn with that mangy mutt, even rolling on the ground as the beast leapt over them. And the ladies! All of them were behaving with thoroughly unladylike manners. Then Miss Hathaway stood in a position of command, and all of the rest of them sat, eventually including the dog.

When he sat, Miss Hathaway poured praise down upon him and offered him something from her hand, which he ate greedily. The sight shouldn't have engendered any emotion in Aidan whatsoever. But watching her laugh and smile, seeing how she lavished praise upon the beast—it left Aidan in a far fouler mood than it should have done.

Why should he care how she behaved with a hound? He was a man, not a dog. There was no good reason that such a thing should have any effect upon Aidan whatsoever, and yet it did. Why, when she was with him, couldn't she be as at ease?

He was still making his way across the lawn when Sir Henry, Mr. Deering, Morgan, and Miss Weston stood to talk with Miss Hathaway. The baronet moved closer to Miss Hathaway than he ought to have done, and a tight pressure squeezed within Aidan's chest—a fact which made even less sense than his reactions to the chit and the dog. He couldn't be jealous. He did not like Miss Hathaway, so he shouldn't care what other gentlemen paid her any attention.

Yet, regardless of how ridiculous the notion was, Aidan couldn't deny the truth. He was absolutely, unequivocally, decidedly jealous of Sir Henry Irvine at this very moment. Hell, for that matter he was jealous of the damned dog.

It did not sit well within him. A slow, creeping sensation was making its way through his gut, leaving sincere nausea in its wake.

Aidan hated it.

They kept working through the process several times with Mr. Deering, Miss Hathaway, and Miss Weston each taking turns giving the commands, with Aidan still crossing the broad lawn. But then it was Morgan's turn.

When Aidan was halfway there, she stood and lifted her hand high above her head. This was not what the others had done. What was she doing? Aidan didn't like that she'd taken it upon herself to try something different. God only knew what the mutt would do.

"Stand," she said loud enough, and with sufficient weight in her tone, that Aidan could hear her. The dog let out a loud bark and leapt straight at Morgan.

That was when all sense of reason fled from Aidan—or at least any semblance of reason he might have still had up to that point— and he took off at a run.

But when he got closer, after shouting Morgan's name at the top of his lungs, he drew to a sudden stop, bewildered by what was taking place.

The dog jumped up on its rear legs, standing tall and trying to get something from Morgan's hands. And all the while, she laughed. Laughed like a loon, actually, in the way she had when they were children and something had struck her in just the right manner, and she would giggle until she made herself sick to her stomach from it all, and still laugh some more.

Aidan hadn't heard such a delightful sound from his sister in so long he'd feared he might never hear it again.

Miss Hathaway had turned sharply at the sound of Aidan's shout, and now stood staring at him in no small amount of shock as he drew close enough he could restrain the beast, should it be required.

"Mr. Cardiff! We understood you'd taken ill." She looked slightly panicked at the sight of him.

In his haste to rush to Morgan's rescue, he hadn't paid even a moment's thought to what reaction his sudden reappearance might cause.

Her gaze roved over his person with such great confusion it left him reeling. But he deserved no less, not after the callous manner in which he'd handled her last night. Indeed, he deserved far worse than her confusion.

This was unbearable, all of it. His jealousy. Her confusion when she ought to be irate with him. The fact that he wanted, even now, to repeat what he'd done last night.

"Why are you staring at me?" he bit off, returning to the callous demeanor which had always been comfortable for him.

"Have you rolled around in white powder for some reason, sir?"

Only then did he look down upon his own person. Good God, he was covered in marble dust from his day's work. Despite their gowns being marred with mud and grass stains, and the fabric clinging to Emma in a most indecent manner, he was perhaps more disheveled than the lot of them combined.

"White powder?" Morgan asked, still laughing. Her eyes held a serious air when she faced him, still holding something in her hands that the dog was trying to reach, and her tone turned almost reverent. "Have you been sculpting again, Aidan?"

He didn't want anyone to know he had been. Not yet. Aidan didn't know why the desire to keep it a secret was so strong in him. He just knew that it was.

And yet, how could he deny telling Morgan when it so clearly pleased her? Under normal circumstances, he would do anything that would cause his sister joy. Anything that would bring a smile to her face or warm her heart.

He brushed aside the notion that allowing her to do as she was with the dog was that very thing. But he found he could not tell her the truth about what he'd been doing all day, however confounding the realization may be. For so long, he'd given up this part of himself. For her.

He didn't begrudge her that time, but he wasn't ready to share his art with anyone. He needed to let it settle over him again first, to allow it to become part of him and he part of it.

Aidan met Miss Hathaway's eyes when he spoke. "Just moving some marble. Burington set it up for me, but he had it all wrong."

The dog finally bit into whatever Morgan had been holding up for him, immediately lowering to the ground and consuming his prize.

"Good boy, Kingley!" Morgan ruffled the fur on top of his head, then returned her attention to Aidan. "Does this mean you plan to sculpt again soon?"

He hated the hopeful note in her voice. It made him feel like a cad for not sharing this part of himself with her, by keeping it only to himself. But he wasn't ready to share it with anyone. Certainly not Sir Henry Irvine, who so easily earned Miss Hathaway's smiles whilst all Aidan rightfully earned from her was censure.

He wasn't entirely certain he was ready to experience it all himself—the way he would completely lose himself within his work and forget everything else, the way the entire world seemed to slip away, and all he could see or think about was whatever project he'd set for himself.

"Not any time soon," he said tersely. "I should go back inside. Not feeling myself." Aidan ignored the dejected manner in which Morgan's eyes fell upon his pronouncement and took several steps away from them toward the main house. "If you let that animal hurt my sister, Irvine, you'll answer to me," he called out over his shoulder.

But as he stalked away, the only thought that continued to plague his mind with each step was this: *How can I be jealous when I hate Miss Hathaway? And why in God's name do I lust after her?*

Everything about her left him more vexed than before. Particularly this last bit.

Devil take it.

CHAPTER ELEVEN

Over the course of the last three days, Emma had spent an increasing amount of her time with Sir Henry and Kingley. Sometimes Morgan and Serena would be with them. Mr. Deering had become a frequent member of their party, since Kingley seemed to react to him better than he did to Sir Henry. Occasionally, Lord Muldaire, Lord Trenowyth, Lord Burington, or some of the other gentlemen would take part in their training activities. It wasn't uncommon for a group of the ladies to bring out blankets and parasols so they could watch the proceedings from a shaded spot on the lawn.

The only person decidedly absent was Mr. Cardiff.

Emma did not mind that he was not playing a role in Kingley's training. On the contrary, she was delighted each time he neglected to make himself known. Every time Mr. Cardiff did join the rest of the houseguests, he would sit off to the side, glaring, and his demeanor as sullen and brooding anything she'd ever experienced before.

Ever since the day he'd emerged from the woods covered in marble dust, his demeanor had made even Lord Jacob Deering appear the very soul of levity—which, inexplicably, only drew her to him more than she already had been. Emma could only imagine it was due to the fact that he was perhaps the greatest outcast of them all.

The longer the house party went on, the less she saw of Mr.

Cardiff. Whether he was off carving his sculptures, or chopping down trees, or simply brooding alone in his chambers and feigning illness, Emma couldn't care less. Without Mr. Cardiff's dark cloud casting a pall upon the proceedings, she and Sir Henry had begun making excellent progress with Kingley.

And with one another, truth be told.

Their time spent together out on the lawn seemed only to draw Sir Henry to her side more often than he already had been during other events. Whenever they would split into groups for a game or an outing, Sir Henry easily worked his way to her side to be sure they could be together.

He sat with her in the drawing room during tea each afternoon, listening to tales of her childhood with Vanessa when they would help Father on the farm, or he'd wait eagerly for her to tell him which book she'd read the night before.

At the breakfast table each morning, he situated himself near her, perhaps not right by her side but close enough they could converse, always smiling at any anecdotes she might offer and hanging upon her every word.

Just last night at supper, Vanessa had arranged for Lord Jacob to be to Emma's right, but Sir Henry somehow maneuvered himself into that position, sending Lord Jacob down to take his seat next to Morgan.

All things considered, Emma believed Sir Henry might be forming a bit of an attachment to her—perhaps even a tendre. Thank heavens for that. She was spending so much time in his company that any chance one of the other gentlemen might develop an interest in her was quickly falling by the wayside. More and more, Sir Henry Irvine was looking to be her only possibility at leaving Vanessa's house party with a gentleman admirer.

Even better than that was the fact that Emma did not feel overly fond of Sir Henry. Not like she'd begun to feel toward Mr. Cardiff.

Yes, she did enjoy his company. He was a very kind man, and he'd done her an immeasurable favor by taking on the task of training

Kingley. But Emma had no fear that she'd fall in love with him any time soon. She did not believe there to be any great likelihood that she'd lose her head and devote herself to him before he was well and truly her husband, if that were to happen.

The beginnings of this relationship couldn't be more perfect, as far as she was concerned. He was a baronet, and so a perfectly respectable gentleman with whom her father would be unable to find fault, while also not being of such a lofty position he would look down upon her family. He had a thriving hobby with his dog breeding and training, but one would not truly consider it to be an occupation, so he could mix within the higher echelon of society.

It was true that Sir Henry did not incite any great emotion within her. He didn't stir her lust or cause tingles to flutter through her core like Mr. Cardiff had done when he kissed her. But that was what she wanted, wasn't it? To have a friendship of sorts with a gentleman, to respect him and admire him, and only after he had promised himself to her completely, only then did she wish to have anything deeper.

Yet, tiny seeds of frustration kept niggling at her, trying to convince her of something else. Each time they did, she mentally brushed them away and reaffirmed her determination to love only after marriage.

Emma tried to reinforce this thought within herself time and again as she and Sir Henry worked with Kingley Sunday afternoon, trying to help him adjust to walking on the leather lead the baronet had fashioned with the aid of the grooms in the stables. It was shorter than what he used with most of the dogs he trained, but he said that should help with Morgan, allowing Kingley to guide her instead of the other way around.

"Stay," Emma said, tugging gently at Kingley's lead.

He settled beside her left leg, plopping his bottom down on the ground and looking up at her with his tongue lolling out of his mouth. While everything in her wanted to give him his bite of chicken right away for being so smart, she resisted, just as Sir Henry had repeatedly emphasized was necessary. Kingley must learn that rewards didn't come immediately—that the best reward was earning their praise.

When he'd sat there happily wagging his tail for at least thirty seconds, Emma glanced over at Sir Henry, raising her brow in question. He gave her a nod, and she instantly bent to reward Kingley with his treat. "Good boy! You learn so well." He gobbled it up while she scratched behind his ears—easily his favorite thing in the world, until whatever the next favorite might be came along.

She only granted him a moment of her effusive flattery before once again straightening and turning serious. Kingley responded to her change in demeanor, sitting up at attention.

"Walk," she said, and then waited for him to take off. She wanted to rely on her eyes and guide him around the obstacles that Sir Henry and the grooms had devised—crates here, and barrels there, that sort of thing—but that wasn't the purpose of this exercise. Instead, she waited for the simple signals that Kingley was to provide.

He moved a little too fast at first but slowed when she refused to allow him such free rein. A moment later, he settled at her side, keeping to her precise pace. But this was the easy portion of the course. Greater barriers lay in wait for them ahead. Indeed, just when she was certain she would have to take over and guide him lest she run headlong into a barrel, he nudged her leg.

She moved to the right, as he'd directed, and they kept walking. Moments later, the two of them drew too close to a bale of hay for her skin not to crawl with trepidation of the impending contact. He tugged her left with the lead just in time, and she went with him.

It didn't take Kingley long to guide her through all of the obstacles they'd set for him. When he came to a stop at the end, Emma dropped to her knees to deliver him his chicken and a series of scratches. He let out a happy bark before licking her on the cheek, which only led her to giggle like a schoolgirl.

"I think," Sir Henry said, reminding her that she and Kingley weren't alone, "perhaps we can put a blindfold over my eyes and see how he does. It wouldn't surprise me in the least if he's ready for that. Kingley has been quite the efficient learner."

Emma couldn't help but note the sound of surprise in Sir Henry's tone each time Kingley exceeded his expectations. A small part of her wanted to shout at him that she'd told him Kingley would be the perfect dog for the task, but such a reaction wouldn't be terribly ladylike. Not only that, but it would likely eliminate any interest the baronet might have in forming a connection with her.

Instead, she kept her thoughts to herself and smiled at him when she rose to her feet. "And do you have a blindfold with you, sir?"

He pulled an un-starched cravat from the pocket of his coat and started to tie it himself, but he was making a muck of it. After three attempts, he let out a laugh. "I do not know why this is proving such a problem for me."

Emma held out her hand. "Allow me, Sir Henry."

"Gladly." He handed the material over, brushing his fingertips over her knuckles in the process, drawing out the contact more than was proper.

She flushed and hastened to move behind him, making quick work of tying the cravat in a knot behind his head. "There we are." She stepped away from him rather more quickly than was necessary, but couldn't seem to stop herself from trying to put as much distance between them as she possibly could.

That was not the sort of reaction she ought to have with a gentleman whom she might agree to marry, should he make such an offer. She bit her lip to stop the thoughts that were racing through her head and trying to make themselves known, such as the fact that there had been none of the friction, none of the heat in his contact that she'd experienced when Mr. Cardiff had touched her.

That thought had no place here. Not now. Not ever.

Sir Henry reached a hand out, groping into the ether. "Miss Hathaway? Might you put Kingley's lead in my hand?"

But that would mean she had to move closer to him again—and he would have an opportunity to touch her.

Emma bit down on her lip, raced over to take Kingley's lead, and

Catherine Gayle

pressed it hastily into Sir Henry's grip. Without giving him the opportunity to prolong the contact, she dashed aside to watch the proceedings from a safe distance, trembling all the while due to the lack of—well, anything save panic—she'd felt at the baronet's mild flirtation.

Kingley safely guided Sir Henry through the course two times in a row before the baronet suggested they rearrange the obstacles and try again. They kept working, praising Kingley when he did as expected and having him repeat when he did not, for another half hour.

Finally, Sir Henry removed the cloth from his eyes and smiled at Emma. "I think he's ready to attempt the course with Lady Morgan. She'll need one of us with her, of course, so we can be certain she learns to respond to his guidance and that he'll respond to her commands...but we're certainly progressing farther than I'd imagined for this stage of our training sessions."

With that, Emma couldn't hold back a giddy exclamation of joy, which only served to have Sir Henry look upon her even more fondly.

"Oh, she'll be delighted."

He took a step closer to Emma, fumbling with the cravat in his hands. "There is little in this world I find as delightful as you, Miss Hathaway."

Her breath caught in her throat when he closed the distance between them more than he already had done. She knew she should be flattered and that she should welcome his attentions—she should even encourage him. But all she wanted to do at that moment was run as fast as she could in the opposite direction because of the lack of charged air between them.

Blast, but she frustrated herself. Why now, of all times, must she compare Sir Henry to Mr. Cardiff? It wasn't fair to either of them. Each man was something the other could never be. Most of all, it wasn't fair to her.

Emma forced herself to stay where she was, making sure to keep her eyes focused upon Sir Henry. She would not give in to the temptation to make her escape. She would not ruin this chance, this opportunity, which fortune had seen fit to grant her.

He was a handsome man. His light brown hair curled slightly at the ends, and he had a certain warmth to his eyes that was inviting. She could learn to welcome his attentions, should they marry. Surely with Sir Henry she could learn to feel the same sense of excitement, of need, as she'd felt with Mr. Cardiff. Couldn't she?

Emma leaned in as he drew closer, bracing herself for the kiss she knew was coming and berating herself for the very fact that she must brace herself for it.

But before Sir Henry's lips met hers, Kingley let out a growl at her side that made her shiver from the ferocious intent behind it.

Sir Henry jerked back and spun around, trying to see what had roused Kingley's hackles. Emma did not have to look far, however. Lord Jacob Deering was walking across the clearing toward them, all cocksure swagger and sullen defiance. While it had taken Kingley a few days to accept some of the men at Heathcote Park, he had never warmed even slightly to Lord Jacob.

That did not stop the man from attempting to goad Kingley in return. He bared his teeth and growled right back at the dog, which so incited Kingley's desire to attack that Sir Henry was forced to make a dashing grab for his lead.

Lord Jacob merely laughed. Then he turned to Emma and gave a sardonic bow. "Lady Burington requires your presence at tea, Miss Hathaway."

Of all the people at the house party, the only one Vanessa would have been less likely to send to fetch Emma than Lord Jacob was Mr. Cardiff. She couldn't help but wonder what his true intention for coming to fetch her might be, but there was no manner in which to question his motive without rousing his suspicion about her own.

Sir Henry smiled at her and offered his arm. "Shall we? I shouldn't wish to keep your sister waiting."

Shaken all the way to her core, and unable to truly explain even to herself why she ought to be, Emma reached out her arm and placed her hand upon his sleeve. She didn't trust her voice, so she merely nodded and quirked a slight smile.

"Coming, Deering?" the baronet asked, still holding tight to Kingley's lead.

But Lord Jacob looked out across the expanse of the lawn, staring off into the woods nearby. He let out a sigh and shook his head. "I don't believe so. I need to go for a walk far more than I need tea." Without waiting for their response, he took off in the direction he'd been looking, tossing another growl over his shoulder for Kingley's benefit before he was out of earshot.

"Well," Sir Henry said when Kingley finally relaxed and stopped pulling against him. "To tea?"

Emma nodded again, despite her sincere doubts that tea would be enough to calm her jangling nerves. Perhaps she could slip into David's study and sneak a bottle of something stronger, like the apple brandy Mother often gave her, without being noticed. It would certainly be worth the effort to try.

Blast Mr. Deering for being out and about in the corridors before tea. Emma had been on her way to David's study to borrow a bottle of apple brandy when he'd come upon her and offered, ever-so-kindly, to escort her in to the drawing room to join the rest of the houseguests. He hadn't really left her with too many options, and so she'd had to try to calm herself without the aid of spirits.

She hadn't done so effectively.

Not only that, but he had begged out of the tea early, claiming he must see if his cousin, Lord Jacob, was feeling quite the thing yet. Lord Muldaire had accompanied him, and off they'd gone.

It seemed everyone, at this house party, was prone to feigning illness. Vanessa might well think they had an epidemic in the great house.

At least now, she, Morgan, and Serena had made their escape.

They were out on the lawn with Kingley…and without a single gentleman there to interfere in their plans. The servants had left all of the obstacles in place.

For the first time since her afternoon lessons with Sir Henry, she could breathe again. It felt as though a great weight had been lifted free from her chest, like it could finally expand and release as normal.

"Should we talk about it?" Morgan asked.

Emma blinked, taken aback. "Talk about what?" she hedged.

Morgan smiled then, kindness etched into the scars around her mouth. "About whatever has you balled up in knots."

But she didn't even know how to sort it out in her own mind, let along how to speak with her friends about it all. She bit her lip and glanced over at Serena, who held the same look of concern. Emma took Kingley's lead and placed it into Morgan's hand. "There's nothing to talk about. It's all been sorted out."

But it hadn't. Not in the slightest.

Still, this was about Morgan, and Kingley, and teaching the two of them to work together. Not about Emma and her silly problems. Hers were nothing in comparison to what Morgan must face for the rest of her life. One look at her friend was all Emma needed to remind herself of what was truly important in life.

Morgan's lips turned down in a frown, then, and Serena let out a bit of a harrumph. But they didn't press the matter any further.

For the next hour, Emma and Serena worked to teach Morgan how to walk with Kingley by her side, how to trust him to guide her through the barriers set up across the lawn and keep her away from harm. Upon successful completion of each lesson, she rewarded him with a bite of chicken. Kingley pranced around between them, yapping happily.

"Shall we try something to test us a bit more?" Morgan suggested after a moment. "We could take Kingley through one of the walks and see how he does with leading me…and how I do with following him."

The thought was tempting, but Emma felt her uncertainty growing by a wide margin. Shouldn't they practice more with the current obstacles, making certain that both Morgan and Kingley were well acquainted with what was expected of them?

"Oh, that sounds lovely," Serena said, clapping her hands.

It did. It sounded lovelier than Emma knew how to handle, because the entire purpose of teaching Kingley what they'd been teaching him was to give Morgan more freedom, more ability to move through the world on her own.

Both ladies turned to Emma, and Morgan's eyebrows lifted expectantly. "Well?"

She opened her mouth, fully prepared to regretfully inform the other two that it wasn't a good idea for them to push Kingley so much at this point, when the doors of the great house opened and several of the other houseguests came out—Sir Henry at the front of them. Then she snapped her jaw closed again. "Yes, let's take him for a walk."

The three of them turned and took off at once, Morgan holding Kingley's lead in her right hand and letting the animal guide her steps.

Almost immediately, Emma regretted her impetuous decision. Truly, she wasn't prepared to spend more time in Sir Henry's company at the moment, because she didn't like the fact that she felt almost nothing in his presence. But was that a good reason to toss good reason aside and trust that both Morgan and Kingley were ready for the next step in their training? Although, Serena and Emma were both along, too. It wasn't as though they were sending Morgan and Kingley off on their own with no one to assist should they encounter problems.

They'd been walking for twenty minutes or more, with Morgan and Serena keeping up a constant stream of chatter and Emma trapped within the doubts clouding her mind, when several male voices cut through.

Angry male voices.

Emma put her arm out to the side, and Morgan bumped into it but came to a stop. Serena stopped just as suddenly, and Morgan tugged on Kingley's lead.

The three of them stood there for a moment, listening.

"If you need more blunt, perhaps you should take up a profession like Charles has," one of them growled. "You won't get it from me. Not after—"

"Not again!" The new voice was unmistakable as belonging to Lord Jacob Deering. "You can't forget that, can you?"

Emma strained her neck, trying to see through the thick tree branches to where the men stood. Her efforts proved fruitless, though. No matter how she tried, she couldn't see them.

"Why should I, when it was my money? When it tarnished my name?" Once Lord Jacob had been identified, it was easy to conclude that this voice must belong to his brother, Lord Muldaire. "As long as I have breath, you'll never see another farthing from my estate."

"Gentlemen, please," a third voice cut in, leaving no doubt that it must belong to Mr. Charles Deering. "You're brothers. Must you fight like this?"

A loud crack sounded in the distance, like a great log splintering in two, causing all three ladies to jump. Kingley whined, but it was so quiet, Emma doubted the men could hear the sound. Serena met Emma's eyes, hers wide and fearful.

They should walk away. Quickly. But quietly, too, so as to avoid drawing the men's notice. This was not a conversation any of them ought to hear, whether they intended it or not.

"You'll still help Charles, though, when he needs it," Lord Jacob shouted.

"I hardly see how anything to do with Charles matters in this discussion," Lord Muldaire said drolly.

"You wouldn't," his brother returned. "Care to explain, Charles?"

"I...I..." Mr. Deering's voice rose in a bit of a panic as he struggled for words.

"There's nothing he ought to explain!" Lord Muldaire shouted just as another booming crash sounded in their direction.

With that, Emma and Serena acted as one, each taking one of

Morgan's arms while she still held Kingley's lead, and guiding the lot of them away from the three men as fast as they could go without drawing notice. Emma didn't even care where they were headed, as long as it was well away from the three men arguing in the woods. By the time they slowed, Emma was gasping for breath and her pulse hammered within her chest—but she doubted it was simply from her exertions. It likely had more to do with what they'd unintentionally eavesdropped upon.

"I think," Morgan said after a few moments, her eyes as wide as Emma had ever seen them, "it is best if we do not mention what we heard to anyone."

"I couldn't agree more," Serena said. She gave an emphatic nod, which made Emma think she was attempting to convince herself as much as the other two. The expression she bore when she met Emma's gaze was one of sheer panic. "And we ought to get back to the house before we're missed."

They couldn't return soon enough. Emma nodded, then looked around. Their surroundings appeared vaguely familiar, but not really familiar enough for her to have a solid understanding of their location.

"Serena," she started slowly. There was no need to make either Kingley or Morgan nervous about the fact that they were lost, particularly not if they weren't truly lost. "Which direction do you think it would be easiest for us to go?"

Serena's eyes shot up, more wild with panic than they'd been earlier. She shook her head.

Heavens, but Serena didn't know where they were either. Not one of them knew where they were, so they couldn't possibly know how to get back. While Serena was with them, Emma felt certain that Mr. Cardiff would blame no one but Emma if anything were to happen to Morgan. What if she tripped over a tree root or turned an ankle in a rut in the ground? Oh, heavens, this wasn't good.

Serena swallowed, casting her eyes around them. "Why don't—?"

Before Serena could finish her question, another loud hammering sound echoed in the distance, though in the opposite direction from whence they'd come. Kingley let out an excited yap and took off so fast that Morgan was forced to go with him or relinquish her grip on his lead. She giggled as she went, despite the few stumbles she had over tree roots and broken branches.

Emma and Serena followed behind them, and after a brief time, Emma started to recognize the recently broken limbs. Kingley was taking them to the abandoned building that she and Morgan had chanced upon with Mr. Cardiff and Lord Jacob last week. This wasn't precisely where Emma would like to be, three ladies off in the woods alone with a dog, but at least she knew her surroundings and could get them back to the manor house.

Well, she could if Kingley would stop leading them in the wrong direction.

With each step they took toward the building, the hammering grew louder. In fact, as they came upon it, it became perfectly clear that the hammering was coming from inside it.

Morgan stopped suddenly and turned, her eyes alight with such joy more intense than Emma had ever seen. "He's sculpting!"

With that, she reversed herself and nudged Kingley forward. They raced to the door, she fumbled for the handle, then threw it open.

"Damn and blast, Deering, I told you to leave me be," Mr. Cardiff shouted.

CHAPTER TWELVE

It was the dog's bark more than anything else that finally got through Aidan's frustrations and alerted him it was not Lord Jacob Deering interrupting his work yet again, but someone else altogether. He spun around, chisel in hand, fully prepared to berate Sir Henry or Miss Hathaway, or whoever it was who'd brought that beast out to the hermitage and decided to intrude upon him unannounced.

But it was Morgan, not Sir Henry or Miss Hathaway, standing before him with a smile fit to light the heavens.

Aidan dropped his chisel and bit back the oath that had been on the very tip of his tongue. "What are you doing here? How did you—?"

"You *are* sculpting again. Why didn't you tell me?" Morgan rushed inside, holding tight to the blasted dog's lead in her right hand.

Miss Hathaway and Miss Weston cautiously stepped inside, each bearing sheepish expressions. Miss Weston at least had the decency to blush. Neither would meet his gaze, instead casting their eyes about the floor.

"I didn't want—" Didn't want what? To share this part of himself with anyone else, including Morgan. At least not so soon. He couldn't say that, whether it was the truth or not. It would break his sister's heart into a thousand pieces, and that was something Aidan could never bear to do. Never mind the fact that just this once, he wanted to live his own life, to do what he wished without worrying about how it would affect his sister. It seemed entirely too self-indulgent. "I couldn't—"

"What is it?" Morgan asked. "What are you working on?"

Aidan scraped a hand over his face. "I—"

Morgan dropped the dog's lead and moved closer, reaching out with both hands to touch the marble. She moved her fingers over the piece with deliberate purpose, dipping them into the crevasses and gliding over the smooth expanses—exploring the sculpture as she did anything unfamiliar. Since her blinding, she'd had to learn to see the world through touch instead of sight. Her palms and fingers, the tips and the length of them, helped her to recognize what was before her in a way Aidan's eyes never had been able to do.

He watched her now: the studious crease in her forehead, the glimmer of recognition that added a sparkle to her gaze, in awe of how she had not only accepted her new lot in life, but instead had almost embraced it. Instead of wallowing in misery, as he'd done for so long, she reveled in learning and becoming more than anyone ever thought she could be.

This realization struck him as if a horse had kicked him in the chest. His sister was far from incapable. She was no longer the fragile girl whom he must constantly oversee, to be certain she didn't shatter like a vase knocked to the floor. Morgan had moved on from that stage of her life. For that matter, Mother and Niall had, as well. Only Aidan felt the need to remain permanently in the past—no one else.

What an arse he was for trying to protect her so much he was preventing her from living. Preventing himself from living, as well. Damnation.

In quick succession, Morgan proceeded to lean in, stretch up, bend almost to the floor, all the while exploring the piece with her hands. "Aidan, it's beautiful." Her voice was hardly more than a breath, a reverent whisper of adoration. When she lifted her face, bright tears pooled in her eyes and fell freely down her cheeks. "It's been so long. Too long."

In that moment, he could no longer see the scars that had so long marred her delicate beauty. He could see the beautiful girl she'd once been, unmarred, unbroken, unfettered.

A sniff sounded behind Morgan, and Aidan's head shot up. Miss Hathaway brushed away a tear and stared at the floor—the perfect image of the marble angel before him, all the way to the angle of her head. Until that very moment, he hadn't realized he'd been sculpting her. It had only been an angel. The angel he'd begun before had never had a face. Now he saw every resemblance, right down to the tears streaking their faces—the long nose, the too-wide mouth, the downturned corners of their eyes.

How could he not have known? And yet, it had simply happened, his hands knowing how to create what his head had not yet fully embraced.

What in God's name did it mean? Why would he, whether he knew what he was doing or not, create a sculpture of the woman he'd hated for so long. Marble wasn't a medium he could toss into the hearth and watch it burn. It was more permanent.

It was absolutely, undeniably *her*.

He couldn't speak. With all the blasted emotion roiling through his veins, he couldn't possibly trust his voice not to crack and betray him. So he stood there, watching and waiting as his sister experienced his artwork for the first time in years—the possibility of which he'd long ago denounced in his own mind, in order to bury the deep seated ache in his gut over her loss of sight.

I'm a blithering idiot. There was no other explanation for how he could have himself been so blind as to think Morgan couldn't experience his sculpting. For so long, he'd been utilizing a different medium—one which she had no possibility of sharing in with him— and trying to convince himself he couldn't sculpt any more.

He'd deprived her of the one part of his artwork she could have shared with him, all along.

And why?

To spite Miss Hathaway? She knew nothing of this part of him, so why should it matter to her if he'd been sculpting or working with pastels, or doing nothing at all?

If he had thought, for even a moment, that his art could help Morgan, he would have started sculpting again in the span of half a second. But now, as her hands slid rapidly over the many contours as though she were trying to memorize every bit of it and store it in her memory forever, he could see how it might have helped her. How it *was* helping her even now. Her eyes sparkled with such joy, he felt like the greatest cad ever to walk the earth.

So he waited, allowing his sister to examine it as long as she wished without interruption. Alas, that mangy dog let out a yap after a few moments. He'd never know how long she might have gone on were she not distracted. Morgan dropped down beside the dog to scratch his ears with such earnestness it was as though spoiling the beast was the only thing she was meant to do in this life.

Then Miss Hathaway cleared her throat.

His head shot up almost, and he locked his gaze with Miss Hathaway's. The sun had started its descent, and streaks of pink and orange came into the hermitage around the two ladies, making it difficult to see them other than their silhouettes. After a moment, her eyes became clear in the dark shadows of her form. They were huge and almost black, forced wider than was their wont. Bewildered and dealing with his own shame, and indeed anger with himself, he knew his expression must be wild and terrifying.

She flinched and took a half step back, which only confirmed his suspicions. "Morgan," she ventured a moment later, her tone betraying none of the fear in her eyes, "shouldn't we return to the main house? They'll send a search party after us if we aren't back soon."

"Why did you bring my sister here?" Aidan demanded. He couldn't seem to stop himself from becoming far more aggressive with the chit than was called for. There was simply something about her that brought out the very worst in him, and he had not come close to discerning a way of stopping that change within himself.

"Did they know this was your destination?"

Miss Weston smiled, her auburn hair shimmering like flame in the setting sun. "Kingley was ready to lead Morgan, and so we all went for a walk with him. We didn't truthfully know where we had gotten to."

Kingley was ready. Of course he was. Their absurd behavior could only be related to something equally as absurd. "How could you know the dog was ready? And why did Sir Henry allow you to go without his assistance?" When he saw Henry Irvine next, he'd demand an answer as to why the deuced baronet would let the three of them go off on their own, but that would be between Aidan and Irvine.

Miss Hathaway pursed her lips tightly together and crossed both arms over her chest. "Berating us after the fact will hardly change anything, Mr. Cardiff. If you'll excuse us." She took the dog's lead and pressed it into Morgan's hand, then started to guide the lot of them out of the hermitage.

But the sun was already setting, and it could be quite dark by the time they returned to the main house. That wouldn't do. Niall would never let Aidan hear the end of it. Not if Aidan allowed them to return alone, and if Niall ever got wind of the situation.

Especially not after what had happened, with Miss Hathaway stalking off alone through the woods the last time they'd been out at the hermitage.

"Wait a few moments for me to clean up my work, and I'll come with you."

His directive seemed to do the trick with Morgan and Miss Weston. The two of them—the reasonable ones of the bunch—stopped and waited. Miss Hathaway continued stalking off, tromping down the almost nonexistent path and stumbling occasionally. Blast, but she was going to hurt herself. Not only that, but she didn't even have the damned dog with her this time.

There was no time to sort out his mess. Aidan marched out the door and chased after her. When he reached her side, he took her by the elbow and forced her to stop. "I said to wait."

"I realize that," she bit off. Her glare was fit to level a man at fifty paces. "I chose to ignore you. Kindly release me."

Never in his life would he understand his reactions to this woman. One moment, he was in awe of his sister and her appreciation for his artwork, and the next he felt ready to spit fire. And all because Miss Hathaway didn't just annoy him, but she consumed him. His every thought was of her. Her image was in his mind even when she wasn't present. For God's sake, he'd even turned his sculpture into her likeness. It was more than he should have to bear.

Before he allowed himself the time to think, Aidan picked her up and tossed her over his shoulder, ignoring her gasp of outrage, then turned to the other ladies. "Miss Weston, would you be so kind as to fetch the lantern by the hearth and then close the door to the hermitage?" Without waiting for her response, he whistled for the dog and started off back toward the manor house.

This was not how he'd envisioned the completion of his day.

After Miss Hathaway had voiced her displeasure with him the entire way back to the manor house, right up until the moment he'd set her upon her feet just before they broke through the line of trees into the clearing, he finished making certain the three ladies arrived safely and more or less intact. Aidan then went in for supper and attempted to go about the rest of the evening as usual.

Such a thing was easier said than done, however. Particularly when he could not remove the image of his sister exploring his sculpture from his mind—the sense of wonder in her eyes, the pure joy alighting her features.

For that matter, he couldn't remove thoughts of Miss Hathaway either. She'd squirmed and struggled against him the entire way back from the hermitage, despite the teasing censure she received from Morgan and Miss Weston, and he'd been forced to hold her legs more tightly against him in order to avoid dropping her. Those legs were long and lean, as was the rest of her. But they weren't bony and hard—there was a softness to them, one which sent his thoughts traveling to an entirely inappropriate place. No matter how hard he'd tried, he couldn't remove the memory of how well she'd fit against him, how her very shapely, very long legs were nearly begging to be wrapped around his waist.

He had no business thinking of taking her to his bed. There was no situation in which it would ever be befitting for him to think of delving between her thighs.

And yet, that was essentially all he could think of throughout their entire jaunt.

His thoughts ought to be focused instead upon the fact that Morgan was by his side but her hand was not upon his person as they walked through the woods. He ought to be marveling that, however unlikely he'd thought such a prospect, the dog truly was guiding her as Miss Hathaway and Sir Henry had intended.

How could he think of such things, though, with Miss Hathaway's entirely too enticing derriere situated over his shoulder, in perfect view? Well, in perfect view should he turn his head to the side. (An act which he discovered, much to his dismay, he was completing rather more frequently than was necessary.)

He couldn't possibly think of those things of which he ought to be thinking. He was a man. He thought like a man. As such, his thoughts invariably turned to those of bedding shapely females and the delightful sounds those very females would make in the process.

Even now, sitting across the drawing room from those same three ladies as the houseguests conversed all around him, he couldn't force himself to think in such a clear manner. The path of his thoughts inevitably turned to the slight downturn of Miss Hathaway's eyes when she smiled, as she was doing just now for Sir Henry. It ought to make her look sad, despondent…but instead it simply made her appear intriguing.

And that made Aidan want to look at her more than before.

He watched her, noting how she crossed her ankles just so, when Niall came and took the seat across from him, blocking the lady from his view.

Aidan bit back an oath.

"How did Morgan fare with Kingley?" Niall asked. "Was she able to handle him? I know Miss Hathaway and Miss Weston say they had no problems at all, but…"

"But you want to hear it from me," Aidan finished for him. But damn, if he hadn't really paid much attention. Still, they had made it all the way from the hermitage back to the main house, without anything involving either Morgan or the dog catching Aidan's notice. That had to mean she'd managed quite nicely, didn't it? He ought to have paid Morgan more attention, and paid less to Miss Hathaway's derrière. "They did just fine together."

Speaking his approval aloud ought to have grated upon Aidan's last nerve. It all came back to Miss Hathaway, after all. But instead of annoyance, a flicker of pride started to work its way through his body, warming his veins.

"Miss Hathaway's idea might not prove to be as disastrous as you first thought, then?"

"I think perhaps she is not as careless as I'd initially thought her to be," he said.

"Indeed?" Niall smugly lifted a single brow. "So your opinion of her is beginning to change? Perhaps you could behave in a civil manner toward her after all."

Aidan coughed on a sip of brandy. "Don't let's take this too far, now."

"But you could, at least, stop depicting her death in your artwork."

After what he'd witnessed earlier, when Morgan had come so alive while exploring his marble, Aidan couldn't imagine ever creating those fiery pastels again. Not with the same rage fueling it, at the very least. The realization almost hurt.

"I could," he finally conceded for his brother's benefit, not that Niall seemed to be paying attention any longer.

Aidan turned his head to see what had caught Niall's attention. He was staring in the direction where Morgan and Miss Hathaway were seated with Miss Weston. The auburn-haired lady was tittering with laughter, her lips pressed together in a mischievous manner—and she had Niall's full focus.

Interesting. In the last many years, neither Aidan nor Niall had spent much time thinking about women for their own personal pursuits. All of their time and energy had been taken up with worrying about Morgan and how to convince her to live.

Sure, Niall had said he was ready to move on since Morgan had obviously done so. But Aidan hadn't thought about it being the truth—hadn't thought about the fact that Niall must find a bride and procure heirs for the earldom. Aidan had thought only of himself and Morgan. Never of his brother.

But the look in Niall's eyes made it perfectly clear what he wanted.

Blast, but that might only mean having Miss Hathaway in his life more fully, since Morgan and Miss Weston both seemed to be attached to her at the hip. His breath hitched at the thought, damn it all.

Aidan pushed back from his chair, walked to the sideboard, and refilled his drink. Confusion always gave him a headache, and nothing could ease a headache quite like spirits.

CHAPTER THIRTEEN

Emma had not played—or even thought about—the game casino since Vanessa and David's last house party three years ago.

So often during that party, many of the guests had sat around the dainty gaming tables in the drawing room in groups of four, one pair playing against the other while Emma and Morgan had sat off to the side. Despite the fact that she'd often been fully absorbed in whatever book she'd been reading at the time, Emma had always been very aware of the card players, much as she'd been aware of everything Morgan had done. She'd just found far more enjoyment within the pages of her books than she did in the deck of cards. And if she sat with Morgan, then at least Morgan wasn't alone.

But, with the drawing room once again filled with all two dozen houseguests, save Mr. Cardiff again, and with Sir Henry and Serena waiting expectantly for her answer as to whether she would join them for a game, her avoidance of it must now come to a close. Much as her penchant for reading at every opportunity had done already during the course of this fortnight.

After all, she was here to catch a husband, even if she was also helping Morgan when she could. How could she possibly do that if she avoided all opportunities for socializing? As it was, she had been busy with training Kingley rather a lot of the time, and Sir Henry had been with them much of that time as well—but after her lack of fluttering sensations while in the baronet's presence, Emma's doubts about whether they would suit had only intensified.

Had she been wrong in refusing to fall in love with the man she would marry until such time as they were married, believing it the only way to avoid a broken heart? It had seemed the right course of action, considering Morgan's lot, but now every time Emma turned around, she felt less certain of herself than before.

Whether she felt flutters around the baronet or not, she could not afford to spurn any gentleman's attentions.

So she smiled for Sir Henry's benefit. "I'd be happy to be your partner for casino tonight." True, that would yet again put her alongside him…but at least she would be involved in the goings-on. The others would see and take note of her participation, which would prevent her being seen as sullen or standoffish.

He looked relieved, as though he'd doubted whether she would agree.

Serena let out a happy sound at Emma's side and clapped her hands together. "Wonderful. Miss Hathaway, you and Sir Henry can play against me and Lord Trenowyth."

For a brief moment, Emma hesitated. What would Morgan do all evening if both Emma and Serena were otherwise occupied with a game she couldn't play?

Morgan must have sensed her reticence. "Oh, lovely." She leaned forward and smiled. "You'll both be occupied. Miss Goderich wanted to try to teach me to play the pianoforte like you suggested, Miss Hathaway, but I didn't want to agree unless you both had other plans."

Lord Trenowyth came over to stand beside Sir Henry, tugging lightly at the front of his coat. The image took Emma's thoughts straight to that night outside, when Mr. Cardiff had kissed her and both of them had needed to repair their appearances. She fought the urge to flush.

He cleared his throat. "The pianoforte? You haven't touched one in a very long time. I daresay Mama gave up the thought of you taking after it again quite some time ago."

"But Miss Hathaway was right in suggesting it. Miss Goderich swears she can teach me to play by touch. She says my fingers can learn where the keys are, and there won't be any reason I should avoid it." Morgan tittered lightly. "Well, aside from the fact that I can't read the music. But the *playing* part I can do."

Emma had no doubts at all on that score. She reached a hand across and took Morgan's, then squeezed lightly. "You certainly can. You'll just have to learn your own music." Every day, it seemed there was something new Morgan learned she could do.

Lord Trenowyth studied his sister for a moment, then nodded. "Very well."

Emma caught a look of amazement upon his countenance, but there was also a hint of pride—much like she'd seen in Mr. Cardiff's eyes when Morgan discovered his sculpting. She seemed to astonish her brothers at every turn. It wouldn't surprise *Emma* in the least if their moments of awe continued to mount for years to come. Morgan was far more capable than her family gave her credit for being. More capable than Emma had given her credit for, as well. They'd all continued to discount Morgan's abilities.

Miss Goderich came to collect Morgan and took her off to the corner of the drawing room where the pianoforte awaited them. Emma and Serena rose and walked with Sir Henry and Lord Trenowyth to a gaming table near the hearth to begin their game of casino as the somewhat discordant sounds of the instrument echoed throughout the room.

Lord Trenowyth picked up the cards and dealt out their hands.

When the cards had been placed, Sir Henry lifted his hand and studied it. "Lady Morgan and Kingley are making excellent progress, my lord. Wouldn't you agree, Miss Hathaway?" He captured the queen of hearts.

"I would."

Serena played an eight, and then built to eight with a five and three. "They seem as though they've been working together for years, not days."

While Emma set down a two, for lack of anything better to play, Lord Trenowyth met Serena's gaze. The look which passed between them was heated enough to warm Emma through to the bones. She flushed with embarrassment and glanced up at Sir Henry, who merely passed her a congenial smile, much as he always did. Should the same sort of heat be coming from the two of them? Blast, but why did it all have to be so very complicated? The heat seemed to go along with the flutters, and she felt neither in his presence. The baronet smiled more deeply upon her examination in what could only be considered a warm manner, but his warmth could not possibly compare to that which was already surrounding them. This heat, between Serena and Lord Trenowyth...it could only compare to one thing in Emma's memory, and that was the heat she'd felt when Mr. Cardiff kissed her. How blasted infuriating.

"I'm pleased to hear that," Lord Trenowyth said. He played a seven and built to nine with Emma's two. "How much more training will the dog require?"

"It's not a matter of Kingley requiring more training, at this point," Sir Henry said. "It's more about having him and Lady Morgan practice together, until everything they must do becomes innate." He scowled at his cards for a moment, then played a four.

"And you're certain that Kingley will not harm my sister?"

The baronet shook his head. "Dogs are very loyal creatures, quite protective. He's already coming to understand she is his responsibility." He stopped as Serena played a nine. "Not only will he not harm Lady Morgan, I would wager he would do anything to be certain no harm comes to her."

Lord Trenowyth nodded while Emma studied her cards. It would help if she had actually paid attention when the others played cards at gatherings, even if she didn't join them. But, instead of watching, she usually just knew that they were playing something. Often, she wasn't even cognizant of what specific game they were indulging in.

At the moment, she honestly didn't know what move to make.

Pursing her lips, she took out a jack and laid it upon the table, looking up to see if Sir Henry reacted to her choice at all.

He didn't. Not that she could tell. He still bore the same benign smile he so often did in her presence.

They continued playing, and it soon became apparent that Emma and Sir Henry would lose the hand in rather dramatic fashion to Serena and Lord Trenowyth.

"I must apologize, Sir Henry," Emma said after playing another seven, which Lord Trenowyth then captured. "You couldn't have possibly expected to be partnered with someone so lacking in skill."

A clatter sounded behind her, and the foursome turned as one to see what had caused the commotion. Mr. Cardiff had finally made his appearance, though at least he'd taken the time to don clean clothing after a day spent with his chisel. He stood just inside the doorway, yet again setting a chair to rights after he'd knocked it over. Emma lifted a brow. While it was true that she could be rather clumsy, *he* could hardly be considered graceful. Good heavens, had a chair wronged him at some point in his life? He seemed to have a great distaste for them.

Lord Trenowyth sighed. "It seems I must once again apologize for my brother."

"Not at all," Serena murmured.

Mr. Cardiff passed a sullen glare over the room, his eyes resting on Emma far longer than was comfortable before moving on to encompass the rest of the houseguests. The drawing room once again resumed a polite din, of a similar strength to before Mr. Cardiff's entry, and Emma's companions returned their attention to their game of casino. She did not find it so easy to redirect her thoughts.

Taking a wide berth around their party, Mr. Cardiff ambled through the drawing room until he found an empty chair next to the Bornholm clock against the far wall. He sat down, picked up a book from the occasional table beside him, and started to read. Rather contradictory of him, if anyone should ask Emma, since he so readily took her to task for doing that very thing. Or perhaps he was merely pretending to read. Every few moments, his head would lift and his gaze would meet hers, and he glared.

But, well, glare wasn't quite the correct term. Always before, when he would look upon her with such depth of emotion, it was rage or anger she felt pouring from him in waves. This was different. No less forceful, certainly, but…different.

His eyes left her for a moment to settle upon Sir Henry. Then his stare was most decidedly a glare, which caused Emma's chest to constrict. After a moment, he returned his gaze to her, and she shuddered. Mr. Cardiff's expression was so heated she felt certain it would consume her, incinerate her, leave her nothing more than a melted puddle on the floor.

The sudden need to swallow became overwhelming. She tried frantically to catch her breath—which was almost impossible, with the vise that had somehow crushed her ribs moments ago—only to discover that she'd been holding it in. And then she did experience the same sort of heat she'd felt coursing between Lord Trenowyth and Serena earlier, but it was because of Mr. Cardiff and not Sir Henry.

She tried to force the sensations at bay, turning back to the card table. Her hands were shaking and moist, and her cards felt as though they would slip free from her grip at any moment. Impatiently, she set them down and pushed back from the table so suddenly that her chair wobbled.

"Emma, are you feeling quite all right?" Serena asked. At once, she also rose and took Emma's hand.

"I don't—I need—" She didn't have the first inkling what she needed, only she was fairly certain it *wasn't* Sir Henry, or card playing, or even well-meaning friends. Good heavens. "I think I should go lie down. I'm so very sorry."

She rushed from the drawing room and out of the house to get some air, racing as though the hounds of hell were upon her. For all she knew, Mr. Cardiff was one of them. She didn't slow until the footman closed the door behind her and cool, evening air filled her lungs, and then she bent over at the waist with both arms clutched over her stomach, trying to force her reaction to the man to subside.

As silly and mad as it seemed, Emma feared she needed *him*.

For longer than was healthy, Aidan stared at the empty chair Miss Hathaway had just vacated, fully at war with himself. He wanted to continue to hate her, but that wasn't possible. Not anymore. Not now that she was doing so many things to help Morgan, things which he and Niall and Mother had been unable to do for her. Not now that every time he saw her or thought of her, the direction of his thoughts turned to taking her in his arms and kissing her as he had before on the lawn. Not now that jealousy had become an unnatural, constant companion in his mind. Why should Irvine be granted time with her when it was so plainly obvious to any observers that Miss Hathaway felt nothing at all for him?

Deuce take it! How could he ever be free of her, if all he saw when he closed his eyes to sleep at night were her downturned eyes and broad lips and silky skin? How could he focus on finding ways to encourage her assistance for Morgan if every time he saw her, she was beside Sir Henry Irvine? Interfering lout.

He had been staring for so long that Niall lifted a single eyebrow in question. Damnation, the last thing Aidan needed was to deal with his brother at the moment. He shoved the book back onto the occasional table, not that he'd read a single word in his current state of distraction, and stood without a thought as to what excuse he would make for departing so early again.

His excuse came to him much easier than he'd ever anticipated. Along the opposite wall, Morgan rose from behind the pianoforte with…well, with one of the young ladies whose name he'd neglected to remember. It hadn't seemed important, but perhaps that had been an oversight on his part.

Aidan stalked to his sister's side and placed his hand on her elbow.

"Is there something I can help you with, Morgan?" In all honesty, his tone sounded a bit frantic, but there was nothing he could do about that. He *was* a bit frantic. Damn.

She turned her face up to him with confusion, or maybe frustration, bunching her brow together. "Miss Goderich was just going to walk with me to the kitchens."

Goderich. Yes, he remembered, now that it had been mentioned. He'd have to make a better effort, in case his memory was ever put to the test. At the moment, the only thing he cared to remember was Miss Hathaway, which was quite the troublesome thought.

"I was going to fetch Kingley's supper…"

Morgan's voice trailed off since Aidan started to tug her along with him. "Thank you so much for your kindness, Miss Goderich, but I'll be happy to help my sister with this task."

"But you hate Kingley," Morgan protested.

By then, they were past the footmen manning the doors and out in the corridor. Aidan kept going until they couldn't be overheard before slowing. "I don't hate Kingley. I just don't like him." What surprised him more than anything was that this admission was the truth. He *didn't* hate Kingley. He didn't like that someone or something other than him was helping Morgan. He especially didn't like that it hadn't been his idea. He plainly loathed the fact that he'd been proven wrong. But he didn't hate the dog. The bloody mutt just made him think of Miss Hathaway, since she was the one who'd essentially made him a pet and a part of their lives.

Morgan scoffed at his statement and rolled her eyes, a trait she hadn't lost when she went blind.

His breath hitched like it always did when something reminded him of how she had been before. Or maybe it was a reminder that she wasn't gone—the same Morgan resided within the scarred body, no matter how many changes had taken place.

"I just—" Aidan shook his head, though she couldn't see it. "I was worried about Miss Hathaway. I came out to…to see if she's all right."

"Miss Hathaway?" She sucked in a breath. "Oh, Miss Goderich said she looked quite ill when she left the drawing room. But—"

"Please don't ask me questions now...particularly questions I don't even know the answers to myself."

Morgan nodded curtly with an impish scowl. "So what are we doing? Where are we going?"

Hauling Morgan along while he followed after Miss Hathaway hadn't been in his plans. Granted, he hadn't truly had a plan. For that matter, he still didn't. "*We* are going to the kitchens, so you can get your meal for Kingley. I'll have a kitchen maid stay with you to help you return afterward, and then *I'll* go make certain nothing is amiss with Miss Hathaway."

That brought out his sister's fiercest frown. "Should you really be alone with her? I hardly think—"

"I don't want anyone else to worry about her, Morgan. Most likely, she's perfectly fine and I'm concerned for no reason. Please?" This was not a conversation he'd ever imagined having with his sister, and particularly not when it concerned one of her dearest friends.

They walked in silence, with Morgan biting down upon her lip. They'd nearly reached the door to the kitchens when finally she nodded. "Fine. But if I hear—"

"You won't hear a thing. Nothing will happen. I just want make certain she is quite well."

He deposited his sister with a scullery maid who agreed to ensure Morgan returned to the drawing room upon completion of her task, and then Aidan excused himself.

The only problem was he didn't know where to go. Where might Miss Hathaway have run to when she'd departed so hastily? He knew he was the reason for her sudden need to escape. There could be no mistaking the heated glances they'd shared.

Aidan sincerely doubted she would have gone above stairs. That didn't seem to be her normal escape route when confronted with a situation she didn't know how to handle. No, it was far more likely she'd gone outside even if Kingley was Morgan's responsibility now.

He started in the west garden, since it would be well-lit by the revelry inside and the brightness of the moon tonight. After going through it thoroughly, however, he hadn't discovered even the slightest hint of her. Fighting back the tension in his jaw, Aidan methodically made his way through the Heathcote Park grounds.

After half an hour, he'd scoured everything in close proximity—every part of the grounds he could imagine she would dare to go alone after dark—and was about to head into the woods, when a strange sound caught his attention: a tiny cry. He spun toward it, off near the stables but not quite in them, and headed in that direction.

It was her gown that he saw first in the moonlight, the soft rose calling to him like a beacon against the inky darkness around her. She was down on the ground, just beside a hedgerow. Of course she was. Surely she'd tripped and fallen over a root sticking up out of the ground, or her skirts had become trapped in the brambles, or the toes of her slippers had found a hole in the terrain. This was Miss Hathaway, of course, a woman who had never been known for her grace.

Aidan moved closer, preparing to deliver her a talking to that she would remember for quite some time when the odd noise reached him again. Louder this time. More insistent.

Was it Miss Hathaway crying in pain?

No, it couldn't be. He'd heard a fair bit from her tongue, and she'd never sounded so tiny and fragile. It wasn't her. But it was coming from where she sat upon the ground.

He took a few more steps in her direction, and the sounds came more frequently, and then he knew.

A kitten.

It was a kitten. A tiny one, by the sound of its cries.

As he drew closer still, the soft, calming tone of Miss Hathaway's voice carried over the night air, though he could not make out her words. Then more cries met him, one on top of another, until there could be no doubt that there was more than one kitten. Finally, he distinguished a panting sound.

Good God, a cat must be birthing at that very moment. What did she think she was doing? And how on earth did she always find these people and animals in need?

He ought to leave Miss Hathaway to her task. Her talent for attracting broken and helpless things to her seemed to know no bounds, and he was no use in such situations. Amidst the crying mewls and pants of the mother cat, and Miss Hathaway's gentle murmurs, Aidan backed with the good intention of returning to the manor house without looking back. None of this was any of his concern. *Emma Hathaway* was none of his concern.

Until his plodding foot snapped a twig beneath him.

Her head shot up at once, and she met his eyes. In the moonlight, hers were dark, almost black, and shining with excitement. They locked onto him, rooting him to the ground.

He should go. He should turn around and return to the house, and forget that he'd ever come after her in the first place. That would be the intelligent thing to do—the rational thing.

Instead, he closed the distance between them. "You just can't seem to help yourself, can you?" God only knew when he'd learn to act rationally again—not so long as Miss Hathaway was in the world.

CHAPTER FOURTEEN

Just can't help myself. Emma tamped down upon her anger, firming her resolve not to allow Mr. Cardiff to have such control over her emotions. How did he so easily incite her anger?

What was he doing out here? Could she not escape his interference no matter what she did or where she went? It seemed, no matter how little encouragement she gave him—and for that matter, no matter how frequently he sent indecipherable looks in her direction—he turned up in her general vicinity every time she batted an eye.

It was infuriating, even if it was a little bit thrilling.

And here, of all places? The thought that he could possibly hold an interest in birthing kittens was ludicrous, so what other excuse might he have for his sudden appearance?

Emma forced a calm expression upon her face—or at least she hoped she was successful in doing so—before she turned to face Mr. Cardiff. "I suppose you can't help yourself, either. Or else how would you explain your penchant for following me, when you can never bear to be in my presence?"

She winced slightly at the coldness of her words, the crass bite pouring from her tongue. So often, he brought out the absolute worst in her. It perturbed her to no end how she became an icy, cantankerous miss every time he opened his mouth in her general vicinity. That reaction was easier than letting herself give in to the intoxicating flutters and breathtaking heat he inspired.

His shoulders jerked back, and even without the aid of a lantern, his scowl was visible across the brief span between them. "You shouldn't be out here alone."

She shouldn't, but that was beside the point. And it was none of his business whether she was out alone or not. He ought to be looking after Morgan, not worrying about anything Emma was doing. Oh, heavens. What if he'd finally decided to leave Morgan to do as she would, and now intended to repeat the coddling process with Emma?

Emma opened her mouth to let him know her thoughts on such a thing just as the mother cat, a calico, let out a soft sound of distress. Another kitten must be on its way. Instead of delivering Mr. Cardiff an earful, Emma cooed softly into the night and ran a soothing hand over the poor dear's back.

"Can't the cat manage without your assistance?" he grumbled. "Cats must birth kittens all alone in the wild all the time. How else would the infernal creatures be so pervasive everywhere?"

"Just because they *can* doesn't mean this one *should*," Emma replied, spinning to glare at him before returning her full attention to the cats. "Not while I can sit here with her and ease the way. Would you want your sister to experience childbirth without someone with her to assist the process?"

"My sister isn't having a child, and she is a human, not a cat."

He had a point, but Emma had no intention of conceding hers. She bit her tongue to keep from lashing out at him again.

The first bit of the sac pushed through while the mother cat panted. Moments later, the kitten was free and the mother was hard at work cleaning it up. This was the third of the litter, but Emma was fairly certain there were more still to come. Her belly had been far too large for only three little kittens. If she had to guess, she'd imagine there were five or six, in total. And she had every intention of staying right where she was until such time as every last one of them had been born, no matter what Mr. Cardiff's thoughts on the matter might be.

He started making impatient noises behind her again, little grunts and heavy breaths. But there was no cause for impatience. The kittens would come when they were ready. All in due time. Mr. Cardiff could not increase the pace of the process, no matter how much he may want to do so. Nevertheless, she stole glances at him to see if he would leave.

His sighs and groans were liable to drive Emma to the brink of madness. She could well imagine he was adding to the mother cat's stress, which just would not do.

"Feel free to return to the party at any time, sir." She looked up at him for a moment, nodding her head in the direction of the door to the great house. "You wouldn't want to be missed."

He scoffed. Loudly. "And leave you alone? Again? I can assure you, Miss Hathaway, there is nothing I would rather do, but it is also something I *cannot* do."

"Of course you can. Turn around to face the other direction, put one foot firmly before the other, and keep going until you reach the door. I'm certain your hands will remember how to open it when the time comes." The hefty dose of sarcasm in her voice seemed to coat the air between them, as heavy and pervasive as it was.

"Touché," he said, the sarcasm dripping just as heavily from his tongue. "And if I should not remember how to open the door? What then, Miss Hathaway? What brilliant suggestion do you have for how I should return to the party in that instance?"

"A strong man such as you ought to be able to figure it out without my help. But if you do require my assistance, I'm certain I can open the door for you. Even I can manage that without causing someone harm." She could return to the cat and her kittens as soon as he was gone. Surely they could manage that long without her.

He fell silent then, blissfully so, and Emma allowed herself to hope it an indication that he would finally leave. She took up one of the cloths Cook had allowed her to bring outside—she'd gone back in to beg for some after she'd discovered the mother cat in distress—and used it to assist the mother in cleaning her babies.

No matter how long she sat there waiting for the sound of his retreating footsteps, it did not come. Mr. Cardiff seemed to have no plans to leave.

"Can you not remember how to turn around, sir?" she asked, amazed that she'd removed some of the sarcasm from her tone. It had not been an easy feat.

"Why in God's name can you not allow me to act as a gentleman with you?"

"Not allow you?" Emma set the cloth down on the ground beside her and painstakingly stood, then turned to face him. "How, pray tell, can I possibly have such control over you?" While she didn't know *why* he was so fascinated, she knew, without a doubt, that she fascinated him to no end. It both fascinated and perplexed her.

"If only I knew!" Mr. Cardiff closed the distance between them in two brisk paces, taking her upper arms in a solid grip as though he intended to shake a naughty child. "I have done nothing in three years but try to burn you forever from my mind, and yet I cannot possibly stop thinking about you no matter how hard I try. I dream about you. I find my thoughts straying to you at every turn. And, as much as I have hated you in the past, I find that I can't continue to do so."

His eyes burned through her, scorching her very soul. She shook her head, tried to piece it together in her mind.

He took deep, rapid breaths, and his eyes kept moving over her, as though memorizing every feature of her form. "Not when you have taken my sister under your protection," he said raggedly. "Not when, even though I have objected to the blasted dog at every turn, you have made it possible for Morgan to become more independent again by working with him. Not when every time I look at you, you have taken some new helpless and broken creature into your care."

His impassioned diatribe left Emma shaken to her core and breathless, as though he'd stolen all the air from the night. The rapid pulse pounding in her throat felt ready to burst if she couldn't take a solid breath soon. What was he trying to tell her? That he loved her? That couldn't be. Even if it was, she didn't *want* it to be. Did she?

Blast, but the flutters were back and more intense than ever before. Perhaps she *did* want it.

"I don't…" She didn't know how to respond. Not in the slightest. The only thing she could think at the moment was that she needed to put more space between them, because when she and Mr. Cardiff were so close together, it never ended well. She pushed against him, to no avail, the corded muscles of his arms and chest like steel beneath her fingertips. It was impossible to escape his grasp. Some small part of her reveled in the feel of his strength enclosing her. "I don't go off in search of animals in need of help. They just find me."

She tried to take a step back, but his grip remained firm and unyielding.

"And people," he added, more softly, and yet with a certain deep power in his tone. His expression was the same as it had been in the drawing room earlier, when he'd left her so flustered and overheated she'd sought refuge from its penetration outside. "They find you, too. Broken and helpless people. They gravitate toward you in droves, and you help them. *All* of them."

Emma swallowed, and yet it didn't seem enough. Being so close to him, she couldn't think clearly, and her body reacted in strange and confusing ways. Her breasts felt full and heavy, and she could almost sense the weight of his lips pressing against hers. The flutters in her belly changed, almost pulling her closer to him against her will. It was downright infuriating, especially since he still seemed so in control. "Yes," she finally said. Her voice cracked on the word, and so she wet her lips and said it again more firmly. "Yes."

Mr. Cardiff's eyes fell immediately to her lips, studying her so intensely she trembled beneath his gaze. "Then help me," he said with his voice breaking like pea gravel under carriage wheels.

Her breath escaped her mouth in a great whoosh, but no words. Help *him*? Emma shook her head, at a loss. He didn't need her help, and even if he did, he would never accept it. What help could she possibly give him? And why should she?

The hands upon her arms tightened to a near-punishing hold. Never taking his eyes from hers, he inched closer and closer to her, until his heated breath fanned over her cheeks and warmed her skin. She licked her lips and could almost taste the spiced port on his…and she wanted to taste it more. She wanted the swollen, tender sensation his lips had left before. She wanted his hands to rove over her again, teasing and exploring, inciting her body to react in whatever way it would. Each second which passed with him staring at her, holding her so close left her trembling harder, pressing closer, aching in places she never knew could ache.

"Help me," was the last thing she heard before he kissed her.

His lips pressed against hers, warm and soft despite the slight stubble along his jaw line that scratched her flesh. She let out a gasp at the contact but angled her head to renew the scratching instead of retreating from it.

Emma expected him to do as he'd done before. She braced herself for the sheer force of his heated kisses. But it was different, somehow. Gentler. There was no lack of heat, but instead of his physical force keeping her involved in the embrace, it was his force of emotion. His need was palpable, like something she could reach out and touch—like something she could stroke and soothe, as she had the mother cat's back only moments before.

The need to soothe his aches, to calm the storm of his frayed nerves nearly overwhelmed her.

He left her mouth to rain sweet kisses over her nose and cheeks, her eyelids, her jaw. "Help me. God, I need—"

"How?" Emma's breaths came in sharp bursts, and she felt lightheaded, like she might swoon if he didn't kiss her again.

What help could she possibly give him? He was a man who had never wanted anything to do with her, and while she might consider him a great many things, broken and helpless were two terms she'd never before had any inclination to connect to his person.

"Kiss me." It was almost a growl from his lips—a curse. "Kiss me, Emma." Or perhaps a prayer.

He'd never called her by her Christian name before. She didn't even realize he *knew* her Christian name. It left her strangely energized. Pushing up on her toes, Emma stretched her neck until her lips could meet his once more. She placed her hands upon his chest, the superfine fabric of his coat smooth under her fingertips, leaving the hard muscle beneath it as a sharp contrast. On a sigh, her lips parted and his tongue slipped between them.

His arms moved behind her back, drawing closer into the warmth of his embrace until she felt completely surrounded by him, enveloped, consumed. He angled his head and deepened the kiss, and his hands roved almost frantically over her back, her shoulders, her neck, her bottom. With every touch, she wanted more. With every breath, she felt more alive than she ever had before in her life, tingling, electric energy bursting through every inch of her body—the lobes of her ears, the soles of her feet, the small of her back. With everything he touched, everywhere they were connected, a growing ache built within her body.

How was this possible? What sort of trance had she fallen into? Or had he enchanted her with some strange magic?

This was precisely the sort of overwrought emotion Emma had been trying, with every ounce of control she possessed, to avoid. Wasn't it? Was she so mistaken about what she wanted? She had no intention of losing her heart so completely to any man, let alone one so perfectly wrong for her as Mr. Cardiff. And yet, not only was she losing her heart, she was losing her head as well.

"Touch me," he said, his voice no more than a rasp. His strong hands moved up her arms, the calluses on his fingers and palms catching on the fine silk fabric.

So she did. With her hands, she mimicked his exploration, marveling in the contrast of their two bodies. Her hands were delicate and soft, traversing over hard muscle and rigid planes. His hands were rough and broken, molding against her curves and soft flesh.

He tugged her cap sleeves down, easing the silky material away until her breast was freed in the cool, night air. "So beautiful," he murmured just before covering it again with his hand.

Emma jumped slightly at the contact, knowing it was wrong but unable or unwilling to stop him. Heaven. It felt just like heaven when he flattened his rough palm against her, then moved back to let his fingers glide over her taut bud. Her knees wobbled beneath her, and she would have fallen to the ground without the bands of his arms holding her in place, and the ache in her center intensified to the point she thought she might explode.

She sucked in a breath, and his lips settled over the rapid pulse at the base of her throat. He breathed in deeply, as though he were trying to memorize the scent of her. "Emma. I need you, Emma, more than I know how to handle."

It was only a whisper in the silence of the night, nothing more than a breath, and yet it echoed in her mind over and over again. He needed her.

"Mr. Cardiff, I—"

"Aidan." He pulled away from her for a moment, his clear eyes shining in the moonlight. "Call me Aidan."

Oh, how she wanted to. Her heart hammered away, swelling within her chest until she was sure it would soon burst if she didn't do what he asked of her.

But she couldn't do that. She didn't want this with him—not really. She wanted to find a nice, respectable gentleman who would marry her, and only then did she want to experience such depth of feeling, such wealth of passion. Only then did she want such familiarity.

Heavens, but that was a lie. She'd been lying to herself, trying to convince herself of that, but why? Fear?

This sort of passion before she was well and truly married would mean allowing the possibility that she could end up as heartsick and devastated as Morgan had been three years ago. That couldn't happen. She couldn't allow it, but she didn't know if she could stop it either.

And Mr. Cardiff was anything but a nice, respectable gentleman. She knew him too well to believe such falsities. For that matter, she shouldn't believe he wanted her now in any way that involved anything more than pure lust. He certainly didn't *need* her no matter what he said, not for anything more than relieving a…well, an itch of sorts. If she allowed this to continue, then she was absolutely setting herself up for exactly the sort of heartache she'd been trying to avoid.

She shoved against him, harder than before. "*Mr. Cardiff,* I—"

An oath sounded in the distance, and both Emma and Mr. Cardiff froze in place.

"I should have trusted my inclination."

It was Lord Trenowyth. There wasn't a doubt in Emma's mind. Mr. Cardiff spun around to face his brother, and Emma scurried to straighten her gown and put herself back together before the earl saw her as she was. In her frantic need to hide her state of partial nudity she fumbled with the fabric, which only made it take longer than it ought to have done.

With one hand, Mr. Cardiff reached behind him and nudged her more fully behind him so she was well hidden from his brother's view. "Go back inside, Niall."

"Do you really expect me to ignore what I just saw?"

"I expect you to do what is best for the lady's honor. She came out to help with birthing the kittens. I came to help her when she hadn't returned soon enough. Nothing more. Nothing untoward has happened."

Emma tugged the silk sleeve again, and finally it moved into place. She was mussed, certainly, but not really much more than anyone would expect from her. Especially if they believed she'd been out near the stables helping to birth kittens, or any number of the other things she so often indulged in.

Lord Trenowyth hefted a sigh. "I wish I thought anyone would believe that, anyone at all, but everyone in that drawing room saw how you two were looking at one another all evening."

In the stillness of the night, the soft tread of his footsteps echoed like the closing of a tomb. Each step brought him closer to delivering a sentence—Emma could feel it all the way to her bones—the very sentence that would seal her fate. She fought down her panic, tucked the hair that had escaped its knot behind her ear, and moved to stand beside Mr. Cardiff.

Now was not the time to attempt to hide. They'd already been discovered, so it wouldn't serve any purpose.

Lord Trenowyth passed his gaze solemnly over her and then pressed his lips together in a tight line, like a disapproving papa. "I do sincerely apologize, Miss Hathaway, but I'm afraid both you and my brother are fully aware of what must be done."

What must be done? She shook her head, as though such a simple action might possibly alter what his words implied.

"There's no reason we have to marry, Niall." Such a horrified tone carried in Mr. Cardiff's voice, a gasp escaped Emma's lips.

She jumped back slightly. He hated her. He had always hated her, and he always would, and he certainly did not want to spend the rest of his life married to her. She ought to have trusted her initial instincts, not allowed herself to be fooled by overheated emotion. There was no need or love on his part. Merely lust.

She couldn't bear to spend her life tied irrevocably to a man who so plainly loathed her mere presence. She shook her head but before she could speak, Lord Trenowyth moved closer to them.

"There's *every* reason. Every reason in the world." He crossed his arms over his chest and leveled his brother with a commanding stare. "If you don't marry her, she's ruined. Do you really think Burington will ever forgive you for such a thing? Do you think *Morgan* would forgive you? Miss Hathaway is one of her dearest friends in this world."

"She doesn't have to be ruined if you don't say anything," Mr. Cardiff nearly shouted. He dragged a hand through his hair, glaring at his brother. "If it stays between the three of us, no one will know.

Not Burington. Not Morgan. Not any one of those blasted people in the drawing room who can't mind their own matters to save their lives."

"The whole house will know soon enough if you keep shouting like that," the earl shot back. "For that matter, half the countryside is probably well aware of the fact that you've compromised Miss Hathaway right this very moment."

"If you would have just stayed inside—"

Lord Trenowyth advanced on Mr. Cardiff and poked a finger into his chest. "Stayed inside? You can't think to blame this on me, Aidan. I came after you because you're my brother, and I thought it would be better if I were to find you than—"

"Than who?"

"Better than me."

When David came around the corner of the house, his sandy-brown hair shining in the moonlight like a beacon and disappointment etched into his brow, Emma couldn't stop the tears from pooling in her eyes.

How had this happened? How had she *allowed* it to happen? It was devastating enough that Lord Trenowyth had found them, but with him, there was a possibility he might agree to his brother's suggestion. But David...David would never let something like this pass.

"David," she started, but her words were hardly more than a blubbering, gibberish sort of sound coming through her tears.

"You'll make this right, Aidan," David said, ignoring Emma's protestations. "You were warned what would happen if you mistreated my wife's sister in my home, and yet you have done worse than I ever would have imagined."

"Which is precisely why I can't marry her," Mr. Cardiff growled. "Do you really want your sister-in-law to be subjected to me for the rest of her life?"

"Oh, no you don't." David's eyes narrowed to slits as he advanced toward Mr. Cardiff. "You don't get to escape this one." His hands were fisting at his sides, his jaw hard and unyielding.

Emma had never seen him so angry before, with veins bulging in his throat and violence in his eyes. He had such intent purpose in his stride, she feared he might actually rip Mr. Cardiff's head from his shoulders. She couldn't allow that to happen, not on her account, so she stepped between the two men and put out her hands as though she could stop David's intent.

"Let him," Mr. Cardiff spat out. He took her by the arm and forcibly moved her out of the way before closing some of the distance himself.

They were going to come to blows, if something didn't stop them…or someone. Emma tried to move between the two men at the same time as Lord Trenowyth attempted to do the same, but it was no good.

But instead of either of them landing a blow upon the other, David put a hand around Mr. Cardiff's throat and nearly lifted him from his feet.

Emma took half a step forward, nearly stumbling from the tears blurring her vision. "Put him down," she begged. Her voice cracked, more of a warble than anything.

"You'll marry her. You'll marry her so she's not subject to public censure, but then you'll leave her here with me and Vanessa so we can protect her from you."

Emma shook her head. She didn't want to love the man who would be her husband *until* he was her husband, but she did want to love her husband eventually. The thought of being married to a man whom she would never see? She couldn't even fathom such a thing. As ridiculous as it seemed, the thought of being kept away from Mr. Cardiff—or rather of *him* being kept from *her*—left a hollow feeling in her gut, stinging like an open wound.

"No," she said, but none of the men heard her. She swallowed, but her tongue felt too large for her mouth. After trying to swallow again, she cleared her throat to repeat herself, but nothing came out.

"No," Lord Trenowyth put in, and Emma's gaze shot to him.

"The censure of such an arrangement will be almost as bad as if he weren't to marry her at all. Miss Hathaway deserves a better fate than that. After all she's done for Morgan…"

"Yes." David released his grip on Mr. Cardiff's throat and gave a curt nod. "What would you suggest then?"

Mr. Cardiff massaged his throat, his eyes mere slits which never left David.

"My brother will marry her, and she will come to live with my family. Then at least it will appear they have a normal marriage. Morgan and I can—"

"Protect her from me?" Mr. Cardiff drawled. He straightened his coat and neck cloth, smoothing his hands over the superfine fabric, but it did little good. Emma could well imagine her gown was in a similar state, which caused her to blush.

"Precisely," his brother answered.

Mr. Cardiff tossed his hands in the air, but the other two men eyed one another thoughtfully.

"That could work," David mused aloud. "To the outside world it would appear they were perfectly content together."

"But we will not be perfectly content together," Mr. Cardiff shouted, then winced and returned his hand to his neck, "because we won't be marrying."

Lord Trenowyth turned on his brother. "You will."

"Or you'll answer to me at dawn," David added.

"This is outside of enough." Emma couldn't stand there and listen to any more of their arguments without having her voice heard. She stepped forward into the middle of them, planted her feet firmly into the ground, and put her hands on her hips. "He will not, and we won't be marrying, because I won't have him."

It took every ounce of fortitude she possessed to keep from blanching at the brief flash of pain that swept through Mr. Cardiff's eyes. But she swallowed hard, steeled her spine, and managed it somehow.

David took her hand, his gaze filled with compassion. "Emma, you don't really have a choice. And you did come here to find a husband, didn't you?"

Vanessa had told him that? She must have, or how else would he have known? Every moment she didn't spend with Morgan and Serena, she was with Sir Henry and Kingley. Emma pressed her eyes closed, saying a silent prayer for an excuse they would accept to come to mind.

Her prayers were in vain. "I did, but—"

"Excellent," Lord Trenowyth said. "We'll announce your betrothal to the party tomorrow then."

"We'll do nothing of the sort, since I haven't agreed to anything," Mr. Cardiff said.

"But you will." David's hand clenched over Emma's, almost hard enough for it to hurt, then released. "You will, and you'll be happy about it tomorrow when we make the announcement. After that you'll never again do anything to harm my wife's sister." Then he looked down to where their hands were joined. "I'm sorry, Emma. This isn't what Vanessa and I wanted for you, but…"

Mr. Cardiff spun around to go back to the house. "But I've left her with no other choice," he spat out over his shoulder. After standing still for a moment, he turned to face Emma. For the first time in their acquaintance, he seemed almost apologetic. And broken, just as he'd claimed to be. "They're right. I've left you with no other choice. As much as you and I both hate the thought of it, you have to marry me."

Then he spun again and stalked back into the house, grumbling beneath his breath the whole way.

Dragging a hand down over his face, Lord Trenowyth sighed. "I must apologize for my brother, Miss Hathaway. I promise you, this is all for the best. It will be all right."

For the best. All right. Those words bounced around in her mind, but none of them felt like they would settle and become reality. She nodded for the earl's benefit, and he left her alone with David.

"Will it really?" she asked him, though she knew he couldn't possibly answer her question. Not with the truth, at least.

None of them could foretell the future.

He stared at the empty space where Mr. Cardiff had disappeared moments before. "At least, if you marry him, you can keep your parents from worrying."

"True. But then you and Vanessa will worry in their stead." She made her way across the lawn to go back inside, her tears now falling freely down her cheeks. David started to follow her, but she stayed him with a hand.

Once she was out of his sight, she bent at the waist and cast up the contents of her stomach in a hedge.

Emma waited until the worst had passed, then made her way up to her chamber alone, unable to stop her body from shaking.

CHAPTER FIFTEEN

As the houseguests all filed out of the breakfast room the next morning, Emma left Morgan and Serena to seek out Sir Henry. She found him standing by the great Bornholm clock in the front foyer, deep in conversation with Lord Jacob and Mr. Deering.

Emma briefly caught Sir Henry's notice. After he nodded in acknowledgement, a question in his gaze, she stood off to the side in the corridor pretending to study a painting of a garden. Such an inane thing to be doing, when her thoughts wouldn't slow down for long enough for her to examine even the frame. A moment later, he was by her side and the other two gentlemen had moved on to some other diversion.

"Exquisite detail in the rose bushes, isn't there?" he said amiably, then lifted his hand to run along the side and point out a particular area. "I quite like the use of yellow just here. You can almost feel the warmth of the sun."

She smiled, though she didn't feel even remotely like being happy. What she was about to do was hardly something she could feel joyful about...and yet, it must be done. "I could use a bit of the sun's warmth, myself."

"Shall we go out to see to Kingley, then?" Without waiting for her answer, Sir Henry turned and offered his arm. "I'm certain he would be glad to begin today's lessons. He's doing so well, now that he has a purpose and plenty of affection."

If she went along with him, it would give them a bit of time to themselves, and it shouldn't arouse anyone's suspicions about their activities. Not like last night when Mr. Cardiff had followed her out.

So she took his arm. He led her out to the lawn, and Kingley came running to them almost as soon as they were outside.

After they spent a moment scratching him behind the ears, Sir Henry took up Kingley's lead. "So, Miss Hathaway, what has brought us out here so early?"

She stumbled from his directness but regained her footing and kept going. Before answering, she looked back over her shoulder to be certain no one was within earshot of them. This was not the sort of conversation she had any desire to have overheard, not even by Morgan and Serena, or by Vanessa.

Sir Henry deserved at least that much consideration.

"There is to be an announcement this afternoon," she finally said when she was certain they were alone.

He squinted off into the distance. "Of Lord Muldaire's betrothal to Miss Weston? Yes, I know."

Emma stumbled again. "Miss Weston?" Of course, Serena's father had been pushing her toward Muldaire, but Emma had thought that he would change his mind once he saw the level of affection his daughter held for Lord Trenowyth.

And Serena hadn't mentioned a word of it this morning at breakfast. How very odd. But then, perhaps they'd all been caught up in Emma's news about her own betrothal.

Sir Henry faced her. "That's not...? There is to be a different announcement then?"

Emma's mouth felt parched, no matter how many times she attempted to swallow. "Yes," she murmured. She really ought to look him in the eye. It would only be right. But every time she attempted to turn her face upward, he was staring at her with such ardor it was impossible to continue looking upon him.

Hurting him had never been her intention, and yet she couldn't see any way around that eventuality.

He shook his head and a small smile stole over his face—not a smile of a man who was content, but more the smile of a man who dreaded what he was about to hear. Bother and blast. "Go on," he said when still she hadn't begun to speak.

Steeling herself, Emma took a breath and then the words rushed out of her mouth. "I am so very sorry, Sir Henry, but they are to announce my betrothal to another gentleman, and I never wanted to cause you pain or give you the wrong impression about a possible connection between you and me, but I fear that it has happened anyway. I do not know what I could ever do to make it all right. No, I'm certain there's *nothing* I can do to make any of this all right, because I *did* give you the wrong impression. I allowed you to think there could possibly be a future between us, and it was very badly done of me to do so."

When finally she stopped to take a breath, she chanced a glance up to gauge Sir Henry's reaction. Instead of anger or scorn, she found stunned apprehension in his gaze.

"Please tell me you haven't accepted Cardiff."

She stopped breathing abruptly. "You know?"

The baronet gave Kingley a gentle tug on the lead, and the two of them stopped beside her. He turned his pained eyes fully upon her. "Of course I know Mr. Cardiff has been trying—he's been trying to catch you alone in some way, to compromise you, though I don't know what his aim might be in doing so. Everyone here knows. We've all seen the way he watches you, the way he follows you."

Emma took a step back, blinking rapidly. Was that his plan? Had Mr. Cardiff been intentionally attempting to ruin her, as his final retribution for her perceived faults?

True, Mr. Cardiff was capable of just such treachery and worse. Emma had no reason to doubt that, and she had every reason in the world to believe it. Yet she wanted—almost desperately so—to believe anything else. Her stomach clenched in knots.

But why did she want to believe better of him? He *had*

compromised her. He *had* trapped her into marriage. He had acted dishonorably toward her more times than she could count, and had seemingly made it his sole purpose during David and Vanessa's house party to be alone with her when he shouldn't. There was no reason at all to believe he wouldn't jilt her, leaving her as thoroughly and utterly compromised as she could possibly be.

Nonetheless, there was the matter of his words before they'd been lost in their lust. He claimed he could no longer hate her even though he'd tried. Granted, that was no grand declaration of his undying affection and devotion. But if he no longer hated her, why would he blatantly and purposefully try to ruin her? She'd thought that what they shared had been genuine for him, as it had been for her...but was it truly only lust on Mr. Cardiff's part? Was he as cold and calculated as Sir Henry would have her believe?

"But—"

"Has he finally done it, then? Has he done something to trap you?" Sir Henry reached out a hand as though to offer a consoling touch, but Emma evaded it. "Please, Miss Hathaway. Please don't go through with this. Don't marry him. Don't announce anything—at least not anything related to Mr. Cardiff."

Her mouth fell open, but for long moments nothing came out. A thousand thoughts raced through her mind. "I appreciate your concern, Sir Henry, but—"

"Marry me. Marry me instead of him." He dropped to one knee before her and took one of her hands in his, despite her startled gasp. "Even if he has compromised you, I can give you a comfortable life. I would not see you suffer at his hand, Miss Hathaway, not when you could avoid such a fate with me." His thumb traced an absentminded path over the back of her gloved hand." My estate is worth a thousand pounds a year, which is modest but still more than respectable. My hounds account for a larger income each year than the year before, and I expect that business to be worth another five hundred pounds a year or more within the next five years. I know you do not feel such ardor for me as I do for you, but I believe that can come later. You can grow to love me."

Which was precisely what she'd been telling herself for the duration of the house party—what she'd been attempting to convince herself of. Of course, her attempts had been rather unsuccessful in that regard.

Emma swallowed hard. She should accept him. That would be the reasonable thing to do, because he was a good and honorable man, and he clearly *wanted* to be married to her. She wasn't entirely certain the same could be said for Mr. Cardiff, and in fact, most likely the opposite was true. This was her entire purpose in coming to Devon—to find a husband, the sort of gentleman who would ease her parents' worry about her future.

Yet, no matter how much her pulse raced through her veins at the moment, no matter how short of breath she had become, none of it was due to any wealth of emotion Sir Henry Irvine engendered within her. She still felt nothing but friendship toward him. Regardless of the fact that this was what she thought she wanted in a relationship with a gentleman, she couldn't convince herself of the truth of it.

She wanted more. She wanted the grand passions she felt when Mr. Cardiff came near, even when it was wrought with animosity at times. She wanted to feel as though her body was alive when she was in her husband's presence, to have electric shocks screaming from her pores and fire burning in her veins. She wanted to feel as though a kiss could mean everything—could mean more than any words which might come from his mouth.

With Mr. Cardiff, those things were highly possible. Emma couldn't see such a thing ever taking place between her and Sir Henry.

She tried to pull her hand away, tried to take a step back, but he did not release his hold.

"I'm so very sorry—"

"Don't apologize," he interrupted with more fervor than she'd ever heard from him before. "And don't say no. Miss Hathaway—

Emma—Mr. Cardiff is not good for you. He will only hurt you, and you deserve so much better."

When she continued to tug, he let out a sigh and finally released her hand.

"Please, reconsider," he said. "I have no desire to see you end up with a broken heart, and that is all I can imagine will happen if you agree to this farce. He *will* hurt you, if not physically, at least emotionally. I know it will happen."

Would it not hurt just as egregiously to marry a good and kind man whom she knew, without a doubt, she could never truly love?

She brushed aside a tear and took a step back, feeling a keen need to place more distance between them. "I cannot marry you, Sir Henry. I cannot in good conscience subject you to a lifetime spent with someone who does not feel devotion for you of equal measure to what you feel for her. It would not be right."

Standing, he adjusted his beaver hat upon his head. His jaw clenched so hard a muscle jerked within it. "In time, you could come to feel—"

"I assure you, I could not," she cut in, making certain her tone was firm so he would not doubt her sincerity. "I do hold you in great esteem, and I treasure your friendship…but that is all there can ever be."

His brow furrowed, forming a deep crease over his nose. He lifted his chin. "Very well. But if you should change your mind—"

"I won't."

"*If* you should, my offer still stands. I assure you, I am quite earnest."

On that, she held no doubt. She only wished she were so certain about the decision she'd made.

He held out his arm for her to take, keeping Kingley's lead firmly in the other hand. "For that matter," he said after they'd started their return to the manor house, "I have no intention of giving up quite so easily. Until you are well and truly another man's wife, I will not stop my pursuit."

His pursuit might not stop, but her heart did. What had she gotten herself into? She'd been hopeful she might find one gentleman upon whom to set her cap, but now she had two vying for her attentions.

Aidan stood next to Emma in the drawing room, her gloved hand upon his arm causing it to tingle erratically. Or perhaps it was the fact that the entire houseful was staring at them, cheering for them, as though what had just been announced was a blessing. He had to physically force himself not to grumble aloud, because he hated every blasted moment of this so much that even his teeth were on edge.

A man ought to feel his impending marriage was to be a blessing. Aidan could only feel that his was doomed from the start.

Yet he wasn't sorry in the slightest that they were to marry—which was a thought that shocked him straight to his core. Now that the deed was done, or at least now that it had been agreed upon and announced, he would no longer have to feel guilty about looking at Emma with lust, or about his libidinous thoughts, or even about sneaking off to steal a kiss (or more) from her.

How such a change in his thinking came to be, Aidan could never say. He'd tried to discover the origin of the shift last night, as he lay awake for hours in his bed, thinking about what had taken place in such a short time.

In some small degree, it had likely started when Emma had defended Morgan at supper that first night. How could she possibly be the hateful, loathsome creature he'd made her out to be all that time and then also be such a true friend to his sister? It wasn't entirely possible for her to be both at the same time, so perhaps his initial impression of her was unjust.

And then, over the course of the house party, Emma had continued to prove herself the kind and thoughtful woman who had championed Morgan, and *not* the inattentive chit who'd supposedly *allowed* Morgan to hurt herself all those years ago. She'd befriended

Morgan and made certain to include her at every turn. She'd found a way to give Morgan more freedom to do things on her own than any of them had ever dreamed would be possible. And Morgan had been thriving like Aidan had long ago stopped allowing himself to believe would ever happen again.

All of the things he'd held to for so many years, it seemed, had been a figment of Aidan's imagination. A falsehood he'd allowed himself to believe—but why? Why would he have spent such time and effort, so many years of his life, hating a girl for something she could never have prevented in the first place?

Sometime before dawn this morning, it had finally hit him like a gale—he'd blamed her all this time because he couldn't bear to blame the one person in this world who truly was at fault. Not Emma, not himself, not Niall, and not even Stoneham could be faulted for the state of Morgan's misery.

The only person in the world who bore responsibility for Morgan's repeated attempts to claim her own life was Morgan herself.

Aidan supposed he'd finally recognized it that day in the hermitage, when the ladies had discovered him at work with his sculpture. With Emma standing next to the angel, it was as clear as the sky on a cloudless day—the angel he'd been sculpting was Emma. He'd crafted her long nose, her downturned eyes. But her hands were reaching out. Down. Into the water, toward Morgan, trying to rescue her.

The angel's tears and the reach of her arms were a permanent reminder of who Emma truly was as a person—always helping those who needed help, heedless of her own needs and safety.

He'd watched Morgan explore the marble with her hands, running her fingers and palms over every contour and crevice he'd created, and her face had come alive. He knew then that she would forever bear the reminders of how deeply she'd been wounded—but she had moved on. She *was* living again, and taking all life had to offer her with open arms.

He, however, was stuck living with his anger.

Or he had been. That didn't mean he had to continue with his life in that way.

The problem now was that he didn't truly know how to go about letting it go. Not entirely. Aidan had no intention of redirecting it onto Morgan, but he couldn't very well continue directing it toward Emma. Especially not since now, he had to marry her.

But in some odd way, it seemed only fitting that he would. He'd spent three years of his life wishing her to Hades. Now he would spend the rest of his life in making up for it.

There was only one problem. As they stood there, surrounded by the rest of the houseguests, by his siblings and hers, Emma didn't seem all that happy about any of it. In fact, she seemed downright morose, staring across at Sir Henry Irvine with a queer combination of anxiety and embarrassment. Before he spent much time in attempting to decipher why she would look upon the baronet in such a way, Aidan caught Sir Henry's expression—sheer, unadulterated desperation. Likewise, the man couldn't seem to take his gaze away from Emma, aside from those moments when he turned to glare at Aidan with what seemed to be a decisive threat.

Had he been so caught up in trying to determine what he felt for Emma Hathaway and why that he hadn't noticed a growing tendre between Sir Henry and her? Had he forced Emma's hand, and all the while her heart belonged to another?

And now that he thought of it, another realization struck him— for all that he lusted after Emma, and all that he admired her for how she had been with Morgan, he really didn't know her at all. That didn't seem the best grounds upon which to begin a marriage, so he would have to do something about it. And soon.

Not to mention the fact that he would have to get to the bottom of whatever was taking place between his betrothed and Sir Henry.

Damnation, why did everything have to be so bloody complicated?

Aidan waited while David announced the other betrothal between

Muldaire and Miss Weston to the gathered crowd, doing his best to avoid glowering or sulking over the fact that his intended was looking at another man instead of him.

Finally, after the crowd came forward to offer them all their congratulations and well wishes, they dispersed to take part in other pursuits for the remainder of the afternoon. Lord Muldaire and Miss Weston stood with the marquess's brother, Lord Jacob, off to the side, speaking in hushed voices.

With a smile as wide as the Thames, Morgan excused herself along with Miss Selwyn, Mr. Deering, and Sir Henry in order to go out to the grounds to find Kingley. He wanted to speak to Morgan, to see how she felt about the recent changes, but Emma caught her breath at Aidan's side. She looked up at him as the group made their way out of the drawing room. "Would you mind terribly if I joined them? I had hoped to work with Morgan and Kingley today."

Allowing her to run off with the very man who appeared to be competition for her affections didn't seem the wisest course of action, but Niall and David were making their way across the room to speak with him. Reluctantly, Aidan nodded. "Go on. I'll join you all later."

He might have focused a bit too long on Sir Henry when he promised to join the group, but he couldn't really be faulted for that. Could he?

The five of them left, and Aidan tried to settle his thoughts so he could focus on David and Niall. That wasn't as easy to accomplish as he might have liked, because the image of Emma and Sir Henry's mutual glances kept invading his mind.

David came to a stop and scowled at Aidan. "You'll have to meet with her father, of course. I promised Sir Phillip I would only send those men worthy of his daughter his way, and believe me, I'm having difficulty in convincing myself you are, but he will have to be the one to work out the marriage contract with you."

That caused Aidan's head to snap around. He'd been staring at the empty space Emma had vacated, but the thought of meeting her father and talking about the terms of their marriage returned him to the moment.

"I thought we could stop by Kingsbridge and work all of that out before taking Morgan back to Tavistock Manor." Niall's lips were pinched together, and his posture was even more erect than normal.

Aidan wondered for a moment what had come over his brother, but he couldn't seem to force himself to think about it for too long. Niall was an impenetrable fortress, more often than not. If he wanted Aidan to know what was bothering him, he'd bring it up. Otherwise, there was no point in wasting thought on it.

So he nodded. Short of racing Emma off to Gretna Green, there really wasn't an alternative to speaking with her father. It would be better to do it sooner rather than later. Procrastination had never really served him well.

"You should be aware that Trenowyth has agreed to my terms on the matter," David said.

Aidan looked up at that, unable to miss the steel behind David's words. "Your terms?" How the man thought he would have any right to insisting upon terms in regard to *his* marriage, Aidan would never know.

"Yes. Emma will stay at Tavistock Manor and you'll remain in the dower house as you have been. If you decide to leave, she'll still be with the family, so the gossip won't be as bad as if she stayed here."

"We've already discussed this," Aidan grumbled. His patience would only hold out so long, and Emma was outside with Sir Henry while they stood there talking about inane things.

David crossed his arms over his chest. "There's one bit you haven't heard yet, though. If your brother sends me word that you have hurt her in any way, I will find you, and I will make certain you can never hurt anyone again. Am I clear?"

"You realize you're being ridiculous, don't you? Once I marry Emma, she'll be my wife, and you won't have any right to be involved in our affairs in any way."

Aidan turned to stalk off, but Niall grabbed his arm.

"This isn't about what the law allows, Aidan. It's about what's right."

As always with Niall, everything was black and white. Never a shade of gray. And now, David was starting to act exactly the same way.

How charming.

CHAPTER SIXTEEN

Emma was still in a daze from the announcements while she and Morgan made their way across the lawn.

"I couldn't have asked for something better if I'd had the chance!" Morgan said. She linked her arm through Emma's and nearly skipped in her excitement. "Sisters. I've never had a sister before, and I can't think of anyone I'd rather have for my first sister than you."

Emma laughed at her friend's enthusiasm, wishing all the while she shared in it. "I'm sure we'll get on rather well."

Being sisters with Morgan was easy to be enthusiastic about. What was a bit more difficult was the fact that she'd be married to Morgan's brother...and she wasn't certain she'd made the right choice in refusing Sir Henry's offer.

Even as her thoughts turned to the baronet, he came back across the lawn with Mr. Deering, Miss Selwyn, and Kingley. He waved happily as they came.

"I must say, though, I'm rather surprised by it all still." Morgan slowed when she heard Kingley's bark, and her tone turned more serious. "I never in a hundred years would have imagined you would be marrying Aidan. Why, you've hardly spent any time with him, and Sir Henry seems quite fond of you..."

There was no opportunity for Emma to respond. The others were upon them, and the day's lessons got underway.

They'd only been working together for a few minutes when, of all people, Aidan made his way across the lawn in their direction. He'd said he would join them, but she hadn't really believed him. Every day, he went off to work on his sculpting in the hermitage. He hadn't taken part in any of the daily activities since only a day or two into the house party.

Now that they were betrothed, did he intend to behave more like a gentleman? Emma was half-tempted to place a wager on how long such behavior would last.

By the time Aidan arrived in the clearing, Kingley had led Morgan halfway to the wood, skirting her around various barricades with Mr. Deering and Sir Henry alongside the pair of them. Emma and Miss Selwyn had stayed behind.

"Lovely day," Aidan said when he reached Emma's side. He placed his hand in the small of her back.

She couldn't decide if his action was possessive or protective. Bother, why did this all have to be so confusing? Her muddled head only grew more muddled by the heat he put off. It rolled from him in waves until she felt like she might suffocate from it. And yet she couldn't help but want to draw closer to it, which only left her frustrated with herself.

"It is," Miss Selwyn agreed when Emma remained silent for so long it was becoming uncomfortable. "We've had delightful weather through the whole house party, haven't we, Miss Hathaway?"

"Quite," she bit off. Her stare remained firmly affixed upon the lawn, but her thoughts didn't budge from the entirely too enticing warmth coming from Aidan's body.

Miss Selwyn looked over at Emma shyly, her brown eyes blinking rapidly. Bother and blast, she hadn't meant to be rude to the lady, and it was all Aidan's fault.

"Dear me," Miss Selwyn said, leaning in closer to Emma, "you and I will both be spotted if we aren't careful."

Aidan tensed at her side. "I could go inside and fetch a parasol—"

"That won't be necessary. I'll get one." The girl gave Emma a conspiratorial look then, as though she were doing Emma a favor by leaving her alone with the man she was to marry. "I'll be back before you realize I'm gone."

That wasn't even remotely possible. Before Emma could voice a complaint, the sweet girl had scampered off, leaving Emma alone with Aidan while watching Morgan and the two gentlemen work with Kingley.

Aidan drew her closer, his hand almost curling around the far side of her waist. She sighed in resignation. Well, she had *intended* to sigh, at least. The truth of the matter was it came out more like a huff, which only caused him to chuckle.

And *that* gave Emma quite the start. The clenching in her stomach turned to flutters at the sound. Heavens! In all the time she'd known him, she had never once heard Aidan Cardiff laugh in any way. Oh, he certainly always bore a half-grin of sorts, but there was always a sneer beneath it. Always a snide remark, something biting and boorish. He had to be the least cheerful man she'd ever in her life known.

"Have I amused you, sir?" she asked when she'd regained her wits—no small task.

"Aidan," he corrected. "And yes, you have."

"I'm so glad to know I can provide you with such a diversion."

"You couldn't possibly be as glad of that fact as me." He tugged her closer still—close enough it bordered on being scandalous. "It's a relief, considering we're soon to be married. I like the idea of having a wife who can keep me entertained."

The trio with Kingley took another turn and headed back in their direction. The baronet kept his focus firmly on Kingley as they traversed the course he'd devised for the day's lesson. Such pure and honest joy lit Morgan's face, one almost couldn't even see her scars. Mr. Deering's effusive praise for Kingley would be enough to cause one to blush, should it be directed at a person and not a dog.

How would Aidan react if Emma were to grant him such praise? She flushed at her own silliness and tried not to think about it.

Morgan's reaction to their betrothal couldn't have put things into perspective better than it had. The entire house party knew there was *something* between Emma and Aidan, but that something couldn't possibly be more than lust. There was no love. There was no great affection.

The other revelers had offered their congratulations, of course, but they all knew there would never be anything more between Emma and Aidan than what there already was. How could there be, especially with the pervasive heaviness that pressed upon her even now.

Emma tried to put more of a respectable distance between her and Aidan, but it was no use. His hands were as hard as the chisel and hammer he so often wielded, and his arms were as solid as the marble. "I wouldn't think it should matter how much I entertain you, *sir*. Since our marriage will only be in name—"

"It doesn't have to be only in name."

"It does!" This time, she spun on him. Only he didn't release his arm, instead pulling her more fully into an embrace and securing the other arm behind her back, holding her in a manner that stole her breath and forced her pulse accelerate so drastically she thought she might expire on the spot. Emma pushed against the brick wall that was his chest. "It does have to be only in name, because Lord Burington will murder you—"

"If I hurt you. I know." He smiled, but it wasn't his usual knowing smirk. It was more seductive, and even a bit disarming. "But if I don't hurt you..."

His charm was addictive. Intoxicating. She wanted, with every part of her being, to believe he could truly be this laughing, smiling man and not the brute he'd always been before. But one afternoon could not change the entirety of their past, despite the wobbling of her knees.

"You will," she said firmly. "You've given me no reason to believe otherwise."

Aidan's blue eyes narrowed, and he stared at her for a long

moment. "You're right," he said at long last. "I haven't. And I don't know how to change your mind on that score other than doing everything in my power to prove to you that I won't hurt you."

Morgan's laughter rang out over the lawn, and Emma tried to turn and see what had so amused her friend, but Aidan wouldn't release his hold upon her.

Instead, he grinned with sly intent. "I won't hurt you, and we can have a true marriage...in every way sense of the word."

When he pulled away finally, she shivered from the sudden loss of his heat. He released her and took a step back, and the smirk had returned once again.

She pursed her lips and turned to see Morgan and Sir Henry, only to have the baronet look away as though he'd been caught staring.

Once more, Aidan wrapped one arm gently but possessively around her waist, then he bent down to whisper in her ear. "He might be the safe choice, Emma, but safe is overrated." His breath warmed her ear and cheek. "And then there is the small matter of you having already accepted me."

"Did I?" Emma mused aloud. If memory served, she hadn't agreed to anything. She had merely been told what would take place, as was so often the case when men were involved.

"Whether you've agreed verbally or not, you know why you're going to marry me." Again, his warm breath brushed her ear and fanned over her cheek, leaving tingles in its wake. "Whether you like it or not, I stir something inside you. Something Sir Henry Irvine doesn't come close to rousing within your soul. Something you want more of. Something you desperately need, though you can't give it a name or reach out and grasp it."

Even as he spoke, a needy ache settled in her belly and her body felt aflame, as though his very words were enough to cause the sensations his hands and mouth had awakened on more than one occasion. When he trailed the callused fingertips of his free hand down the length of her arm, barely more than a tickle against the fabric of her sleeve, she couldn't stop the shudders from coursing through her entire body.

"I can give you that and more."

There was no denying that Aidan sparked her passions, something Sir Henry did anything but. It was not love, but it was at least *something* upon which to build. Wasn't it? Could it be enough? For the first time, she allowed herself to feel a sense of hope at the prospect.

"Have I missed anything exciting?" Miss Selwyn called out from behind them, startling Emma with her intrusion into such an alarmingly intimate. She trudged back out to where they were standing, a parasol in one hand and a blanket in the other.

"Nothing at all," Aidan replied, stepping away from Emma to take Miss Selwyn's accoutrements from her.

Emma's gaze followed him and his eyes shot up to meet hers…his eyes that were filled with all the heat and promise he'd just roused within her.

This was turning into everything she'd decided she didn't want, and everything she'd promised herself she would avoid. And yet, for some reason, she couldn't make herself care.

She feared she might just be forming some form of attachment to the man. Not love. Not yet. But there was something more...

After supper, Emma was finally able to pull both Serena and Morgan off to the side of the drawing room, just the three of them.

"Thank heavens," Serena said as she dropped onto a silk brocade covered armchair. The Pomona green muslin of her evening dress fluttered lightly before settling around her. "I've been desperate to talk to you, but I haven't been able to get away from…"

"From Lord Muldaire?" Emma put in for her. She kept her voice down, so no one could overhear. Granted, the only people nearby were a grouping of matrons with rather poor hearing, who were entrenched in a game of loo. They would never hear a word.

"Indeed." Serena gave a rueful smile, but her tone was enough that surely even Morgan could make out her expression.

Morgan reached across and took Serena's hand in hers. "Why did you accept him if you don't wish to be married to him?"

"Father didn't give me a choice. They'd worked out the details of the marriage contract, and it was signed before I was even told of the matter." With her free hand, Serena fidgeted with the lace flounce on her gown. "And since I haven't yet reached my majority…"

"You have to do what he wants you to do," Emma deduced.

Morgan chewed lightly on her lower lip, deep in thought. Then she frowned. "I suppose you'll just have to make the best of it. There's little I can imagine I'd enjoy less than spending my entire life married to a man I didn't like."

"But I—" Serena cut herself off, but her eyes flitted across the room to where Lord Trenowyth stood. He crossed to stare out the window after passing a longing glance in Serena's direction. Then she met Emma's gaze and shook her head, pressing her lips together.

So everything Emma had suspected was true. Serena was stuck in an engagement to a man she didn't love…and the man she *did* love, the man who loved her in return, was one she couldn't have.

Emma gave her friend a consoling smile. "Morgan's right," she said. "You'll just have to make the best of it." She cringed even as she said it, but what else could she tell Serena to do? There weren't many options available.

Was that what she would have to do with Aidan? Make the best of a less than ideal situation? This was not what she'd planned when she'd come in search of a husband.

How very naïve she'd been, to think that what she really wanted was to marry a man she didn't love. She *wanted* to love her husband…but she also wanted *his* love in return. She still didn't know if she'd ever have it.

Unlike Serena, Emma had reached her majority. She didn't have to marry a man simply because her father told her she must. Yet it still felt like she was being forced to marry against her will.

The next day, Aidan slipped off to his hermitage to work on the angel for a few hours, but *only* for a few hours. He had to force himself to ignore the fact that at this point in time, when he was so close to finishing the piece entirely, the artistic side of him desired to do nothing but work on it.

Yet he was more than simply an artist. He had other needs, which couldn't possibly be served at the moment by losing himself entirely in his work.

Even he didn't understand why he was so determined that he and Emma should have a true marriage and not the farce of a union that David and Niall seemed to think best. But the thought of spending his days in the dower house while his brother and sister *protected* his wife from him did not sit well. In fact, it left him seething.

He had no doubt David would come to her rescue if needed, that he would do everything he could to defend her honor. And so that meant only one thing—if Aidan was going to have a normal marriage, he would have to convince Emma to love him.

That had seemed like an easy enough proposition at first, except yesterday on the lawn, she had been so adamantly against the idea that Aidan was now experiencing doubt about his capability to succeed at the task.

If he were to have any chance of making theirs into a true marriage, he would have to put in a valiant and sincere effort toward that end.

And so he had decided to give up time working with his chisel in order to convince her how very much in love with him she would be. He could only hope she would, at least someday, recognize the degree of effort he put in to make this work.

When he returned to the main house, once again, Emma and Morgan were out on the lawn with Kingley, but at least this time they were working without Sir Henry's interference. Or aid. Whichever.

Convincing Emma she loved him would be a decisively easier task if he didn't have competition for her affections at every turn. The baronet was around altogether too often for Aidan's comfort. Mr. Deering seemed to be around rather a lot, as well, but at least he seemed more interested in spending time with Kingley than he did with Emma. The affable barrister was not someone Aidan felt was a threat…not like Sir Henry could potentially be. Alas, there didn't seem to be any real way to keep the baronet away from Emma until such time as the house party came to an end and the man returned to whatever part of the country he called home.

After the house party, Aidan could deal with meeting Emma's father and the details of the contract, and calling the banns, and all that other nonsense.

In the meanwhile, he must convince her she loved him.

When he came over the hill and Emma saw him, she reacted visibly. She stopped in mid-stride and nearly fell over, which led to Morgan laughing freely.

"And who has startled you so?" his sister asked. "Kingley? Who is it?"

She asked it as though the dog could actually give her an answer. That would be as likely to happen as fish growing legs and walking upon the land.

Since Kingley couldn't answer her, Aidan called out, "It's me."

Morgan's face lit with a smile. "Oh! But it's still so early today. Shouldn't you still be hard at work?"

Emma said something beneath her breath, which, sadly, the wind neglected to carry to him. Whatever she said, it elicited a wry grin from his sister and a scowl from his betrothed. That left Aidan with no doubt that it was directed at him.

"I thought I'd spend some time with Emma this afternoon," he said, never slowing his gait. After a few more steps he stood directly beside the lady in question, where he could admire her scowl from a better angle.

Indeed, with her lips which had always been rather too wide for the rest of her face, the scowl made quite the impression.

Aidan bit back a grin. "Does this displease you?"

"I'm sure you can see I'm busy with Morgan and Kingley."

"Actually," Morgan cut in, "I believe Kingley and I are ready to attempt some lessons on our own. If you'll excuse us." She dipped into a brief curtsey and tugged on Kingley's lead. They headed back toward the main house—leaving Aidan and Emma alone on the lawn.

Emma had her hand up in the air and her mouth open, as though she were trying to call the two of them back to her rescue. Then her hand dropped to her side, her shoulders slumped, and she turned her scowl back on Aidan. "Did you and Morgan plan that, sir? Her excuse came far too readily."

"Aidan," he corrected her again. "Since we are to marry, I would prefer for us to be less formal."

She ground her teeth together and her brown eyes flared in pique, but perhaps the most delightful thing he'd ever seen was the manner in which the end of her nose tugged slightly to the right. It only made him want to spark her temper far more often, which was probably the wrong reaction to have. He sincerely doubted she would be amused by such a thing, no matter how amused he might be.

Still, he couldn't help but think all of this would be so much simpler if she would just tell him what was on her mind. "What have I done now?"

"It's what you haven't done. What *none* of you have done." With that, Emma spun on her heel and stalked away from him toward the orangery.

Aidan had no intention of allowing her to just walk away from him. He started after her, his long legs easily matching her stride. "And what, pray tell, might that be? I can't very well make something right if I don't know what I've made wrong."

She turned unexpectedly, leading them off the main trail toward the orangery down a path he hadn't noticed before, though it did seem well worn. He had little choice but to go with her.

"What you haven't done—" her sarcasm, in this instance, knew no bounds— "is ask what I might prefer. *You*, along with Lord Trenowyth and Lord Burington, decided there was nothing to be done for it but for us to marry. *They* decided we should marry but have it be for propriety's sake. *You* then informed me that our marriage would not be merely in name, but in earnest." Emma touched the gnarled wood railing of a bridge that led over a creek, spinning around to lean her back against it. "No one asked me what I want. You haven't even *asked* me to marry you—and yet it has already been announced to everyone in attendance."

"If you think I'm going to drop to my knee, take your hand in mine, and profess my undying love and devotion—"

She tossed her hands into the air. "That's precisely the problem! You don't love me, and I am quite certain I don't love you." She blanched when the words left her lips, but she didn't retract them.

Aidan crossed his arms over his chest. This wasn't quite what he'd expected, and he didn't know how to proceed. "Do you love Irvine? Is that what this is all about? You love another man and feel like I've trapped you into something you don't want."

"What?" Emma's jaw dropped and her mouth formed a ring. "No. No, I don't love Sir Henry."

A great whoosh of air left Aidan's lungs at her denial. That, at least, was one less obstacle. It didn't ease the ache that was building in his temple. It would be just his luck that it would only continue to grow. "Then what is the problem?"

She nibbled on her lower lip, which was a definite distraction from the conversation at hand. Aidan had to force his thoughts to remain on her words and not on the decisive bulge forming within his trousers from imagining other things she might nibble.

After a long moment, she hefted a sigh. "We don't love one another, Mr. Cardiff—"

"Aidan."

Emma shot him a glare. "*Aidan.* We don't love one another, and I thought that was what I wanted. For these last several years, I thought I wanted a gentleman to offer for me with whom I had at least a passing friendship—and only after we married did I want to love him. That way, if something should happen before we were to marry..."

Several years. Aidan would stake his life on the fact that the several years she mentioned would mean the three years since Morgan attempted to drown in the river. "You don't want to end up as heartsick as my sister was, if the gentleman in question should not follow through with his promise to you."

For the first time in his memory, Emma looked into his eyes whilst something of a mutual understanding passed between them—not lust, not anger or hatred.

"You've sparked something within me," she said, "and now I'm not so certain of my plan anymore."

"Why not?" It all appeared simple enough to him.

"When Sir Henry kissed me—"

Something snapped within Aidan, and he grasped her upper arms. "He kissed you?" Then he remembered himself and gentled his touch.

"He did. Once, a few days ago." Emma tugged, and he reluctantly released her. "When he did, I knew he was precisely what I'd convinced myself I was looking for: a man whom I could respect. A gentleman I held in great esteem. But his kisses didn't elicit within me any of the passions that yours do. And I think..."

She turned away from him and crossed the bridge, the heels of her half boots clicking along the wood. When she reached a honeysuckle trellis, she stopped and plucked a fragrant bud, holding it near her nose and mouth for a long moment.

Aidan followed her, not rushing her along or drawing so close as to worry her, even though he felt an almost desperate need to touch her.

Finally, she turned to him again. "I think I was wrong. I want more than that. I *need* more than that. I need to know the man I'm going to marry loves me, and not just hope that someday he will. I need to love him, too, and not just hold him in great esteem."

How on earth was he supposed to be able to give her such a thing? He'd moved on from loathing her very existence, and he was no longer attempting to devise the means of her death in his artwork. But with this revelation, she might be asking too much of him. "You might as well ask me to fetch the moon and the stars from the sky, put them in a little box, and then tie a ribbon around it for you."

"I can assure you, I recognize the impossibility of what I'm asking. Nevertheless, it is what I need."

"Is it not enough to know there is something more—something exciting and fiery and perhaps a bit dangerous—between the two of us?" he asked. "I can only imagine there was none of that when Sir Henry kissed you, or else why would we be having this conversation?"

This time, Emma frowned and very nearly rolled her eyes. "If it was enough, we *wouldn't be* having this conversation, would we?"

"Touché." Aidan paced, grinding the slightly damp grass into the earth with the soles of his Hessians. How in the blazes was he supposed to concentrate on making her fall in love with him when all he wanted to do was convince her to let him take up where they'd left off when Niall interrupted them? "So what do you suggest is our next step? What am I to do to convince you that you're head over ears in love with me, Emma? Do you require poetry? Serenades in the moonlight? Grand, public displays of my eternal devotion?" None of which sounded even remotely appealing to Aidan, but he'd do them all if it would help him find a way to get her into his bed.

She didn't answer.

Finally, he spun around to face her again. She simply shook her head with a downcast expression.

"You don't understand," Emma finally said. "I don't want words. I don't want you to simply *tell* me you're madly in love with me; I want you to *be* madly in love with me. And I don't want you to convince me I love you if it isn't the truth."

"You ask for the impossible."

"Does it have to be impossible?" Without waiting for a response, Emma crossed the bridge and headed toward the main house.

He should let her go. There was no way—absolutely, unequivocally no way—he could give her what she wanted. A man couldn't go from hating a woman with every fiber of his being one week to becoming a besotted fool for her the next. The world didn't work that way. *Life* didn't work that way, and anyone who said differently—well, no one would say differently, so it didn't matter.

What did matter was that, like it or not, he had to marry her. If he didn't, there wasn't a doubt in his mind David would call him out. The thought that one of them might hurt or kill the other, all over Emma Hathaway—the maddeningly entrancing, impossibly giving woman that she was—well, it was unthinkable. Aidan couldn't allow his thoughts to go there, or he'd end up in a far worse state than Morgan was in not so very long ago.

If he had to marry Emma, it apparently meant he was going to have to convince her she loved him and he loved her, whether it was the truth or not.

He sprinted after her, catching her before she reached the lawn. "So how do we go about it?" he asked, trying to regain his breath. "How do we fall in love with one another?"

"I—" She shook her head, questioning him with her eyes. "Well, I suppose we might start with spending time with one another—doing those things that the other enjoys."

Aidan nodded. That didn't sound too horrible, despite the potential for his lustful urges to intensify painfully. "Very well. When do we begin?"

Bloody hell. What had he just agreed to?

CHAPTER SEVENTEEN

It was such an odd sensation, this whole *falling in love with one another* thing they were attempting to do. Aidan wasn't quite sure what to make of it all, and yet he'd promised Emma he would try—so try he would. Likewise, she had promised to do the same.

Because of her dedication to the idea that they must truly love one another, and because of his discomfort with the notion of having a marriage with her in name only (and his complete dedication to getting her in his bed), Aidan vowed to avoid his hermitage and his art, making a point of being with Emma every moment he could.

And so it was that he had gone out on the lawn today, helping Emma to work with Morgan, Mr. Deering, and Kingley. Sir Henry had also been present, damn his eyes. Aidan would have preferred to ignore that fact, but had found it increasingly difficult to do with the baronet issuing decided glares in his general direction at every opportunity.

Perhaps tomorrow, when they repeated the process, he might find it an easier proposition. Or mayhap Sir Henry would suffer some ailment or another, causing him to miss the morning session.

I can hope.

But at the moment, he stood with Emma in the library even though most of the rest of the house was out on the lawn for an afternoon of archery. This had to be as sure a sign as any that he was devoted to *falling in love* with her, because he couldn't remember the last time he'd read a book for pleasure…or the last time he'd allowed the opportunity to practice his skill with a bow and arrow to pass him by. He'd never quite had the knack for shooting with a pistol, but the string of a bow required a certain finesse he likened to painting with oils. Every curve and angle could change the entire thing, making the painting something else entirely, or sending the arrow in the wrong direction.

She walked along the far wall, nearest the window, drawing her hand along the spines of the books she passed, whispering the names of the authors. "Chaucer. Shakespeare. Milton." Her voice had taken on a lilting quality once they'd arrived in the library. It seemed to flounce through the air, almost in the same manner as the blue silk of her day dress flounced as she walked. In here, in this room, she seemed as light as a cloud in a clear summer sky.

When her hand settled on a singular title and she pulled a monstrously large tome from the shelf, it reminded Aidan that he, too, was supposed to be selecting a book to read. That was how they'd chosen to pass the time this afternoon, the way they were to share themselves with one another. He wasn't entirely certain how, exactly, they were supposed to get to know each other better if they spent all of their time with their noses buried in books, but it would make her happy. At the moment, that was more important for his aim than just about anything—keeping Emma happy. If she was happy, then she was far more likely to believe herself in love. And if she believed she was in love, perhaps she might also believe *he* was— whether either of them was or not.

Alas, it was much more entertaining for him to watch the sway of her hips beneath the silk fabric of her gown than it was to select reading material.

"Have you settled on something?" she asked a moment later as she hauled the heavy thing she'd selected over to a striped satin armchair near the hearth. Her eyes didn't come up from the page she'd already opened to—not really surprising, given what he remembered of her from their last visit to Heathcote Park three years ago. Thus occupied, she nearly took a tumble over a matching ottoman.

Aidan reached out to stop her fall, but she managed to straighten herself without his help. He put both arms back by his side, but she'd seen his attempt to rescue her.

She flushed with a shy smile. "I'm afraid I'll never be very graceful."

"I don't believe I'd know what to do with you if you were."

A single brow arched above her eye. "Touché." Then she sat, her skirts falling into lines that perfectly outlined her legs. The heavy volume fell to her lap with a thud. "I thought I'd read Pope. I haven't read any of his works before." She opened the cover and flipped to the first page.

"Pope?" Aidan repeated, having great difficulty taking his eyes from the curve of her knee.

"Yes, Pope. Alexander Pope?" When he didn't respond, she lifted her head. A dark curl pulled free from her knot and fell to drape over her shoulder, just at the base of her neck. "The Rape of the Lock?"

"Ah. Yes." He remembered one of his tutors going on about it once, but those memories were long since suppressed. At present, he couldn't imagine why anyone would willingly choose to read such a treatise, particularly when he could otherwise think about her legs and how they might feel holding tight to his waist.

"And what will you read?" she asked him again.

Damn, but he didn't want to read anything. Aidan turned to the nearest shelf and reached for the first book he found. "I'll read the 'General View of the Agriculture and Minerals of Derbyshire; with Observations on the Means of their Improvement'." Good God. He wouldn't be able to get through that no matter how hard he tried. He'd likely be asleep before he finished the second page.

Emma snickered. "I never imagined you were one for such dry choices in reading material."

"Nor did I," he muttered beneath his breath. Nevertheless, he took his book to the chair across from her and flipped it open. Even the first sentence had him wishing he could simply nod off instead of attempting to get through such drivel. After he'd finished the first page, he chanced a glance up to see if Emma was yet absorbed in her selection.

She was staring straight at him with a cheeky grin plastered firmly upon her face. "Bored senseless yet?"

"I do not understand how you can possibly find enjoyment from reading—"

"I sincerely doubt there are many people in the entire country who would find enjoyment reading something like *that*."

"Then why was it written, if not for someone's enjoyment?" Aidan slammed the book closed and set it on the occasional table beside him.

The corners of her lips quirked upward. "Oh, I don't know. Maybe for edification instead of enjoyment?" Her sarcasm was almost enough to make him smile.

"But we were supposed to be spending time together doing something you enjoy this afternoon."

"I do love reading," Emma said, "but no matter how much I enjoy it, I'd never be able to sit down and read something like that. I like reading novels. Plays. That sort of thing."

Aidan nearly grimaced at the thought. "I haven't touched a novel since I left school. Even then, I only read the things because they made me do it."

"You might be surprised. If you choose a book because you want to read it instead of having it forced upon you, you might just discover you like reading better than you thought you would."

It took great pains and sincere effort for him to avoid scoffing at her suggestion. He put the effort in, however, because he doubted she would react well to him openly reacting in such a manner. "Is that so?"

Emma closed her book and set it on the same table. "It is." Then she stood and returned to the shelves near the window. "Hmm. Let me see." After a few moments, she pulled out a brown leather-bound book and tossed it in his direction.

"*Robinson Crusoe?*"

"Have you read it?" she asked tartly.

Aidan scowled but didn't reply. He flipped open the cover and thumbed through the pages. At least it wasn't as massive as the Pope tome Emma intended to read.

"I thought you might enjoy it better, to start with, than one of Jane Austen's novels, though I do think someday you could come to appreciate her work."

"I'm not reading a novel written by some chit."

"She's not *some chit*," Emma retorted.

There was such vehemence in her tone, Aidan's gaze shot up from his book. Her eyes blazed, and yet again the end of her nose tugged to the right. The sight was so fascinating he experienced sincere difficulty in convincing himself he shouldn't intentionally goad her temper more often.

That would be counter-productive in terms of his overall goal, so he fought the urge to give one more little jab. Now was not the time. Once they were married, then he could incite her to pique as often as he liked.

"Quite so," he finally conceded. "Shall we read?"

Emma pursed her lips and gave a tight nod.

Aidan inclined his head, and then they each returned their focus to the books in their hands. The thought of being married to Emma Hathaway grew more appealing by the moment.

Maddeningly, the smirk on Aidan's face remained ever present. Emma hadn't discovered a means for removing it, but at least occasionally it changed in tone.

So often in her experience, it came across as meaning *I'm higher in the instep than you and I know it* or possibly *Everyone in this room is a crashing bore and I wish to escape at the first opportunity*. But throughout all of yesterday afternoon, when she'd looked up in the library and caught him smirking across the top of his book at her, it had said something different.

Emma wasn't entirely sure yet *what* it said. Maybe *I am actually enjoying reading a book but I don't wish to let anyone know it*. That seemed altogether more likely than the other thought that had crossed her mind—the one which said it might mean *I like spending time with you, despite myself*. While such a sentiment may come eventually, now was too soon for such a change to have occurred. Wasn't it?

When the sun had started to wane and they could no longer read without straining their eyes in the candlelight, she'd been amazed to discover he didn't immediately rush off to do something else. She'd held every expectation that he would dash off at the first opportunity, desperate to escape her and the humdrum pastime she preferred—but he hadn't. Instead, he'd sat with her in the library, discussing what they'd read.

It had turned into a rather rousing discussion, as Aidan had vehemently agreed with Robinson Crusoe's attempts to become the master of all around him. They debated the finer merits of his reading to that point for well over an hour. All the while, Aidan refused to concede that one could not simply declare oneself a master and have it be so. Likewise, Emma refused to believe a man such as Aidan could believe such a thing, considering the fact that he had likely decided he was the master of all around him (as only seemed logical, given his temperament) and yet his sister had taken her fate into her own hands—an act which, undoubtedly, as the master of all around him, he would not have allowed.

It was only after their discussion had grown so heated that David poked his head into the library to see if he should come to Emma's aid, which garnered yet another smirk from Aidan, that it became clear to her.

Aidan wasn't arguing with her because he believed the point he was so desperately trying to beat into her head. He was arguing with her because he found some sort of perverse pleasure in the act of arguing.

Emma wasn't entirely certain whether this propensity for discord spread so far that Aidan would enjoy arguing with anyone at all, or if he merely took pleasure in arguing with *her*, but it didn't particularly matter. Once she'd discovered the reason for his belligerence, she'd stopped trying to prove her point.

One could not convince a donkey to do what a donkey did not want to do, after all. Why bother trying?

Except, she *had* enjoyed herself in debating with him. A bit too much, actually. While most gentlemen would only speak civilly, making certain never to rouse a lady's ire, he seemed to take great pleasure in piquing her temper. It was exhilarating to be able to speak her mind and not have it instantly dismissed as being mere drivel, simply because it came from the mind of a woman.

The pleasure they each took from their argument didn't mean they were falling in love with one another, but at least they were finding some common ground.

After they'd ended their time in the library, they'd gone about the remainder of the evening with the other houseguests. Aidan had sat with her to play whist, and if she was not mistaken, he even flirted with her a time or two. It was slightly difficult to tell for more than one reason. Of course, there was his ever-present smirk, which masked whatever lay beneath. But there was also the fact that Emma had so rarely been flirted with, so she wasn't entirely certain she'd recognize such behavior if she saw it.

Then this morning, he'd come out to help with Morgan and Kingley's lessons. Sir Henry had begged off, claiming a headache, but Mr. Deering had gladly taken over anything the baronet would have done. He focused so much on his interactions with the dog, however, that it almost felt as though it was just the three of them working— Emma, Morgan, and Aidan. Emma had found herself more than just a little charmed by the manner in which Aidan so willingly helped his sister whenever he could. His desire to be at her service was almost problematic, as he wanted to do things for her which clearly, she and Kingley could manage without Aidan's interference. Yet, over the course of their lessons, he began to relax and allow his sister to prove how capable she was.

It would take time—for all of them. Morgan and Kingley must learn how to work together, but Aidan and Lord Trenowyth must learn to trust them.

After they'd completed the day's lessons and were making their way across the lawn to the house again, Emma received her greatest surprise yet.

Her hand was upon Aidan's arm, and Morgan and Kingley were several paces ahead of them. Aidan slowed, allowing his sister to put more distance between them. After Morgan took several more steps, he spoke. "I'd hoped we might try artwork today."

"Artwork?" If she'd had a drink, Emma was certain she would have spit it out from shock. "I can assure you, I'm a dreadful artist. No governess my parents hired could bear to look at the atrocities I created."

"You can't possibly be as bad as all that."

She was certain it was amusement she heard ringing through his tone.

"I can assure you, it is even worse than you can imagine."

"While that may be," he said slowly, allowing a chuckle to come through, "perhaps you simply haven't had the right teacher. Or maybe you haven't tried using the right medium."

"Father hired six governesses and a painting master. Not one of them could find any use for me. We tried watercolors, pastels, coal— even embroidery."

At that, he stopped and stared at her with disbelief. "You can't even embroider?"

"Why do you think I spend so much time reading?" Emma shook her head with a laugh. "It isn't that I try to be abysmal at artistic endeavors. I just am."

With narrowed eyes, Aidan's smirk widened to a smile.

"Nonetheless, we read yesterday. Today, we shall attempt artwork. Unless…"

"Unless?" She raised a single eyebrow. "Are you suggesting I'd prefer to go hawking with the others? Because in all honesty, while I'm a poor shot, I think I stand a better chance in that endeavor than I do in creating what anyone might term as being *art*."

"I would never have imagined you as a falconer, Emma." Then Aidan chuckled. He bent lower to whisper in her ear. "What I'd hoped to imply was, unless you have changed your mind and no longer require love." The arm she'd been holding wrapped behind her waist, drawing her closer until the musk of his cologne wafted over her nostrils. "I'd be perfectly content to forgo your requirement and whisk you off to the hermitage instead—where we could continue where we were interrupted before."

He barely touched her, his fingers just tickling against her ribcage and his arm only brushing her side, and yet she couldn't stop the goose flesh from rippling over every inch of her flesh from the slight contact. Or perhaps it was more from the dark intent of his words.

His eyes had turned the shade of the midnight sky, and the heat of his lips hovered near hers.

It would be easy to become lost in his silky promise.

Emma shook her head and pushed her hands against his chest until he backed away. "We're falling in love, and that's that."

"All right." The smirk had returned, unsurprisingly.

Of course it had. She shouldn't have expected anything else. The thought of seeing his face without the smirk—well, she couldn't imagine it.

A husky laugh escaped her. "Very well. You may attempt to turn me into an accomplished artist this afternoon, but don't say I didn't warn you about my lack of skill in that particular area. Artistry is quite possibly the feminine pursuit in which I can be found most wanting."

He put her hand over his arm again and resumed their journey to the main house. "Why don't we allow me to be the judge of your skill?"

"And you won't regret not going with the others? We could, you know. I wouldn't mind."

For a long moment, he merely stared at her, his head turned toward her instead of looking where they were walking. "Your brother-in-law will allow me to return and go hawking with him any time I wish. I'd prefer to spend the day with only you."

Surprising as it was, even to her, Emma believed him. Maybe there was hope for them to have a love match, after all. Maybe there could be more than just the spark of lust that so readily kindled between them. "If you wish," she replied.

And so, after they took luncheon with the rest of the houseguests, the two of them went together to sit in the rose garden with canvases and easels while the others went off in the direction of the dovecote. Even Morgan went along with Kingley on one side and Sir Henry on the other.

Aidan set up an easel for Emma and gave her a brief instruction on the use of watercolors before leaving her on her own while he started on his own piece. They created in silence for quite some time, but with every stroke of her brush, the canvas before her came closer to resembling a great greenish-black blob. She sighed in resignation.

Aidan looked around his easel. "Problem?"

"I daresay you ought to judge for yourself, oh master of artistry." Emma stepped back so he could come around and get a good view of her mess.

He visibly blanched when he saw it, which had been a regular response from her governesses over the years. "You seem to have muddied the whole canvas as though it were your palette."

"I told you I'm a rather dreadful artist."

Aidan turned to her and lifted a skeptical brow. "Are you certain you didn't do this purposefully? It is so bad it would seem it has to be intentional."

Emma couldn't stop herself from laughing at his accusation, whether he was serious or joking. She *thought* he was joking. Maybe. "I promise I would never do anything of the sort."

"Hmm." Before she could defend herself again, Aidan had removed the canvas from the easel and replaced it with a new one. He turned to her with both hands held out. "Surrender your brush and paints."

"Gladly," Emma said, pushing them toward him as though they were poisoned.

Her relief only lasted a moment, because he quickly replaced them with a box of pastels.

"These will be far more difficult for you to create such a muddied effect. Just use one at a time, blending a bit here and there."

Then he turned and went back to his own easel, picking up another box of pastels and resuming his work. Emma frowned, not that he would see it. He was too absorbed in his own creation to notice her discontent.

Since sulking about it was pointless, she decided to set to work on another attempt.

After nearly thirty minutes of ineffectual strokes with her various pastels, she had what was supposed to be one of the pink roses on the bush next to her but which appeared far more like a mal-shaped parasol. But maybe taking a step back would help it to look better. Didn't artists tend to do that, to view their pieces from various distances? She took a step back, and then another—but now it didn't even look like a parasol. It might seem more like a pink storm cloud.

While she examined her piece, Aidan's grin flashed in the corner of her eye.

"Well?" she said, putting her hands on her hips. "You might as well come and see it for what it is."

He moved to stand beside her and stared at the canvas. After a moment, he cocked his head to the side and stared again.

Emma pursed her lips. "Go on. I promise you can't say anything worse than Miss Throckmorton did when I was thirteen."

Instead of speaking, he nodded—and that same smirk was back on his face. "I suppose now is when I admit you were right."

A great peal of laughter escaped Emma's lips, and she nodded. "I suppose that will do."

When he took the canvas down from her easel, a slight moment of panic hitched in her chest.

"You're not going to ask me to try again, are you?"

He turned to her, but his smirk had fled. Emma recognized the look in his eye. It was the same expression he bore each time he kissed her, the same one he'd had in his eye as he'd unnerved her from across the drawing room. Her breath hitched when he moved closer.

But instead of kissing her, he brushed a finger along her jaw, tracing the curve of it and leaving her trembling from the contact. Then he passed the same finger over her cheek and tucked a stray tendril of her hair behind her ear. When she was almost desperate for him to kiss her, he instead moved the easel to the side.

Then he pointed toward the stone bench behind it. "I had hoped you might sit just there for me while I finish."

"Of course." Sitting and waiting while he worked would be far preferable to making a fool of herself with another attempt, and she sincerely doubted herself capable of completing any task at the moment which would require her to think. Not while her heart was fluttering and her breaths were shallow and she could think of nothing but the gentle yet rough texture of his fingers against her face. Emma sat down upon the bench while he went back behind his easel.

He kept peeking around the side of his canvas at her, though, so often that her cheeks grew warm from his attention.

"Is something the matter?" she asked when he'd looked around it for the fourth time in only a few moments. "Do I have paint on my gown, or—"

"There's nothing amiss," he cut in. "I'm just seeing how the light hits your cheeks."

That only served to fuel the flames of her blush. He was doing her portrait. He *had* been tracing the shape of her jaw, so his hands could know how to form it upon the canvas.

Emma sat as she was, trying not to think about it but unable to think of anything else as he worked. If he was creating her portrait—what would that mean for...for how he felt about her?

And had he been as moved, had he felt as erratic as she did when he was touching her so?

A love match might just be in her cards after all.

CHAPTER EIGHTEEN

Trying to make Emma into an artist might not have been a fully unmitigated disaster, but it certainly hadn't turned out how Aidan had planned. No matter how desolate the possibility of developing her skill in such an area might be, there was no denying the fact that what was issuing forth from his hands onto the canvas was one of the most beautiful things he'd ever done.

Before he'd started this portrait of her, none of his pastels had been what anyone would term beautiful. They certainly weren't something he could ever attempt to sell. Emma's portrait, however, would easily take a hefty profit at auction.

The one he'd burned so many years ago might have, as well, but he would never know.

Not that he could bear to put this one up for sale. Even as his hands formed the lines that made the slope of her shoulders, the soft curve of her waist and hips, he couldn't stop himself from thinking of drawing his hands over her actual skin in such a way. Any man who saw it would be bound to think in a similar fashion, and the thought of that was enough to send Aidan back into a rage. No one would ever touch Emma—no one but him.

So he would never sell this one. He'd hang it in his chamber, where he and he alone could stare at it and think lustful thoughts. Aidan wouldn't seek a profit from it.

At one point in time, he'd thought to make his art into a means of supporting himself and his family. With all the rage that had fueled his creativity of late, that had fallen by the wayside. He'd told himself it was all right, that he could live on Niall's coin, because Morgan needed them all around her.

But she didn't need them all anymore. Emma had seen to that. Aidan's sister was almost as self-sufficient as she had been before her injuries, and her desire to prove herself capable knew no bounds.

Emma had seen what Morgan truly needed—and for that matter, what Kingley needed—and then had found a way to make it all happen. In three years, neither Niall nor Aidan, nor even their mother, had been able to see through their own ideas of what Morgan needed to get to the truth of it all.

She needed to be trusted. She needed to be set free, to make her own way through the world with what she had left. She needed the freedom to fail, and then to try again after she'd failed until she could do anything.

No one but Emma had been able to recognize that…and in less than a fortnight, she'd provided it.

Emma Hathaway was as sweet and genuine a young woman as she could possibly be. She honestly cared for other people, for animals, for everyone and everything around her. It was no wonder she was so often surrounded by those in need.

Everyone needed *someone* to care for them. Why not Emma?

The more time Aidan spent in her presence, the more he found he wanted to be in her presence. Not only that, but he was quickly discovering that he didn't particularly care to share her attentions with anyone else. Not even Morgan.

And, while he wasn't certain he *loved* her yet, Aidan was absolutely, unequivocally certain of something else. He did *not* hate her. He couldn't. It was no longer a possibility.

Lust, however, Aidan found to be in free supply. He wanted Emma more than he knew how to handle—wanted nothing more than to be with her at every moment he could. With *only* her, as if that were even a remote possibility.

Even now, she looked over at him with those lightly downturned eyes—eyes that only made him think of bedding her—and gave him a cheeky grin, her lush lips widening seductively. "Have you finished yet? I am desperate to see it."

She couldn't possibly be as desperate to see the portrait as he was to touch her again. When his finger had moved along her jaw, her cheekbone, it had taken every ounce of restraint he possessed to refrain from kissing her again—and Aidan feared that the next time he kissed her like that, he might not be able to stop himself from doing so very much more than simply kiss her.

Alas, they remained at David and Vanessa's house party. He couldn't very well take her up to his chamber and toss her in his bed. Their betrothal had been announced, and the others were granting the two of them some time alone when otherwise it would not be done, but even then, there were limits.

The image flashing through his mind at the moment, of her in his bed with her long limbs bared for him, did him no favors. If he didn't change the course of his thoughts soon, he might just pull out a blank canvas and attempt to create the vision in his head.

So instead, he swallowed, wishing he could wash the thoughts swirling through his mind down his throat so easily.

"Come," Aidan finally said. "Take a look."

When Emma came to her feet and took a step toward him, a moment of panic clutched his chest. What if she didn't like it? What would she think?

Before he had much opportunity to worry over her reaction, she'd made her way around his easel and stared at the likeness of herself. Silently.

She didn't say a word, didn't take a breath. It was more than Aidan could handle. He turned around and took two steps away. He shouldn't have ever shown her. He should have never opened himself up to her reaction, whatever it may be. If he could, he would reverse time and never let her know he'd been working on a portrait of her in the first place. He wouldn't leave himself so vulnerable as to work on such a thing with anyone around to see it, to know such an intimate part of who he was.

But he couldn't go back in time, and he couldn't undo what had already been done. He could only find a way to live with the regret.

"I don't—" Her breaths were stilted and sharp. "It's beautiful. I've never thought…"

But she didn't finish her sentence. The incomplete thought hung in the air between them so long Aidan feared he might fall over if she did not finish it.

"You never thought what?" he prodded when still she remained silent, save the uneven breaths.

Emma's hand, so small and delicate, hovered near his arm but didn't touch it. He felt her warmth through his coat, wanted her touch, but could not bring himself to ask for more than she would give.

"I've never thought of myself as beautiful. Not until I saw this. I don't—" Then she did touch him, lightly brushing her hand over the sleeve of his greatcoat, her gentle touch as reverent as the awe in her tone. "This is how you see me?"

How could she not see her own beauty? Truly, she wasn't beautiful in the traditional sense. She didn't have a perfect English rose complexion, nor did she have the golden hair so popular amongst a certain set, but if she was in the room, he couldn't look elsewhere if he tried.

"Of course," he finally said, his voice cracking on the words like they had when he was no more than a green youth.

She moved around him until she stood before him, close enough he could touch her if he allowed himself such freedom. With each shuddering breath, her chest rose and fell, nearly straining against the delicate yellow fabric of her bodice.

"Thank you." Her lips remained parted after she spoke, just enough he could see a hint of the whiteness of her teeth.

He couldn't look away. It didn't matter that he knew he mustn't kiss her or touch her. To do so, at this juncture, would be perilous to his plan. Emma wanted more than lust. She wanted love. But if he kissed her now, he knew beyond a shadow of a doubt that he would fall victim to need.

Aidan tried to back away, but she came with him, moving closer with each moment that passed until her lips came up to meet his.

Her kiss was almost wild, and entirely too seductive. Placing a hand on his chest for balance, she leaned in and moved her lips over his in thoroughly untutored fashion. Aidan held himself back as well as he could, but was unsure how long he could go without taking control of the situation before losing that very same control. Restraint had never been a skill he had mastered.

When the soft tip of her tongue flicked out and touched the seam of his lips, he very nearly lost all desire to hold himself back. At that moment in time, all he wanted in the world was to toss her over his shoulder and carry her off to somewhere they could be alone. He couldn't stop the groan that sounded deep in his throat, but somehow refrained from ravishing her on the spot.

Emma seemed to take his groan as encouragement. Sliding one hand up his chest, she wrapped it behind his neck and tugged him down to her, even as with the other hand she grasped his lapel in a desperate clutch. Moment by moment, she grew bolder, her tongue delving between his lips to stroke and explore, her hands nearly frantic as she tried to get closer.

It was more than he could bear. He had to stop her, now, before he forgot why such a thing was necessary.

Aidan broke off the kiss and took both her shoulders in his hands. "We can't do this."

But she didn't take his pronouncement well. She stretched on her toes, trying to kiss him again. "Touch me. Please. Like you did that night. I want—I want to feel you touch me. To feel your hands on me."

Never before in his life had a woman begged him for his touch. He wasn't a libidinous bastard by any stretch of the imagination, but he'd taken his fair share of women to his bed—and they'd all been more than content by the time he was finished with them. He was not a man to deny a woman her pleasure. Not when he could grant it.

But how could he possibly do that with Emma before she was his wife? If David caught wind of such a thing, they'd never make it to their wedding day. Either that or it would occur much sooner than any of them wished. And even if no one discovered what had transpired, Emma would be sure to come to her senses and realize it was only lust between them and not love, wouldn't she?

Once more, she tried to kiss him but he turned his head to the side. Her lips fell upon his jaw, and she trailed a series of kisses along a path to just below his ear.

"Emma..."

He couldn't finish his thought because her hands kept fluttering over his chest and arms, and it was all he could do to remember his name or where he was.

"Please," she repeated. Her lips settled on that spot just below his earlobe, her warm breath fanning over him and tickling the sensitive flesh of his neck.

This was madness. There could be no other explanation for why, instead of taking both her hands in his, putting a good foot or more between them, and telling her precisely the reason what she was doing must stop, he fisted his hand in her hair and lowered his head to capture her mouth with his.

Emma had been happily sinking in Aidan's kiss for what could have been hours when he broke away again. He had both hands in her hair, holding her captive as he trailed wet kisses over her neck, her jaw, her shoulder blade.

Then, just as suddenly, he pulled back. His eyes were nearly black with intensity, and his chest was heaving as erratically as hers. "Not here."

Not here? She barely had, "Wha—" out of her mouth before he'd taken one of her hands in his and started walking, rapidly, across the lawn.

She almost had to run to keep up with him, he was moving so fast. By the time he slowed at the trail through the woods, she was far more breathless than before.

"Where are we going?" Emma finally asked. He seemed to be in such a rush, she couldn't imagine what the hurry might be.

"The hermitage."

The hermitage? "Do you feel the need to sculpt right now?" One minute, he'd been kissing her passionately and the next, he wanted to hammer away at marble. No matter how much she thought she was beginning to know him, she would never truly understand the manner his mind worked.

"I can't very well take you up to my chambers, can I? Even though the rest of the guests are out hawking, the servants are all in the house."

She'd only thought she was breathless before. Now she knew she was, yet she couldn't seem to stop herself from wanting to move faster. As frustrating and infuriating as Aidan could be at times, Emma was fairly certain she loved him. Or at least that she was falling in love with him.

And there wasn't a doubt in her mind that she wanted to be with him, at least this one time. If he couldn't fall in love with her, then perhaps they *would* have a marriage in name only. If that was to be her fate, she didn't want to spend the rest of her life without at least knowing what was missing in her marriage.

Then she could resign herself to her fate, whatever it may be.

But for now, for this moment in time, she wanted to experience all she could with this man. She wanted to know the source of the ache in her core, to see if he could help her relieve it. She wanted to feel his body against hers like it had been that first time he kissed her, when they were so tangled together she couldn't think. And maybe, if fortune decided to favor her, maybe it would be enough to convince him to love her in return.

How could a man, even one as jaded as Aidan, share such an intimate act with another and not give at least part of himself to that other person?

Finally, they reached the hermitage. Aidan hastily undid the lock and threw back the door, and before it had fully closed behind them, he'd hauled her into his arms.

He kissed her and drew her closer, his strong hands pulling against her until their bodies were nearly joined despite the barrier of their clothing.

After that, everything happened in frenetic fashion. Hands and fingers, lips and tongue. Aidan removed their clothing, frenzied and hot and needy in his quest. It was so fast, so new, Emma didn't know what to do or how to react. A rabid need built within her, straining at her core and tingling through her limbs all the way to the ends of her fingers and tips of her toes. A rush of heat fled to each place he touched, and all the while a pervasive ache built higher and higher in her center.

Then he was above her, surrounding her, sliding over and within her. Everywhere. He was everywhere, filling her like she'd never known was possible. Nothing in her imagination could have prepared her for the sensations racing neck-or-nothing through her veins. From head to toe, every pore of her body felt alive. Her mind couldn't contain it all. One thought chased the next, none of them settling or fixing permanently in place.

Then it was as though a dam burst. A flood of heat.

Aidan lay over her, covered in a sheen of perspiration. His weight trapped her between his body and something soft—a settee?

"I'm sorry," he mumbled. "I shouldn't have...that was too fast."

She shook her head. Too fast? It was all a blur, but it had been a wonderful blur.

Lifting his head to look down into her eyes, he kissed her, his tongue delving between her lips and making it impossible for her to speak. Not that she could have anyway. His hands brushed over her, molding against her breasts. With his thumbs, he teased her swollen nipples.

"Ah," Emma cried, and her back arched up to meet his ministrations.

The warm heat of his mouth came down over one breast, and he suckled and licked. That desperate pull, the gathering of wetness and heat started between her thighs again, pooling together and pulsing. Aching.

Aidan moved his attentions to the other breast and slid one hand down between their bodies, lower, until his fingers tangled in the wetness of her curls.

Each time he suckled, he slipped his fingers deeper, searching, tantalizing.

Emma writhed beneath him, her hips driving her closer to his touch. "Oh my."

The pad of his thumb found a nub much like her nipples, swollen and tender, and he rubbed it, circled it, tickled and teased it until she thought she would die from the pleasure.

This time it was a wave, building and gathering speed until it washed over her and she collapsed, sated, against the cushions.

"So beautiful," he murmured, then he kissed her again.

They lay together like that, Aidan atop her, Emma desperately seeking the return of her ability to think, for a long time. She lost track of anything but the weight of his body, the feel of his breathing, the musky scent permeating the air around them.

He repeated something in her ear. But she couldn't hear it. Couldn't make it out. Couldn't focus on anything but the shivery weightlessness the heat left behind.

Eventually, he rolled off her and lowered himself to lie on the floor, then pulled her to drape over him. His hands moved in lazy trails over her back, the rough calluses of his fingers scraping in a pleasant way along her overly sensitive skin.

When once again she felt the effect of gravity upon her person, when the bones returned to her limbs and she was no longer just a limp mass, Emma lifted her head and met Aidan's gaze.

In all the time they'd known one another, Emma had seen countless expressions on his face—but never this one before. He seemed almost confused. Distraught. The urge to comfort him became overwhelming, so she lowered her lips to his and kissed him long and slow.

When she lifted her head away again, Aidan raised his hand to her face. He tucked her hair behind her ear, then cupped her cheek.

"Did you not hear me?" he asked, with a harsh edge in his tone. Then he shook his head, a wave of pain rushing through his eyes. "Never mind. It is probably best this—"

"Hear what?"

His other hand came up, and he held her head between the two of them. The pads of his thumbs repeatedly smoothed over her cheekbones. "I said I love you."

Aidan could hardly believe that the words were coming out of his mouth the first dozen or so times he'd said them, when he knew Emma was in such a fog of sensation that she couldn't possibly know what he was telling her.

But then for him to tell her again, when there was no more possibility that she could misunderstand him? And more importantly, for him to mean what he'd said? It left him shaken through to his core.

He did love her. He loved how she cared so much for her friends that she would do anything she possibly could do to help them. He loved the way her eyes turned down at the corners, and how her nose tugged to the right when she was upset. He loved her awkwardness, and how she was so unaware of her own beauty and the effect she could have on others. He loved that she would argue with him for hours over a book.

More than anything, he loved that she attracted fragile and broken things, and that she never turned them away.

He loved her.

And, most importantly of all, he'd told her so.

Yet, instead of saying that she loved him, and instead of reacting with the sort of unbridled joy he'd felt upon uttering the words aloud, she lay there draped across him, simply staring.

No, that wasn't quite right. There was something decidedly not *simple* in her stare. He couldn't quite make up his mind if it was shock, or perhaps fear.

Shock was a sensation he could well understand, since he felt rather surprised himself, but why would Emma be afraid? She had essentially given him an ultimatum, telling him they must come to love one another or she would not go along with having a normal marriage with him. And now that he truly was in love with her, now that it was not simply something he was feigning in order to get her into his bed, she was afraid?

"Emma?" he said quietly.

Instead of responding, she abruptly removed herself from his grip and stood, reaching for her clothing.

"Stop," he said softly.

But she wouldn't stop. She kept frantically trying to sort out her undergarments and get them on, but she was making a muck of it. Aidan put out a hand and stilled hers, and her eyes shot over to meet his.

At least she wasn't crying. He could handle a great many reactions she might have, but tears—particularly when he wasn't certain of the source of her reaction—might have been too much for him.

Since Emma wasn't talking, Aidan decided he'd better do so or he'd never understand what was wrong. "You wanted us to fall in love—"

"Yes, I did. I do. I want us to love one another." She finally got her drawers on properly and then grabbed her shift, tugging it into place as quickly as she could. Her movements were harsh. Sharp.

Angry.

"What I do *not* want," she rasped, her voice cracking, "is for you to say you love me, try to fool me into believing you love me, only so that I'll be biddable in your bed."

She didn't honestly think he would have said those words if he didn't mean them—did she? But then again, the manner in which he'd always glared at her had to cause her some doubts. *Damnation!* Aidan dragged a hand through his hair, then reached for his clothes as well. Once she was dressed, there was no telling what she would do, and he needed to be prepared to chase after her if she should try to run off.

"That's not what happened."

Emma spun on him and jabbed a finger into his chest. "That is *precisely* what just happened. You can't switch from hating me with every fiber of your being one day, to gleefully picking fights with me another day, to supposedly *loving* me the very next. It doesn't work that way."

By normal standards, she probably had a point. But how was love ever *normal?* It just happened, whether you wanted it to or not, whether you were ready for it or not.

"Love can't just fit into a perfect little box, Emma."

"I'm not trying to fit it into a box," she muttered, fumbling with the ties of her stays. Finally, she got the ties to settle into place and gave them a hard tug. "I'm trying to avoid ending up as heartbroken as your sister was when Lord Stoneham betrayed her trust."

"You're not going to end up heartbroken."

"You're right. I won't." Emma pulled her dress over her head. "I'm not going to let you hurt me. We both know how you've felt about me all this time."

His misplaced hatred.

But of course, she'd known. She had to have known. Aidan hadn't made any effort at all to hide his feelings toward her in all that time. She'd be a fool to believe him now—now, when he finally saw the truth of what he felt for her.

She was almost fully clothed again, though shoddily so, and he had hardly done more than pull on his breeches. Aidan worked faster to make himself presentable.

"I won't hurt you. Christ, Emma. I love you."

Lifting a brow, she said, "Is that so? For some reason, I have a much easier time imagining my own interpretation of what took place in here is closer to correct." She reached for one of her half-boots, tripping over her skirts which were still tangled about her knees in the process.

Aidan caught her and set her to rights, his jaw grinding together all the while. "I don't know what else you want me to say. I've told you I love you. How am I supposed to prove it to you if you don't believe it?"

This time, finally, she looked up at him—truly looked at him—with a tear shining in her eye. "That's just it," she said a moment later. "I don't know that I'll ever be able to believe such a thing. There's been so much animosity, and I swear to you I've never understood a lick of it. How should I believe you've put all that well and truly in the past? How should I believe you love me?"

He knew because of the ferocious pounding of his pulse anytime he was with her. He knew because of the irrational jealousy he felt, which made him want to rip Sir Henry's head from his shoulders any time the baronet was alone with Emma. He knew because even when he wasn't with her, he thought about her and wanted to be with her.

But Aidan didn't have the first inkling what to say in response to her question. None of those things were tangible. None of them were things she could grasp or feel or experience.

When he didn't respond, Emma shook her head. "They'll be back from hawking soon. We should return to the house before we're missed."

As her sure fingers closed the series of tiny buttons along the back of her gown, Aidan felt like she was closing the door on any chance they could have a true marriage. He felt like she was stabbing his heart with a hot poker, over and over again. It wasn't just about having her in his bed. Not any longer. He wanted to spar with her over books, and to laugh together over her attempts at painting. He wanted to watch her collect all of the broken and damaged people around her, fix them, and send them on their way whole again.

Yet he was perhaps the most broken of them all, and she was merely breaking him further.

"Of course," he said. His voice sounded flat to his own ear. Emotionless.

He was about as far from being free from emotion as was humanly possible. It would be a blessing just now, because there were so many of the blasted things coursing through his veins he felt like he might explode from them at any moment. Love, fear, rejection, anger... There were a great many he couldn't even name, but they were powerful and overwhelming, and he worried they might topple him if he weren't careful.

Nevertheless, Aidan finished donning his clothes and helped Emma to repair hers, so it wouldn't appear that anything was amiss. Then together, they left the hermitage and began the silent journey back to the main house.

As they came out of the path onto the main lawn, they were greeted by chaos. The party had returned from hawking, and they crowded the vast expanse: houseguests, horses, and dogs were milling about, with servants rushing amongst them from one to the next.

No, milling about wasn't quite right. They were racing, as though in a panic.

Perhaps someone had been injured on the hunt? But if so, why hadn't they taken the injured person inside and sent for a doctor? No, that couldn't be.

Aidan glanced over at Emma. Her lips were pursed together and her eyes held an intense sense of purpose. She knew something was very wrong, as well. Without a word to one another, they increased their pace.

When they drew near the gathered crowd, Aidan spotted Niall and started to veer them in his brother's direction—but Sir Henry Irvine stepped into his path and blocked his way.

"Miss Hathaway, thank goodness. I've been looking for you—"

That was as far as the baronet got before Aidan's fist landed squarely on his nose. "I warned you to stay away from my intended," he growled, even as Irvine toppled over to the ground with blood gushing past the fingers covering his nose.

He'd had more than enough of Irvine trying to get close to Emma. Every time Aidan turned his back, Irvine was trying to wheedle his way closer to her, like he would steal her out from under Aidan's nose. That wasn't going to happen.

He hauled Irvine up by his shirt and pulled his free arm back to swing at the would-be-usurper's face again.

"No!" Emma tried to rush in, but Aidan jerked Irvine away from her.

"And you," he shouted at her. "You may not love me, but you can damned well honor our betrothal by staying away from him."

He pulled back for another blow and had nearly connected again when Niall caught his arm.

"It's Morgan. She's missing."

CHAPTER NINETEEN

Just as quickly as it had all begun, Aidan dropped his hold on Sir Henry, and the baronet collapsed to the ground. Emma rushed forward to see to him, her heart pounding all the while.

Morgan was missing? How could that have happened?

She ripped off a strip of her petticoat and pressed it to his nose. "Hold that in place, please."

He nodded and kept the cloth where she'd placed it, but instantly pushed himself to his feet then reached down to help Emma up.

When she released his hand, it was Aidan that she focused upon—his face contorted with anguish and pain and fear and anger, all of it so intense and acute she felt it radiating from him despite the distance between them.

She reached for his hand, hoping to feel for broken bones or see to any cuts it might have, but he snatched it away from her.

"We have to organize a search party." He said it to Lord Trenowyth, not to Emma. He wouldn't even look at her. "All too soon it will be dark, and then we'll have no hope of finding her before morning."

Her heart cracked a bit, but now was not the time to wallow in her own pity, despite the fact that this only served to prove what she'd realized in the hermitage. He didn't love her. He might never be able to love her, so it didn't matter how desperately her heart yearned for him. Her love would never be enough. He was like a wounded animal, lashing out to hurt anyone in his path before they could hurt him any more than he already had been. He didn't know how to let her love him.

Emma blinked back tears and tried to focus. All around her, the men were gathering into groups, preparing to go out into the wood. She wanted to with them, but Aidan would never allow her to. Not with as angry as he was.

Besides, he'd already moved away from her, with David and Lord Trenowyth on each side of him. Vanessa came over and put her hands on Emma's shoulders, trying to urge her inside with the other ladies, and Serena took one of Emma's hands in her own.

"Come inside," Serena said. "They'll find her. I know they will."

But she couldn't just sit and wait while Morgan was missing. What if she was in trouble? What if she was hurt and needed help? Wouldn't more people searching be better?

Emma never should have let Morgan go out hawking without her. Sir Henry and Lord Trenowyth were sure to try to help her more than Morgan would have wanted, and so she was bound to try to go off on her own, to prove herself capable as long as she had Kingley by her side.

"Kingley!" The word came out of Emma's mouth so suddenly, it startled even her. She spun around, breaking free from Serena and Vanessa's grips, and raced to where Sir Henry was still standing alongside Mr. Deering.

"Where is Kingley?" she asked frantically. "He would never have left her. He would never have let anyone hurt her." *Not even herself.* The bond between the two had grown immeasurably in a very short amount of time. That dog would do anything for Morgan. He wouldn't ever leave her side.

Sir Henry shook his head, his eyes downcast. "We haven't seen him, either. They're both missing. That was what I was going to tell you."

What he would have told her, had Aidan not attempted to cosh in his face.

Emma blinked back her tears. This was no time for tears. She needed to be level-headed and calm, or she'd never sort out this mess.

Finally, she nodded. "Find him, Sir Henry. Find Kingley, and he'll help you find Morgan."

"I'll do everything I can," he assured her.

Then Serena took Emma's hand again and turned her around. The two of them followed the rest of the women into the main house. To sit. And wait. And feel utterly, completely useless.

Morgan wouldn't try to hurt herself again, would she? It couldn't have all been feigned.

No matter how much Emma tried to convince herself of this, the fear wouldn't go away. Worst of all, she'd been off with Aidan, and they'd been oblivious to whatever Morgan's needs might have been.

His feet felt heavy, like he was wearing stones upon them instead of boots. But he couldn't slow down. He couldn't stop.

Aidan had long ago broken off the main path, with David at his side. If Morgan had somehow gone this way, she wouldn't be able to find her way back to the trail. And if she'd been *on* the main path, there was no explanation for how she would have been separated from the rest of the party. For how she would have gotten lost.

Every step he took, his heart constricted just a little more, his lungs felt a bit smaller, his world seemed a bit dimmer.

What if it wasn't that she'd gotten lost? What if she had intentionally gone off alone somewhere?

Off to hurt herself again.

He shouldn't think that. He shouldn't let his thoughts travel that trail, but there was no stopping them.

Even though it had been well over two years since she'd last attempted to take her own life, the idea that it could happen again made him feel as though he were attempting to single-handedly carry an elephant through the woods.

She could have been fooling them all along, pretending she was happy and ready to live. She could have tricked them all into believing she was of sound mind.

And they had bloody well allowed Emma to teach that damned dog to aid her. For what? So she could escape their notice and hurt herself again? He'd let himself be distracted by Emma, and now Morgan might suffer the consequences of his lust.

Devil take it.

Aidan crashed through a bramble, ignoring the cuts and scrapes on his hands and face. They were minor. He wouldn't die from them.

"Slow down," David called from a distance behind him. "We won't be any good to her if we can't get ourselves out of here."

But he couldn't slow down. If he did, then all of the rambling emotions—both for Morgan and for Emma—would catch up to him, and he'd drown beneath them.

That couldn't happen. *Please, God, let Morgan be all right.* He'd never forgive himself if…

Aidan shrugged the thought aside and kept going, breaking off tree branches as they got in his way and ignoring the orange tint of the sky.

His lungs were on fire, and he couldn't remember the last time he'd felt such an ache in his thighs.

Something snapped off to the left, a twig or a branch, and he stopped so fast he nearly fell over. Aidan swung his head to find her. But it was only David.

He cursed beneath his breath and kept going.

They had to find Morgan tonight.

The men had been out on their search for more than an hour. Emma paced before the bay window in the drawing room, fidgeting constantly with her skirts for lack of anything better to do with her hands.

She couldn't stand this. She couldn't bear to sit idly by, chatting over tea and crumpets and having inane conversation about ribbons while her friend was out *there* somewhere. Alone. Probably scared. Maybe hurt.

It was enough to send Emma to an early grave, waiting and unable to do anything about it.

A man's form came out of the woods. She stood still and strained her eyes to make out who it was. It was the first sign of anyone since the men had gone in.

But once the figure was out on the lawn and free from the tree line, Emma realized it was only Lord Muldaire. Alone.

She started to pace again as the marquess met up with a maid on the lawn, drank something, and then went back into the woods.

"You're going to pace a hole in my new Aubusson carpet," Vanessa said lightly behind her.

Emma spun on her sister.

"I know." Vanessa held her hands up in surrender. "I know you're worried. But there's nothing you can do, and pacing isn't going to help anything."

"Sitting here isn't going to help, either!"

Every head in the drawing room turned to stare at her, as though she'd grown multiple heads like Cerberus.

She hadn't meant to cause a scene, but the longer she just sat here doing nothing, the more she worried—about Morgan, and about what she was going to do about Aidan.

Really, the true problem had been to allow her thoughts to wander to Aidan. The more she thought about him, the more she was left to ponder his reaction to Sir Henry's arrival earlier and what it could mean. It couldn't have anything to do with love—he was merely trying to fool her into believing he loved her. How else would he have switched so easily to glaring at her with such hatred again?

Emma looked helplessly across at the other ladies in the drawing room, hoping to find someone to aid in her cause. "I can't just sit here and wait. I *can't*. I'm going to help them look."

Her pronouncement was met with a handful of scandalized gawks, but she didn't care.

Vanessa tried to take her hand, but Emma pulled hers free.

"It isn't a good idea, Em," Vanessa said. "What if something happens to you, too? Then they'll have to help both you and Morgan."

"Something could happen to any of the men who are out there right now just as easily as something could happen to me."

"It's getting dark! The sun is already starting to set, and it won't take long for it to be as dark as pitch out there. It's too dangerous." Once more, Vanessa tried to take her hand. "The men will be on their way back soon, anyway. We can't search for her in the woods at night."

"I can't leave her out there without at least searching." Emma stalked across the drawing room to the door then turned around to face her sister once more. " Morgan lives in the dark, all the time. If she can live like that, I can look for her in the dark at least tonight. I don't know that it'll do any good for me to go out there, but at least I'll be doing *something*."

"And you won't be alone," Serena said, standing.

Then several other ladies stood as well: Miss Selwyn, Miss Goderich, and even Lady Portia, who had been so rude to Morgan early on during the house party.

Serena moved to stand beside Emma and linked their arms together. "We're coming with you. The more people we have searching for Morgan, the better."

Their show of support nearly moved Emma to tears, but since she'd already established earlier that tears had no place here at the moment, she suppressed them.

"Right. Well, we should be off. The sun will be setting before long."

The five of them went, as a group, out into the corridor and out the side exit, then marched across the lawn.

What if they couldn't find Morgan before the sun set fully? What would happen to her if she was out there alone all night? Emma swallowed the lump of fear that kept trying to rise with the thought.

Fear would have to attack her another day. She refused to give in to it today.

"We can't stay out here much longer, Aidan." David's voice sounded thin, like he was far away.

Aidan spun around and squinted into the shadowy wood surrounding him. A few streams of light were still coming through the branches overhead, but they grew dimmer by the moment. What had been orange and pink only minutes before was now near pitch darkness, and they still had to return to the main trail.

But how could he turn back without finding Morgan? No one had shouted that they'd found her. All he could hear around him were masculine voices calling her name as they searched.

Even those voices had become fewer and farther between, however.

Most of the others had probably already turned back, relenting to nightfall.

David caught up with him where he had stopped. Worry had left a crease in his forehead. "I know you don't want—"

"You know what could happen to her if she's out all night," Aidan snapped.

"I know. What good will you be to her if you hurt yourself trying to find her because you can't see the ground beneath your feet?"

Aidan ground his teetj together, clenched his fists. There was nothing he wanted less than to concede David's point. But he was not a fool.

Well, not entirely. He had been a fool where Emma was concerned, it seemed, trusting her to be in Morgan's presence again.

Convincing himself he loved her. How could he love someone who would treat his sister with such disregard?

And now, he would have to go back to the house—back to where Emma was—without Morgan.

He wasn't certain he could face Emma yet. Facing her would force him to likewise face his own demons, the fault which may lie with him and no one else.

"Let's go back," he finally said, though he nearly choked on the words. It felt like he was giving up on Morgan, like he was leaving her to her fate.

He'd never quit on her before. In fact, he'd sworn when they were children that he never would. Yet now, he was.

They returned to the main path, trudging over above-ground roots and broken tree limbs, ducking beneath low-hanging branches. When they'd covered about half the distance back, a dog barked in the distance.

Aidan's heart stopped. It didn't sound like one of the hounds from the hunt. It was a deeper bark, lower and fuller—like Kingley's.

David stopped moving and turned, his eyes wide in the dim light. "Kingley? Kingley, is that you?"

The barks increased and drew closer. It had to be him.

"Kingley, come here," Aidan shouted as he took off running toward the sound. "Where is she? Where's Morgan?"

"Cardiff?" someone called from the direction of Kingley's barks. In his panic, Aidan couldn't place it.

He kept running like a madman, despite the brambles and treacherous ground.

"I've got Kingley over here," the man called again. Was that Mr. Deering? It must be.

"Where's Morgan?" Aidan shouted. "Where's my sister?"

The dog let out a happy bark just as Aidan toppled through a break in the trees into an opening. Charles Deering was on his knees, scratching Kingley behind the ears like Emma and Morgan so often did…but Morgan wasn't there.

"Where is she?" he growled, desperate for air and answers.

"I found Kingley off over there," Deering answered, pointing deeper into the woods, where almost no light came in at all. "Haven't seen any sign of Lady Morgan, though. He was alone when I found him."

David came up behind Aidan, gasping for breath and holding his right hand tightly over his left upper arm. Something dark glistened in the small amount of light coming through the canopy above them.

"You're hurt?" Deering asked David. "We should head back. We'll all end up injured if we stay out in this much longer. Kingley can help us find her tomorrow."

When Deering stood, Aidan reached for Kingley's lead...but there was no lead. Good God. The lead had been on him when they'd all left to go hawking. And the dog seemed fine, so it hadn't just accidentally come off of him.

Someone had taken it off. It was a good quality leather—it wasn't just going to snap off on a whim.

If it was Morgan...

Devil take it, this had been her plan all along. She was trying to hurt herself. Trying to kill herself. Aidan's chest grew so tight he thought it might burst, and his breaths became shallow.

Damnation, he couldn't think like that. He'd only cause himself more problems if he let his thoughts run rampant, not that he had an inkling as to how he would stop that very thing from happening.

There was the possibility, of course, that someone else had taken off Kingley's lead. This possibility was no less haunting. Why would someone do such a thing?

Standing there in the growing dark wouldn't do any of them any good, and David needed someone to see to the cut on his arm.

"Let's head back," Aidan finally said.

The three of them and Kingley headed out of the trees, making for the main path where they could still hear a lone voice calling out for Morgan on occasion.

They'd almost reached the end of the thickness when he heard something else that set his blood to boiling: none other than Emma Hathaway calling out into the woods.

"Morgan? Please answer me, Morgan."

And then there were other feminine voices.

"We're coming for you."

"Call out if you can hear us."

Aidan cursed beneath his breath and turned to Deering. "Get Burington and the dog back to the house safely. I'll take care of the ladies."

Then he took off in the direction of their voices. They were on the main path, but deeper in the woods. He cut across at an angle, hoping to catch them before they got too much further.

"Keep calling out to her, ladies." It was Emma again. "She'll hear us. I know she will."

"Emma Hathaway, what in God's name do you think you're doing out here?" Aidan bellowed. He didn't care who else was with her. It didn't matter.

"Morgan!" she cried, willfully ignoring him.

"Emma!" He increased his pace, ready to throttle her as soon as he reached her. "Stop where you are."

"I think you should listen to Mr. Cardiff," one of the other ladies said, loudly enough he could make out every word.

He gained ground on them with every step. "She should, if she has any sense of self-preservation."

"I'm trying to find your sister," Emma shrieked just as he came through the bushes upon them.

"You were supposed to stay at the house," he growled. For a moment, he passed his eyes over the rest of them, but his fury at having Emma out here clouded his mind so that he couldn't decipher who else was with her. "All of you. It's dark, and it's too dangerous even for the men to remain looking for Morgan."

"You're quitting?" Emma spluttered. "You can't give up yet. We could get torches or lanterns—"

"It's too dangerous." It took every ounce of restraint he possessed not to take her by the upper arms and shake her until her teeth rattled. It was bad enough *he* knew he was quitting on Morgan. He didn't need Emma to remind him of that fact.

"But we can't leave her alone out here all night."

"She wouldn't even be out here if you hadn't put the idea in her head that she could become more independent."

Emma blanched at his rebuke. As well she should. Aidan didn't truly believe that. He was just lashing out at anything he could. It was just his worry for Morgan, but that didn't mean Emma deserved his treatment of her.

Even in the bit of moonlight shining down over the path, the paleness of her skin seemed to intensify, which only caused Aidan's pulse to race faster than it already was. Cold sweat covered his skin. What was he doing to Emma? He loved her, but he couldn't seem to stop himself from trying to hurt her.

"Miss Hathaway?" Niall stepped into the path beside Aidan. "Are you ladies all right?"

He hadn't realized Niall was there.

"Yes, my lord," she said. But she never took her eyes—her huge, brown, downturned, hurt, heartsick eyes—from Aidan. "We're just worried about Morgan."

There was no one to blame for that but Aidan. He'd put that look in them. He'd caused her pain. After all of these years, finally, Aidan had achieved some small amount of the revenge he'd sought ever since that one day.

He wanted to be sick. Bile rose in his throat, and he was sure he would lose the contents of his stomach at any moment. What had he become? What had he done?

"We all are," Niall assured her. "But we're going to have to trust that she'll be all right until morning."

Emma sniffled, which caused Aidan to hate himself just a bit more than before.

"But…"

"But nothing." Niall put out both arms for the ladies to take.

"Come along. We can't stay out here waiting for someone else to be hurt."

"Someone's been hurt?" one of the other ladies said. "Oh, heavens."

As a group, the lot of them made their way back along the path toward the main house, leaving Aidan behind.

He watched them, debating for a moment whether he should go with them or ignore his own counsel and continue the search. But then Emma stopped and looked back at him, and her tears twinkled in the moonlight.

All he could do was shake his head.

She turned around again and followed after the others, leaving Aidan alone to ponder his descent into madness.

CHAPTER TWENTY

"Did anyone check near the river?"

The silence which fell over the drawing room after Lord Roxeburghe's question was heavy and thick, like syrup. Emma heard every breath taken, every shift of fabric upon a chair, every swallow. She wished someone would say something, anything, so her thoughts wouldn't go back to Morgan at the river.

But no one spoke. No one moved, until Aidan thundered to his feet and stalked from the room, intentionally tossing over a chair as he went.

Emma started to follow after him until she remembered that, yet again, he hated her. He blamed her for Morgan's disappearance, as irrational as such a thing may be. Which only meant that for three years, he had apparently blamed her for what had happened in the river.

The knowledge of why he'd hated her for so long didn't ease the ache that had filled her gut since they'd left the hermitage this afternoon. If anything, it only intensified the sense of emptiness, the hollow pang that had been consuming her. How would he ever come to love her? She couldn't fathom a life without his love now, but it seemed it was to be her fate.

At last, David cleared his throat. "We'll split into teams again in the morning and begin the search anew—starting at first light. We should all try to get a good night's rest, however difficult such a prospect may be."

They filed out of the drawing room, talking quietly in small groups as they went, and Vanessa came over to sit beside Emma on the settee.

"Come," she said. "You won't be any use to Morgan tomorrow if you don't rest tonight."

Emma couldn't calm the thoughts that were racing through her mind. "I'll just go out and check on Kingley once more."

"Kingley is fine," David said from behind her. "We've already seen to that. He doesn't need you."

Kingley may not need her, but Emma needed him. She needed someone or something she could hold onto, someone whose neck she could wrap her arms around and have a good cry, someone who wouldn't think any less of her for doing it. "I'll just be—"

"You'll just be off to bed," Vanessa cut in.

Emma looked from her sister to her brother-in-law, hoping one of the two would see things her way, but neither gave her any sign they would aid her cause. Instead, she let them help her to her feet. Vanessa walked with her all the way to the ladies' wing. After the door closed behind her, it was a few moments before Emma heard the sound of her sister's footsteps heading in the opposite direction.

Of course, now there was Fanny to deal with. She allowed the maid to assist her in changing out of her gown and into a nightrail. For the maid's benefit, Emma even got into her bed, tucked neatly beneath her counterpane...but she had a book with her.

"Leave the candle, please," she said sweetly, so Fanny wouldn't think anything was amiss. "I'm hoping to finish this book tonight." She might have said it too sweetly, because the maid narrowed her eyes before bobbing a curtsey and closing the door behind her.

Emma tried to read for a few minutes, because she couldn't go out so soon. She had to be sure no one in this wing of the house would hear her, or they would surely try to stop her. But reading proved impossible. She couldn't force her mind to focus on the words on the page. It kept jumping around from thought to thought, and in a wildly erratic manner, no less.

She wished she could take Serena with her, but that didn't seem such a brilliant plan of action. Someone might hear her when she went to Serena's door, and that was a risk she just wasn't willing to take.

When finally she heard nothing else coming from the corridor, Emma threw off the coverlet, pulled on a wrapper, picked up her candle, and padded as quietly as she could to the door.

Before going fully out into the hall, she peeked around the doorway to both sides, making certain she wouldn't be seen by a random houseguest who was up too late at night. She didn't see anyone, and the footmen had already been through to extinguish the wall sconces, so she took a full step out.

The risk of being caught and sent back to her chamber like a naughty child weighed so heavily on her mind that she hurried through the corridors and down the stairs faster than she ever would have otherwise. Most times, if she attempted to avoid detection, she would take the servants' stairs and halls in order to get to where she was going. But the servants were the ones most likely to be up and about at this hour, so she used the main pathways.

Finally, she reached the door to the east gardens and escaped outside without being detected. She'd been most concerned, perhaps, about the possibility of Aidan poking his head in and impeding her progress. When she stepped out into the cool, night air, it was as though Kingley had been waiting for her, like he knew she would come. She'd barely closed the door before he let out a bark and ran to her side, jumping up excitedly.

Emma dropped to her knees, set the candleholder carefully on the ground, and wrapped her arms around him, drawing him into an embrace. He let out a series of happy yaps and shoved his head into her hands so she could scratch his ears.

"Where did Morgan go, Kingley?" she murmured, not that she expected him to answer. He was just a dog. He didn't really understand her, no matter how smart he might be and no matter how quickly he'd learned to guide her friend.

But that was just the thing—he might not understand her question, but he *did* understand that Morgan was his responsibility. He would never have left her willingly.

Even if, as had been prodding at her mind, Morgan had removed Kingley's lead and tried to shoo him away, he wouldn't have left her. In their training, it had become increasingly clear that he knew there was something different about Morgan, that he knew she needed his protection in addition to his guidance.

Morgan hadn't tried to hurt herself again. There wasn't a doubt in Emma's mind.

And she hadn't gotten lost or innocently separated from Kingley.

Someone else was involved. Someone else had taken Kingley's lead from around his neck and convinced him to leave Morgan.

Which meant that someone had to have done something to Morgan. Someone Kingley trusted, no less.

She couldn't sit around and try to sleep while Morgan could be hurt...or dead, however grim the thought may be. It wasn't a possibility. Especially not now that she had realized, beyond any doubt, that someone had intentionally meant harm toward her friend.

How could she find Morgan, though? What could she do in the dark, alone, to help her friend? Kingley whined at her side, and she absentmindedly put her hand down for him to nuzzle. He licked and sniffed her, then nudged her hand again, and she knew what they must do. Taking her candlestick again, she raced back into the house and up to Morgan's chamber. Since Morgan was missing, Janetta wouldn't be about—so Emma threw open the trunk in the dressing room and searched for a piece of clothing that would smell strongly of Morgan's scent.

She found a soiled shift, likely one Morgan had worn for one of their outdoor sessions, and then hurried back out to Kingley. "Here, Kingley. Smell this. Smell Morgan."

He sniffed deeply, moving his head back and forth over the

garment.

Then she stood and walked across the lawn, carrying her candlestick and Morgan's shift. "Come on, Kingley. Let's go find her."

He came along by her side, his head low to the ground as they went. He understood.

And they *would* find her.

Maybe then Aidan would see she'd never meant his sister any harm. Maybe then he could believe it.

Aidan dragged a pillow from beneath his head and threw it across the room. It hit the wall with a dull thud and then fell to the floor. The action felt so good, he repeated the process until every pillow from his damned bed was on the floor at the other side of the room. After that, he leapt up and pulled the bedding free, thinking it might give him a similar satisfaction.

But even when the entire bed had been disassembled, its various parts strewn across the Parquet floor of his chamber, he still felt just as angry as he had before getting started on it all in the first place.

The truly perplexing thing was he was no longer angry at Emma.

When Roxeburghe had so casually suggested searching the river, it had been like a hot knife piercing Aidan's heart. But it was a slow thrust, inch by inch, dragging out the pain until he was ready to beg for death, because it only confirmed what Aidan had already been thinking: what if Morgan had attempted to hurt herself again? What if she'd been successful this time?

He'd left to search the river, despite the full darkness of the night, and despite the dropping temperatures, yet there had been nothing to find in the inky-black waters. Morgan's body had not washed up on the bank. He couldn't see her bobbing on the top of the water in the estuary. And with no light but the moon, he'd never be able to dive beneath the surface and see anything. He was a fool to even have gone.

By the time he'd returned to the estate, the rest of the houseguests had gone to bed—including Emma. On his walk back, he'd thought about how he should apologize to her for his reaction. How he should once again try to convince her that yes, he truly did love her, that he hadn't just been trying to convince her he did.

For a moment, he hadn't been so certain—when his thoughts had turned to how she'd supposedly aided Morgan in potentially harming herself again. But even if Morgan had done so, if she'd tried to drown herself or found a poison that could finish the job, Emma couldn't have possibly known that had been her aim.

He knew, without any doubt that Emma only wanted to help people. She was *good*, and *kind*, and would never harm a fly if she could avoid it.

So why would he think otherwise?

And yet again, it all came back to Aidan's inability to place the blame where it truly ought to lay.

For this disappearance, that blame ought to rest with either Morgan, or with someone else who wished to harm her.

But it most certainly was not Emma's fault. None of it was. If anything, Emma had proven by going out into the woods earlier with some of the other ladies that she wanted to help Morgan, yet again.

And he'd treated her like she was an imbecile for doing so.

There was another thing he'd have to apologize to her for. Damn. He'd never been very good at apologizing, but he'd accumulated quite a list—one which only seemed to grow—to increase his skill in that area. He needed to swallow his pride and admit that he wasn't always right, that sometimes others might know better than he.

He needed to start making amends. Now, not tomorrow. Aidan didn't want one more moment to go by with Emma thinking he hated her. Not only that, but if they worked together—if they combined what Aidan knew of Morgan with what Emma saw in her which Aidan was blind to, they would have much better luck with finding her.

They had to join forces. They had to work together. There was no other option, or he might lose his sister forever.

Without truly thinking of the consequences, he stalked out into the corridor, yanked one of the few still-lit sconces from the wall, and made his way to the ladies' wing. He knew which chamber was Morgan's, as he'd helped her settle in when they first arrived, and she'd informed him Emma's was the chamber to her right.

In order to get to Emma's he had to walk directly past Morgan's...so he couldn't help but notice that the door was ajar.

He went in and passed the light over the room. Nothing seemed to be amiss in the main room, but the door to the dressing room had been left open wide, which Aidan thought was more than just a little odd. Janetta always left Morgan's doors closed, because it was what Morgan expected. There was little more important to Morgan in terms of finding her way around on her own than having things be as she expected them to be.

Surprises were not a good thing, when one lived by touch and sound, and not by sight.

Aidan went into the dressing room, and his heart nearly stopped. The whole room appeared to be ransacked, with the armoire doors thrown open, clothing tossed about all over...but the most damning thing of all was that Morgan's trunk had been almost completely emptied.

Aidan tried to think what someone would have been after, but nothing came to mind. Morgan didn't wear much jewelry. Her skin was so sensitive after it had been scarred, that she didn't like the feel of jewels upon it. They'd brought very little else of true value with them.

Had she been attacked in the woods, and when the attacker didn't find what they wanted, they searched her chamber?

But that meant it had to be someone in the house party.

Good God.

Without wasting another moment, Aidan raced out of Morgan's chamber and down the corridor to Emma's. He threw open the door without knocking.

She was gone.

CHAPTER TWENTY-ONE

Truly, Emma's plan to go off into the woods with nothing but a nightrail and wrapper, a half-gone candlestick, and Kingley hadn't been one of the brighter moments of her life.

After being out for what had to have been more than an hour, the chill in the air was biting, easily blowing through the thin fabrics covering her and making her wish she'd taken the time to don something more substantial. Something more practical.

Practicality had never been one of her strengths, much to the chagrin of nearly everyone in her life.

She'd gone too far to turn back now and give up on her plan. And as it stood, every moment which passed could bring them one moment closer to Morgan's death. Emma pressed on, following where Kingley led her and wishing she would stop shivering so heavily.

Kingley kept his nose down to the ground as they walked, sniffing every inch of terrain he passed over. After they'd gone for ten minutes or so, Emma would put Morgan's shift down again, reminding him of the scent they were searching for. Surely, soon he would pick up her trail. Surely they had to be getting close.

But the further they went into the woods, the more the scant bits of moonlight coming through the tree cover waned. Emma wasn't certain if that was because the canopy above them had grown thicker, or if it was a sign of impending rain.

Her feet hurt, and her house shoes provided her very little protection against the rocks and brambles along their path. At least they were still taking the path. Emma feared they might have to veer off into the lesser-traveled areas at some point. There was no telling how her slippers would survive, let alone how her nightrail and wrapper would fare, if she were to get caught in low branches or bushes.

A bit later, a stiff breeze kicked up which extinguished the flame of her candle. It was a miracle the flame had lasted as long as it had.

Now she had nothing to light her way but the thin streams of moonlight that filtered through the trees.

"Kingley?" she said, and he yapped. She bent down and gave him Morgan's shift again, wishing there was a lead for him. What would happen if he got away from her? The thought was more than Emma wanted to allow herself. There was no time for her to panic. "Stay close with me."

Before they took off again, Emma set her candlestick on the ground. With no more flame, there was no point in carrying it, and the metal of the holder was cold upon her skin. She was chilled enough without the additional discomfort.

She stood and Kingley started off, his nose sniffing close to the ground.

Emma followed him, so tired she occasionally stumbled over her own feet, but she would not give in to her exhaustion.

After another stretch of time, she couldn't fool herself any longer. The lack of moonlight wasn't due to the the trees being thicker. It was because of heavy clouds rolling in with the wind.

That brought a new sense of urgency to her step, a rekindled sense of purpose to scanning her surroundings.

"Do you smell her yet, Kingley? We have to find Morgan."

He started to move faster, or maybe she only felt like he was moving faster because she was moving slower. She tried to increase her pace to keep in step with the dog.

After a few minutes, she walked over more uneven terrain, and she knew they'd gone off the main path though she'd missed the change. That had to be a positive sign. Kingley wouldn't have gone off the trail without a good reason for it, would he?

"Is it Morgan?" she asked him. It had to be. There wasn't another explanation.

He kept moving, so she kept following. Kingley barked. Emma tried to run as fast as she could on her battered feet. When she increased her pace, the dog bolted, and soon he was outpacing her by a good deal.

It didn't seem to matter how fast she ran. She couldn't keep up with him, no matter how hard she tried. His barks grew more distant, and she couldn't see him in the few bits of moonlight any more.

And then she couldn't hear him either.

Emma kept going, desperate not to lose Kingley, too, but growing ever more certain that she'd already done so. After a few minutes, she couldn't see him anymore, couldn't hear his yaps or the patter of his feet upon the ground. He was gone, and she was alone.

She stopped and dropped to the ground in defeat, gasping for air and holding the pain in her side. What had she done?

Emma wasn't certain how long she sat there, almost in tears with her arms wrapped around knees that had been drawn up to her chest for warmth. All she knew was that she was cold and tired, and she'd failed Morgan. And Aidan. She'd failed everyone, and morning couldn't come soon enough.

But then she saw a light off in the distance, bobbing up and down it seemed. That couldn't be. She rubbed her eyes, but the light remained. "Hello?" she called, even as she pushed to her feet again. "Over here!" she cried and took off as fast as she could go in the direction of the light.

Something ran into her feet—or perhaps her feet ran into something—and she fell forward, nearly flying through the open air before smacking the entire front of her body hard against the ground.

She moaned, certain she'd done herself significant harm. Her left arm throbbed in pain, and her head felt like she'd cracked it open. Or maybe she only wished she had cracked it open. Either way, it wasn't pleasant in the slightest.

She tried to roll over, but it was no use. Every inch of her body ached like she couldn't remember it ever aching before. Moving so much as a muscle was more than she could ask of herself at the moment. She lay there, moaning but not doing much else.

Oh, heavens. What if that light had belonged to whoever had tried to harm Morgan? Would they come after Emma now? She should have thought before she acted.

Until the light she'd seen came to her, floating above her head as though it were a supernatural creature of sorts. It hurt her head, and nearly blinded her. Emma blinked, squinting up into the brightness.

"Is she all right?"

Emma knew that voice without a doubt, so soft and melodic. It belonged to Morgan. But how was that possible? Morgan was missing, and Emma was supposed to find her—not the other way around.

Then a rough, wet tongue licked the side of her face.

"Kingley?" Emma said on a groan.

"I think she'll be fine, once we get her back to the estate and see to her injuries."

A man's voice. She knew him too.

"Can you carry the lantern for me, Lady Morgan? I'll have to carry her, and you can hold my arm as we go back."

Then his strong arms went beneath her, and he lifted her up into the air. Emma had enough wits about her that she was able to put her arm across his shoulders, to better support her weight in his arms.

Kingley grumbled and growled when Morgan put her hand on the man's arm, as he'd instructed her to do, but the dog didn't attack.

Emma squinted into the man's face as the lantern light swung near.

"Lord Jacob?" she rasped.

"We'll have you back to the estate safely in no time, Miss

Hathaway," he said firmly. "Try not to worry yourself."

Then he took off walking, with Morgan at his side and Kingley at hers, growling his menace at the man he'd never liked with every step he took.

They'd been traveling some minutes, Lord Jacob and Morgan talking all the while, by the time the pounding in Emma's head calmed enough she could concentrate on what was happening around her. The events of the night left her so confused; however, she feared that attempting to sort it all out would only leave her with a more blistering headache than she already had.

"Lord Jacob," she finally asked, her voice far more tentative than she would have liked, "how did you find Morgan?"

He let out a mirthless chuckle. "Your Mr. Cardiff woke the entire household sometime after we'd all taken to our beds. He was yelling about how Lady Morgan had been attacked, and now you'd gone missing as well."

Aidan had been upset she was gone? How did he know? He couldn't have discovered her absence unless he'd gone to her chamber...but why?

"At that point, it was decided as many men who were willing would go out again, with lanterns and torches and whatever else could be found, in order to locate you both."

They were all out looking for her, because she'd been so impatient and irresponsible. What if someone else had been hurt in the dark? Emma would never be able to live with herself if that had occurred. She never should have left her chamber. She should have waited until day, like they had planned.

But she hadn't, and now what?

"Kingley found me first," Morgan said softly. Her voice seemed to calm Kingley somewhat, as his growls lessened in intensity. "But he made such noise that only a few moments later Lord Jacob arrived."

"Lady Morgan was frightened, of course," he continued, "after being lost alone in the woods for so long, but she was unharmed. We started to return to the estate when we heard you crashing through the woods and moaning in pain."

Lord Jacob was beginning to labor with continuing to carry her—his breaths came too rapidly, though she doubted he would ever voice a complaint.

Nonetheless, Emma shifted a bit, to determine if she could walk. Her legs and feet ached, certainly, but she was fairly certain she could manage.

"Set me on my feet," she said after a moment.

"Certainly not. Not until all your injuries have been examined."

"I can walk," Emma insisted, more firmly this time.

Eventually, he relented and set her down. Even so, he put an arm around her waist for support. Once she was walking again, she was glad for it. She couldn't remember a time she felt less steady.

That wasn't entirely true. Aidan left her feeling unsteady at every turn, but she couldn't help but wish it was his arm supporting her now. Lord Jacob's arms were strong and sure, but Aidan's made her feel safe. She felt so conflicted, wanting to get back to him as quickly as possible to reassure him she was fine, and wishing she could delay their reunion as long as possible, since she couldn't be certain of what his reaction would be when he saw her.

The most perplexing part of it all was that, no matter how easily he had blamed her again, she still loved him. She only wished he could love her equally.

But what if he did? What if what he'd said to her had been the truth?

They walked along for some time in silence, aside from the low rumblings coming from Kingley because of Lord Jacob's presence. By the time they returned to the main path, however, the curiosity that had been niggling at Emma's mind for quite some time became too much for her to bear.

"Morgan?" she asked tentatively. "What happened?" There was no need to be more specific with her question. Morgan would know what she meant.

"Kingley and I had been walking along with Mr. Deering, some distance behind the others. One of the men called out ahead of us, asking Mr. Deering to come to his assistance. I told him to go on, that Kingley and I would be along at our leisure. He did, promising he would return to us in short order. He'd been gone for ten minutes or so, and Kingley and I had been wandering around, listening to the sounds of nature, when someone whistled. Kingley took off running, and I was only able to keep up for so long. Eventually, I turned my ankle and let go of Kingley's lead, and then I was all alone. I called for him, but he didn't come back. I had no choice but to wait for Mr. Deering or someone else from the party to find me. My ankle feels better now..."

"Good heavens! Do you know who whistled for Kingley?"

The path before them widened. They were close to the estate. Close to warmth and comfort. Close to Aidan. Emma's pulse roared in her ears from the realization.

"I haven't a clue," Morgan said. "It would have to be someone he knows and likes, or he wouldn't have gone to them."

As though to prove her point, Kingley growled at Lord Jacob again.

"But there is no possibly means of knowing how many people from the village he knows and is comfortable with," Morgan went on. "He'd been on his own until you took him under your wing."

A few minutes later, they emerged onto the Heathcote Park lawn. Lord Jacob called out, "I've found them!" Instantly, the heads of everyone gathered on the lawn spun in their direction, and chaos ensued.

Servants rushed to them with blankets and hot drinks. David wrapped two blankets around Emma and carried her the rest of the way. Lord Trenowyth did the same with Morgan while Lord Jacob rejected the hot tea offered by a servant.

"Brandy," he said. "And keep it coming."

"Here, Kingley," Mr. Deering said, and the dog went straight to him. "I found your lead out in the woods—not a flaw on the thing." A moment later, the leather was back around Kingley's neck. He'd stopped his growling, now that he was with Mr. Deering and not with Lord Jacob.

Everyone kept rushing around, trying to take care of all of their needs at once—but the one person Emma strained to see more than anyone else never appeared. No matter how hard Emma tried to find him, Aidan was nowhere to be seen.

"Mr. Cardiff?" she asked David while he and Vanessa tried to warm Emma's skin. "Where is he?"

David shook his head. "He hasn't returned from the woods yet. He's the last one we're waiting on."

The relief she'd felt at being back to safety once again deflated, and her chest felt tight with worry. The night would not be kind to him. The clouds that had gathered earlier still clung to the night sky, thick and heavy and ominous.

Her thoughts kept returning to one thing: why would a man who hated her so thoroughly be out risking his own life and safety in order to find her?

He does love me. She was sure of it all the way through to her bones.

Emma stood, moving to where she could see the tree line. Until Aidan came out, she wouldn't budge.

Thunder rattled the sky overhead, but still Aidan had found nothing but Emma's discarded candlestick. Still, it meant he was on the right path. She had been there at some point in the night, though he had no way of knowing how long ago—or what direction she'd gone when she left there.

For two hours after finding the damned thing, he'd kept looking, circling around the spot in search of another sign. Something. Anything.

But now, he knew he had no choice but to go back. The heavens were preparing to open up and release a torrent, and he'd lose the bit of light he had from his lantern. Feeling like the worst sort of failure alive, Aidan turned around and made for the main path.

He hadn't just failed Morgan, now he'd failed Emma, too. Somehow, the realization that he'd failed Emma struck him deeper in the gut than he'd been prepared for. It wasn't just tonight that he'd failed her—as long as he'd known her, he had let her down over and over again.

A few cold drops hit him just as he reached the well-travelled trail, so he increased his pace. The entire way back to the estate, Aidan kept berating himself over and over again for his poor treatment of Emma, all the while searching his mind for a plan of action for what he'd do when he finally found her again.

Groveling for forgiveness seemed his best option. Not that he ever groveled. But given the circumstances, this seemed as good a time as any to try his hand at it. And then he'd apologize. Then he'd tell her he loved her, and he'd repeat as many times as it took for her to believe him.

The closer he got to Heathcote Park, the louder the thunder grew overhead. When the wind picked up and blew out his lantern, Aidan ran.

He didn't stop until the end of the path opened out onto the lawn. Lightning flashed in the sky, illuminating the scene before him.

Morgan.

She was huddled in blankets and being carried back to the house by Niall, but there wasn't a doubt in Aidan's mind that it was his sister. Her blonde hair shimmered in the burst of light, a piece of brilliance amidst the darkness surrounding her.

Better yet, she was moving. That meant she was alive. Hurt, possibly, but alive.

He breathed a bit easier, racing toward the mad assemblage trying to get back inside the manor house before the rain drenched them all.

He had every intention to follow Niall and Morgan inside the house, but he changed his mind with the next bolt that hurtled to the ground. On the other side of the lawn, David and Vanessa attempted to drag Emma inside the house but she fought against them both like her life depended upon it.

Aidan changed his trajectory to intercept them. Niall was with Morgan. She would be fine.

Emma needed him now, though.

"Emma!" He doubted she could hear him over the howling of the wind and the rumbles echoing from the sky.

David tried to toss her over his shoulder, but she flailed and kicked against him so much that he was forced to put her down again.

"Emma!" Aidan shouted again. This time, she heard him. In an instant, her head turned toward him, and then she dashed across the lawn to meet him. The blankets they'd wrapped around her fell off and she wore nothing but a nightrail and wrapper, but that didn't deter her in the slightest.

His heart leapt at the sight, but then it froze. Now was the time he'd been dreading, the time when he'd have to apologize and grovel and beg for her forgiveness—a forgiveness which he hardly deserved, but desperately needed.

She didn't stop until she'd flung herself into his arms, her tear-drenched cheek buried against his neck. "You're all right? I've been so worried."

But she shouldn't have been worrying about him. With the way he'd treated her for so long, she ought to have been praying for his demise. Aidan pulled back, prepared to begin what would be his life's work for the remainder of his days—making Emma realize just how deeply he loved her and how very much he needed her in his life— but she stopped him before he could even start by kissing him.

Her arms tightened around his neck and she pressed the length of her body against him so he had to hold onto her or they would topple to the ground. She pressed her tongue between his lips and then drank from him with a desperation near to matching his own.

A new flash of lightning struck through the sky, and the air fairly crackled with the electricity as thunder crashed all around them.

"Get inside," David demanded.

But Aidan couldn't move a muscle. Not while Emma was kissing him with such abandon, like he was her breath and heartbeat and soul, all combined. Or perhaps it was him kissing her in that way. He couldn't tell any more. He didn't much care, either.

The sprinkling of raindrops turned into a deluge, an icy torrent pelting them from above.

Emma trembled in his arms, and he forced himself to pull away. "We have to get you inside," he shouted over the noise of the storm.

She looked up at him, as earnest as he'd ever seen her, and shook her head. "I love you!"

"You're mad!" he shouted. As mad as he was. And yet her declaration warmed him to the core. Still, he took her hand in his and tugged, trying to draw her closer to the warm, dry house.

Emma dug in her heels and put her hand on his chest. "Wait." He couldn't possibly deny her anything in that moment, despite the water plastering her hair to her head and drenching her from head to toe. "I know why you've been angry with me—"

"I'm not angry with you anymore. I was a fool. I blamed you because—"

"Because you couldn't blame Morgan," she interrupted. "I know. But I know that it wasn't really me you were so angry with, and it's all right. It's all right because I love you and you love me and for now, that's enough."

Aidan shook his head. "It's not enough. How can it possibly be?"

She couldn't be serious. He'd blamed her time and again for things which couldn't be further from her fault—and she knew it. Worst of all, he'd done it again after making love to her, and declaring that he loved her. How could she simply brush it aside, like it had never happened? He didn't deserve such devotion.

But standing there beneath the pouring rain, shivering in her nightrail, she smiled up at him with the most radiant smile—wide lips, too-large teeth, and all.

"Aidan," she shouted over the pounding of the rain, "it's enough *because* I love you. And I didn't believe you loved me earlier, but I was wrong. I know that now. Why else would you have come searching for me when it was madness to do so?"

Never in a thousand years would he understand how her heart could be large enough to love all the broken and helpless things that she did. But he was grateful for it—it was precisely what he was. Broken and helpless.

Until she'd fixed him.

EPILOGUE

September, 1819

The wedding had been a quiet affair in Knightsbridge, since Sir Phillip Hathaway was not readily able to travel to see his youngest daughter wed. From what he'd observed, Lady Hathaway had been beside herself with all of those of Quality present. Not only was one daughter a baroness, the other was now sister-in-law to the Earl of Trenowyth, and one of her dearest friends was to marry the Marquess of Muldaire. That happy couple had made the journey to join them, along with Muldaire's brother and cousin, their fellow houseguests from David's house party.

Aidan was not nearly so enamored of all the grand events of the day, but he was more than happy with the end result, particularly since there had been no more talk between David and Niall about protecting Emma from him.

No one would keep him from his wife.

He still worried about Morgan, particularly since they had never discovered the source of the whistle which lured Kingley away from her that day in the woods. But after they'd all been located and none had been found the worse for wear, life had just gone on as before with a few modifications.

The most obvious of those was that Kingley now went with

Morgan everywhere, including back to the family home...and Morgan was granted much more freedom than she had been in years, due to his assistance.

Finally, Aidan was allowing her free rein to fail. He had Emma to thank for such a change, and he did so at every opportunity he was granted. She'd helped him to learn that, while Morgan was blind and had her scars, and had at one point been a bit touched, it was he who was still stuck in the past.

With Emma at his side, however, he was able to move forward with his life.

He'd resumed his sculpting and finished the angel piece, which was now listed for auction. After seeing the portraits he'd done of Emma, he'd begun to take commissions for other portraits, and was attracting quite the attention from this new venture.

For now, he and Emma would live at the dower house. But with Emma's encouragement and Aidan's renewed passion for his art, soon he would be able to purchase a home they could call their own.

Even though it would mean being further away from Morgan, this was something Aidan felt certain he could handle. Besides, Kingley was perhaps better in the overprotective bear of a brother role than even Aidan had been. The way the dog growled at Lord Jacob Deering at every turn was as good a sign as any on that score.

There was nothing left for Aidan to worry about but one thing—getting his bride into bed on their wedding night.

She stood beside her mother, with Morgan and Miss Weston standing across from her. Her smile stretched from ear to ear, and somehow only spread wider when she caught him staring at her.

Aidan hitched a brow, and a moment later she excused herself from the ladies and made her way to his side.

"You've got that smirk on your face again," she said on a laugh. "I never quite know how to react to it."

"I'd say your reaction this time was just about perfect. You nearly came running to me."

Emma pursed her lips and made a poor attempt at a pout. "Am I to be at your beck and call?"

"Mm," Aidan murmured, dropping his voice so no one would overhear. "I rather like the sound of that. Of course, there might be times we could trade roles. You could hitch your finger in my direction, and I would drop my chisel and race to your side...then find other uses for my hands."

She laughed, a hearty sound that warmed him through to his toes. "I might become spoiled if I had such power over you."

"Care to give it a try right now?"

Emma's tongue darted out briefly to wet her lips. Her chest rose and fell with rapid breaths. Then she gave him the tiniest of nods, and skirted out of the room.

Aidan followed after her before she could change her mind. Once they were in the corridor, he caught her from behind, drew her back against him, and nibbled on the spot just below her ear.

"You're wicked," she breathed. She didn't sound overly upset over that fact.

"More wicked than you could ever know." Then he proceeded to show her just how delightful being wicked could be.

ABOUT THE AUTHOR

Catherine Gayle has been an avid reader of romance novels (and almost anything else she can legally get her hands on) for as long as she can remember. Her mother might say it started in the womb. When she is not writing or reading, she can often be found buried beneath her sleeping cat or chasing the Nephew Monster.

OTHER BOOKS BY CATHERINE GAYLE

Lord Rotheby's Influence Series
Twice a Rake
Saving Grace
Merely a Miss

Old Maids' Club Trilogy
Wallflower
Pariah
Shelved (Coming Soon)

Featured in Anthologies:
A Summons From the Castle
The Betting Season
A Season to Remember

Wanton Wives: An Anthology of Erotic Regency Short Stories

Coming Soon—the other books in the Cardiff Siblings Trilogy
A Match Made in Devon
Devon Can Wait

www.ingramcontent.com/pod-product-compliance
Lightning Source LLC
Chambersburg PA
CBHW070659180626
46817CB00006B/2445